Wiregrass Chronicles

Long Rows to Hoe

Glenda Stroud-Peace

ISBN 978-1-4958-2181-3

Copyright © 2019 by Glenda Stroud-Peace

All rights reserved, including the right of reproduction in any form, or by any mechanical or electronic means including photocopying or recording, or by any information storage or retrieval system, in whole or in part in any form, and in any case not without the written permission of the author and publisher.

This is a work of fiction. Names, characters, places, and incidents either are the product of the author's imagination or are used fictitiously. Any resemblance to actual events or locales or persons, living or dead, is entirely coincidental.

Published May 2019

FastPencil
1094 New DeHaven Street, Suite 100
West Conshohocken, PA 19428-2713
Toll-free (877) BUY BOOK
Local Phone (610) 941-9999
Fax (610) 941-9959
Info@buybooksontheweb.com
www.buybooksontheweb.com

This book is dedicated to the memory of two Alabama Wiregrass farm girls — my mother and my Aunt Kate.

The Wiregrass Region, which includes southeastern Alabama, the Florida Panhandle, and a portion of southern Georgia, is so called for the native *Aristida stricta*, generally known as wiregrass because of its texture. Dothan is the heart of the Alabama Wiregrass.

The early Wiregrass settlers of Southeast Alabama understood better than those in more fertile regions that farmers had many a long row to hoe: overcoming the natural barriers of vast forests of pine that had to be cleared, farming soil inhospitable to the cotton seed, and living in uneasy proximity to indigenous people fiercely battling to keep their land. *Long Rows to Hoe* recounts the struggles, the failures, and the successes of the first settlers and their descendants who faced rigorous struggles of their own:

Jackson Knightley, one of the few Confederates who served from Manassas to Appomattox, returns to the Wiregrass; but he may never be able to cleanse his memory of that infamous day at Cold Harbor, when Union troops were slaughtered in a bloodbath that was not war, but murder.

Ephraim Tanner, heartbroken at the death of his Creek wife in Oklahoma, must choose between leaving his newborn son to be raised by her tribe or risking that the infant will be rejected by his white family in the Wiregrass.

Keziah Cates, the daughter of slaves, must balance her distrust and dislike of whites with her love for the Tomlin children, who have won her heart.

The cotton farmers of the new cash-crop era late in the nineteenth century, dragging their long sacks down the interminable rows, hands bloodied by the prickly burs, backs and arms aching, dare to dream of what this long-desired crop can do for them.

And Nora Waldron, healer and preacher's wife, family matriarch, must suddenly take on the parenting of grandchild Theora, a feisty, self-assured handful who defies barriers and may be facing a hazardous future in the segregated South.

These are just a few of the characters who people *Long Rows to Hoe*. This first book in the *Wiregrass Chronicles* series will appeal to lovers of historical fiction, Civil War buffs, and those who admire strong women and men who do not flinch when confronted with danger or adversity. Filled with uplifting stories about overcoming hardship and surviving against great odds, *Long Rows to Hoe* recounts tales, both heartrending and hopeful, with compassion, humor, and an unerring depiction of the people of the Wiregrass from the Creek Wars to World War I.

WIREGRASS CHRONICLES

The Wiregrass Families

Knightley

Josiah Knightley (1817-1910) — Sally Ann Coltayne (1820-1905)

| Ellie (b. 1838) | David (1840-1863) | Peter (1842-1862) | Jackson (1844-1924) m. Sophronia (b. 1851) in 1867 | Maudie (b. 1846) | Micah (b. 1848) |

| Lee (b. 1870) | Rebecca (b. 1872) | William (b. 1875) | Lillian (b. 1880) | Bryce (b. 1883) | Lucinda (b. 1890) | Nathan (b. 1897) m. Abigail Coltayne (1899-1935) in 1919 |

| Bryce (b. 1919) | Letty (b. 1921) | Toby (b. 1923) | Nolly (b. 1927) | Lily (b. 1935) |

Coltayne

Ross Coltayne (b. 1817) — Sylvania (b. 1822)

| Millard (1841-1862) | Grayson (b. 1843) m. Eugenia (b.1847) | Susannah (b. 1845) m. Fraser McFarland | Noble (1847-1924) m. Maisie McFarland | Tobias (b. 1854) m. Victoria (b. 1853) |

Andrew (b. 1879) m. Meg (b. 1885)

Eden (b. 1907)

Abigail m. Nathan Knightley (see Knightley family for offspring)

Note: Josiah Knightley's children are the first cousins of the children of Ross Coltayne. Jackson Knightley's children are the second cousins of the children of Grayson and Tobias Coltayne. This cousinship qualifies Nathan Knightley and Abigail Coltayne as sufficiently unrelated to be classed as "kissing cousins," meaning their marriage would not have been considered outside the bounds of propriety in their generation.

Cates

Keziah Tolliver (1880-1956) m. Daniel Cates (1870-1915) in 1904

Cauley

Stonewall Cauley (1897-1939) — Faye (b. 1893)

| Leonard (1918-1944) | Ruth Ann (b. 1920) | Carrie Sue (b. 1923) | Rodney (b. 1927) |

Long Rows to Hoe

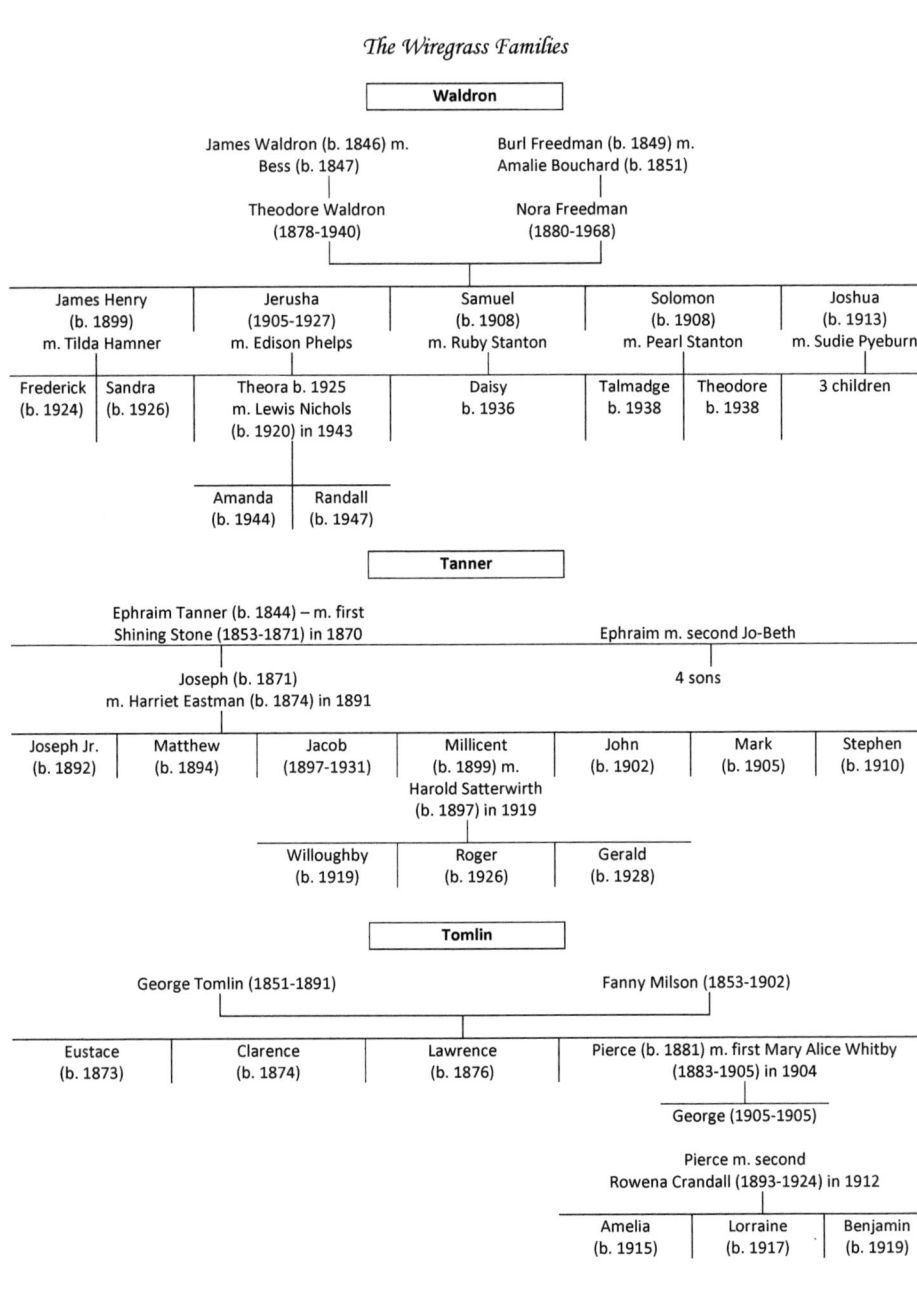

Table of Contents

		Page
1.	Nora and Abigail	1
2.	Ivy	13
3.	Jackson	23
4.	Julia	39
5.	Pierce and Keziah	71
6.	Noble	107
7.	A Precocious Child	131
8.	The Riot	137
9.	Theodore and Nora	149
10.	King Cotton	175
11.	Nemesis	179
12.	The Tanner Family	181
13.	Miss Tenpenny Returns	197
14.	Of Wiregrass Brides and Babies	221
15.	James Henry	231
16.	Love and War	243
	Sources	268

Chapter 1

NORA AND ABIGAIL

THE WAR TO end all wars had been fought and won, and the Great Depression was still two years away. Hitler was a penny-ante politician licking his wounds in the Bavarian Alps after his failed attempt to seize Munich. There was not a single nuclear weapon on the face of the earth. It was a propitious time to enter the world, and in late August of that year, an unborn child slowly, inexorably twisted and turned until its tiny body was upside down in preparation to do just that.

The child kicked. Hard. High up under Abby's heart. It was her fourth, so she knew those were tiny feet, not hands or elbows. The baby had turned. It was almost time.

Abigail Knightley stroked her extended abdomen and shook her head in Nora Waldron's direction.

"It's another boy, for sure."

She was not happy about it.

"No, it ain't. You carrying high. I done told you twenty times, that baby's a girl."

Abby pursed her lips in disagreement as she poured out more tepid tea from the pressed glass pitcher into two jelly glasses. The wrap-around tin porch roof and two large pecan trees shaded them from the early afternoon sun, but the air was stagnant and heavy with the heat.

Nora had walked from home with her son Joshua, hired by Abby's husband Nate to help water and hoe cotton that day. Many of the bolls were beginning to ripen, but it was still too early for the first of two or even three pickings needed to harvest all the crop. Two of the Knightley children, seven-year-old Bryce and six-year-old Letty, were working in the field as well. Nora had brought her granddaughter Theora along, and the toddler was playing in the yard.

Nora welcomed the chance to chat, and she was helping Abby snap beans and shell peas. It was a second-nature activity for them both, performed since early childhood. When had they not snapped beans and shelled peas? In the womb.

They stirred a faint breeze as they rocked in cane-bottom chairs, the snapped and shelled pile steadily growing higher in the blue-speckled enamel bowl on the small wooden table between them. Abby brushed a strand of her board-straight, pale brown hair out of her eyes, reached for a folded newspaper, and fanned herself. They both took a moment to sip the lukewarm tea.

"Sorry we're out of ice," Abby said. "Sweet enough?"

Nora nodded.

"Just right."

Theora was pulling a small red wagon in circles near the porch. Her hair was neatly plaited into multiple tiny braids that stood up all over her head. She wore a short, blue-flowered grain-sack dress and was barefooted. A kitten caught her eye, and she headed for it.

Brilliant patches of goldenrod and deep purple morning glories draping a fence relieved the austerity of the hard clay yard. It was swept clean, but stubborn blades of crabgrass stood in spiky patches where Bryce's fingers could not pry them loose.

"Looka yonder at all them weeds. I cain't bend over to pull them up and my oldest's not strong enough to get them all, and Nate's too busy to pay a mind to it."

"My yard be the same way, Miz Abby. Tee love his flowers, but sometimes he let the yard go."

Nora was nineteen years older than Abby, the wife of a pastor, Reverend Theodore Waldron, known to family and friends as Tee. The Waldrons owned fifty acres of land in the farming community of Chinkapin, nearly five miles west of Dothan, Alabama, and had once owned even more. Tee had sold ninety-seven acres to fund their thriving nursery business, which did not require nearly as much acreage as a cotton farm. Abby's husband was a tenant farmer struggling to purchase the house and 142 acres he was now renting, with little likelihood of achieving this for several more harvests. But Abby's fair-skinned caste trumped Nora's higher social status. Thus Abby was "Miz," while Nora was simply "Nora." Neither of them questioned this pecking order, and it did not in the least affect their cordial relationship or their willingness over the years to help one another.

"Theora's walking real good," Abby observed. "My Toby was slow to walk, but now I have to watch him like a hawk."

Four-year-old Toby was napping in the house. Nate, Joshua, and Abby's older children had just gone back to work after eating the large noon meal she had cooked for them with Nora's help. But for her advanced pregnancy, she would have been in the fields working with them, keeping Toby near by, until time to return home and cook supper.

Theora was trying to force an orange kitten to sit in the wagon while she pulled it around. Every time she started off, the kitten bolted.

"Now you leave that cat alone, baby. You might hurt it," Nora cautioned.

"She cain't hurt that cat," Abby said. "I'm more worried it might scratch her."

The kitten solved the problem by scampering off and climbing a chinaberry tree. To the amusement of her elders, Theora plopped down in the wagon, crossed her arms and scowled, clearly disgusted, and pondered her next move.

Abby lifted the bowl of peas and beans and shook it around a bit, satisfied with the heft of it.

"That'll do for supper, I guess. I've got some boiled rutabaga ready to dice, and there's ham from last night."

The new baby kicked again, and she grimaced.

"By durn it, Nora, that's a boy! Letty never kicked that hard, I know she didn't. I treasure my boys, but I need me another girl."

Then, remembering, she said, "Well, *you* know."

Nora nodded ruefully. Because didn't she have four hard-headed boys and just one sweet girl? Her eldest, James Henry, they had not seen in eight long years, all because of that foolishness in Dothan. And he swore he was never coming back south. Sometimes it seemed he was punishing her and Tee for things that weren't their fault.

The twins had never been as worrisome as James Henry. Solomon assisted Tee in the nursery business, and Samuel was settled with a decent job as a barber in Dothan. But lord, they'd been a handful to raise. And now Joshua, with that horn of his, begrudged every minute of honest work that kept him from that devil's instrument and the rowdy company that went with it. Why today, if he hadn't needed money to buy some sheet music, no amount of nudging could have gotten him over to the Knightley farm to hoe cotton. Not that she wanted any of her children to be farm laborers, but it didn't hurt for him to spend a couple of days in the field. Make him appreciate the soft life he'd led. While Josh frequently worked alongside Tee and Solomon in Waldron's Gardens, tending the flowers, shrubs, and fruit trees that comprised their livelihood, nursery work was nowhere near as grueling as the backbreaking stoop labor required of the average farmer. Tee had stopped farming and become a nurseryman before Josh was born. The nursery business, the modest income from Divine Truth Church, and the money Nora's midwifery skills earned supported them just fine.

Between James Henry and the twins, the Lord had blessed them with Jerusha, their soft-spoken, sweet-acting daughter. To her parents' dismay, after graduating from high school she had set aside her ambition to attend college and become a music teacher to marry, Edison Phelps, a smooth-talking man who could not keep a job. He went north before Theora was even born, promising to send for Jerusha. But he never did. Nora suspected he had taken another wife up there. She knew it was perhaps a selfish feeling, but she was glad he'd left her daughter and granddaughter behind. After the first sadness and distress, as the infrequent letters from the North stopped coming, Jerusha simply loved her baby girl the more, knowing she had to be mother and father both.

She had combined her parents' names to form the name Theora, which pleased them.

Then Jerusha had begun to grow weak for no reason they could see. She was always tired, no matter how much she slept, and was often dizzy. Her face and limbs were swollen, and she complained of a strange metallic taste in her mouth — as if she had swallowed iron, she told them.

Abby broke into Nora's thoughts. "Is Jerusha better?"

Nora shook her head. "She still doing poorly. She don't get better."

Abby touched her arm. "I'm sorry. I wish I could do something."

Suddenly she half raised up from her chair, pushing herself up awkwardly by leaning on the table.

"Theora!" she shouted. "You come away from that chicken coop. You come back here right now!

"Saw a snake down there this morning," she explained as she eased herself back into the chair. "Probably just a rat snake, but best to be careful."

Theora obediently turned the wagon and started back to the house.

Nora got up and carried the brimming bowl into the kitchen, setting it next to the rutabaga, then returned to the porch. She squeezed Abby's shoulder and cautioned, "Now don't overdo, honey. And be sure you sends for me soon as you needs me."

"You know I will."

Nora had delivered each of the Knightley children. Once Nate had tried to get a doctor for her, but Letty was already born by the time he arrived, out of breath, apologizing and explaining that he had just delivered a baby at a neighboring farm.

Abby reluctantly watched Nora and her grandbaby leave, the little girl sitting in the small wagon, Nora stooping slightly to pull it. Nora's presence was a comfort. Abby was blessed with a caring husband and children who were about as well behaved as anyone else's. But in Nora's presence she somehow felt better able to cope, a bit stronger, more inured to pain and discomfort than she otherwise was. Nora had that effect on many people.

Nora Freedman Waldron, a well-known midwife, came from a long line of healers, women who were knowledgeable in every aspect of folk medicine. She knew every herbal and mineral remedy the earth could offer up. She knew which barks were best gathered while the sap was running, that roots should be gathered before the sap rises, and that medicinal flowers must be gathered when fully ripe and dried in the shade. She knew how to staunch blood and stitch up a cut, which ointments to apply, when, and for how long. This knowledge had been handed down to her by her mother, Amalie, a gifted healer, who had been taught by her grandmother, Reba.

Nora's healing touch had been felt by many, black and white, in Chinkapin and the surrounding small communities. And before marrying Tee and coming to Houston County in the Alabama Wiregrass, she had ministered to folks in the rural area north of Mobile where she was born and raised. So she was no novice. But she was wise enough to know the limits of her knowledge and abilities, and she had determined that no poultice or brew would help Jerusha.

When Nora and Theora got home, the child jumped out of the wagon and ran up on the porch where Jerusha was sitting on the swing. She climbed into her lap, and Jerusha smiled and hugged her.

"Hey, baby. Did you and Granny Nora have a good walk?"

Theora nodded as Nora settled on the swing next to them. "She try to boss a kitten around, but it run away."

"Smart kitty!" Jerusha said with a laugh, giving her feisty little girl a squeeze.

"You looking tired, baby," Nora said. "Maybe you best lie down."

"I just this minute got up, Mama. Been sleeping ever since y'all left."

"You still feeling dizzy?"

Jerusha looked down and did not immediately answer. She hated to worry her mother. But she knew Nora would see straight through her if she tried to lie.

"Yes, a little. I – I fell down in the living room on my way out here to the porch."

She turned and looked into her mother's troubled face.

"What's the matter with me, Mama?"

"I doesn't know, sugar. But us gone find out."

THE FOLLOWING DAY, Nora and Tee helped Jerusha into the nursery truck, where she insisted on holding Theora in her arms, and took her to see Dr. Pleasant Ewing in Dothan. Dr. Ewing adhered to the custom of separate waiting rooms for colored and white patients, but he saw them on a first-come, first-served basis, regardless of their skin color. He had known the Waldrons for more than a decade and through the years had earned their trust. He was familiar with Nora's midwifery practice and occasionally purchased flowers and shrubs from Waldron's Gardens.

Today he examined Jerusha, took a urine sample, and then sat the family down in his small office for a grave talk.

Theora clung to her mother as if she understood the awful words. Jerusha sat stone faced, Tee squeezed Nora's hand and blinked away tears, and Nora engaged Dr. Ewing's eyes, letting him know, *I be the strongest, you pour all the bad news into me.* It boiled down to two simple words: kidney failure. Eventually and inevitably fatal.

That evening, Tee led them in prayer, beseeching almighty God to spare Jerusha and to give all of them strength. His deep strong voice had never fit his slight body, but his family was used to it. The powerful voice that easily reached to the last pew in the Divine Truth Baptist Church, admonishing sinners, comforting mourners, praising the faithful, and uplifting the spirits of the overburdened, had also sung to his children, told them stories, commanded obedience, and explained the ways of white folks. More than his bald head, his weak, bespectacled eyes, and his polio-stiffened left arm, the voice was the essence of the man, imbuing him with a presence, a power, not evident in his physical appearance.

At supper, the twins and Josh ate a leftovers meal with Nora and Tee, solemn in the knowledge they would rather not have had. Jerusha was served a plate in her room, barely touched it, and would not let Nora take the sleeping Theora from her arms.

FOUR DAYS LATER, Nobella Knightley entered the world amid the usual stress, pain and mess of childbirth. Because this was her fourth child, Abby's travail was brief, a mere five hours, thirty-seven minutes of excruciating discomfort.

It was September 2, Theora Waldron's second birthday, but as promised Nora was there to assist at the birth. The other children were asleep when Nobella debuted at four o'clock on a Friday morning. As the child took its first breath, wailing with the newborn's outrage at being expelled from the womb, Nora triumphantly declared to Abby, "You gots your girl, honey!"

After Nora cleaned and swaddled the child, Nate lightly touched the child's face, as always awed at the sight of a newborn. He had stoically clasped Abby's hand throughout the birth, despite a strong urge to bolt from the labor room.

He always carefully put by money to pay a doctor or a midwife. The thought of delivering a baby by himself terrified him. And there was always the chance something could go wrong for Abby or the child. Thus far, nothing had. As his pious father Jackson would say, this continued good fortune was surely by the grace of God, and Nate gave thanks for the safe delivery of his newest daughter.

Nora prepared breakfast for Nate, as well as the children, who would soon be awake. Abby reached up to hug her before she left. Nate drove her home in the newly acquired second-hand Model-T Ford, the family's first automobile. He pressed a five dollar bill into her hand and warmly thanked her again as they pulled up before her house. Tee Waldron, dozing in the living room waiting for her, was awakened by the sound of the car and came to the door with the lantern as she wearily walked in and headed for the bedroom. "It be a girl, they both fine," she told him, as he started out the door to congratulate Nate.

Back home, Nate did not offer to take the child from Abby's arms, nor did she expect him to. She knew that newborns made him nervous. Their fragility scared him, and he could never manage the confident baby-handling skills that seemed so natural to Abby and other females. His six-year-old daughter Letty would be happily holding and rocking the five-and-a-half-pound bundle in a few hours, while Nate dared only kiss the baby's face and caress her tiny hands.

NATHAN NAMED THE boys, but Abby felt it was her prerogative to name the girls, and he did not argue the point.

Nate would have preferred to call his first-born son Jackson, after his father, but his oldest brother had already bestowed that name on his son. So Nate named his boy Bryce after his youngest, favorite brother.

Abby chose Letitia for the girl born between the boys because, she said, "It's pretty," and Nate agreed.

Nate generously named his second son after a Coltayne, Abby's father Tobias, a man he liked and admired. But for obvious reasons it would never have occurred to him to name a boy after Tobias's brother Noble, who unaccountably was Abby's favorite uncle. He was also Nate's cousin, but Nate did not claim him. Had the word been in his vocabulary, he would have dubbed the man "Ignoble," and many would have agreed with that description.

But now Abby had chosen the outrageous name of Nobella for the new baby, claiming that it was the girl version of Noble. Nate shook his head in disbelief. First of all, he had never heard of such a name. Abby had made it up. Secondly, how could she name a child after the black sheep of the family?

True, Noble Coltayne, who had died three years earlier, had been a successful cotton agent in Apalachicola and doted on his Alabama nieces and nephews. They all loved traveling by train to visit him and his family at his seaside home. Florida and the warm waters of the Gulf held enormous appeal for children bound to the flat farm land and waterless horizon of southeast Alabama.

Abby had many fond memories of Uncle Noble's place, which faced directly on the Gulf. After a morning of wading in the sea, enjoying the delicious feeling of wet sand squishing between their toes, she and the other children, mud-spattered and soaked to the skin, would dig for clams at low tide, then compete for finding the most seashells. None of them willingly submitted to being splashed with buckets of well water to wash off the brine before retiring to the house for an afternoon nap. But as the sun gloriously set over the Gulf, they enjoyed lolling around a fire on the beach while the grownups prepared a feast of freshly caught red snapper, king mackerel, and shrimp.

Abby and one of her closest cousins, Eden Coltayne, had spent many summers in Apalachicola. Eden's grandfather, Grayson Coltayne, had been another of Noble's brothers, and she and her folks still lived on the family farm up in Barbour County, worked now by her father Andrew and his children.

But there was a shameful reason Noble Coltayne had left Alabama, and there was a dark reason he had never returned. And Abby knew those reasons. Yet she still loved the old man and wanted to name their new baby girl after him.

"Why not Sophronia, after my mother?" Nate suggested. "Or Victoria, after yours?"

"Because your family and mine have already claimed those names for their girls." It exasperated Abby to have to explain this to him. "And the thing about it is, this might be the only other girl we have. And if we only have boys after this, I know you will never name one Noble."

She stroked the baby's soft, down-covered head and hitched her up to her breast.

"So Nobella she is, my darling little Nobella." She glanced up at Nate and smiled her charming, lopsided smile. "After my dear Uncle Noble, God rest his soul."

Chapter 2

Ivy

IT WAS STANDARD practice for Nora Waldron to follow up on her maternity patients several times after they gave birth. She had checked on Abigail Knightley three days after Nobella's arrival, but then a week elapsed without a visit. Knowing how ill Jerusha was, Abby grew concerned. One evening after the children were in bed she asked Nate to drive over to look in on the Waldrons.

He returned so quickly that, observing him pulling back into the yard, she assumed the Waldrons had not been at home. He slowly walked up on the porch as she opened the door for him.

"They gone somewhere?"

Nate took off his sweat-stained felt hat and threw it on a chair and shook his head.

"Well, what did Nora have to say? You did ask about Jerusha, didn't you?"

"I didn't see Nora. Tee come to the door and told me — Jerusha died this morning, Abby. I could see he was in no state to talk, so I just said as how I was very sorry and took my leave."

Abby felt her throat tighten, and her eyes dimmed with instant tears.

"Oh, my dear Lord. I knew she was very sick, but I didn't think — I was hoping — She wasn't but twenty-two years old. And such a sweet girl."

Nate nodded in affirmation.

"Funeral's tomorrow. Younguns can stay home with me, Abby. You go."

"Of course I will," she responded, knowing he assumed she would bring Nobella with her, since handling a newborn was beyond his capacity.

She wiped her eyes with the heel of her hand and thought about what, if anything, she could do for Nora Waldron, who had done so much for her. What comfort could she offer her? As sadness for Nora pulled at her, her practical nature directed her to the kitchen, where she determined there was ample food to prepare a dish to bring for the church dinner sure to follow the service. When she looked into the closet, she was relieved to find that her one formal dress, a purple silk crêpe de Chine cast off by her friend Millicent Tanner (and substantially altered because of Millie's larger size), would not require a nerve-wracking session with the flatiron heated on the stove, trying to iron out wrinkles without scorching the delicate fabric. So from a practical standpoint, she was ready to attend the funeral.

But emotionally, her heart ached for the good woman who had been with her through the pain and joy of childbirth, brought meals to her when she was sick with the flu, watched the children for them in the emergency of Nate's broken leg, and sent her sons to help them through the wrenching necessity of moving into rental property when their farm failed.

What do you say to someone like that in her hour of need? What do you do?

As Nate silently observed her busy preparations for a sad tomorrow, Abby thought, wiping away more tears as an image of Jerusha's bright smile flashed through her mind, *Well, I can cook for her. And I can be there for the funeral, even though my preference would be to pretend Jerusha was still here and that Theora was not now a motherless child.*

THEORA LAY IN NORA'S arms as her grandmother hummed a lullaby, fighting sleep but gradually giving in to the low humming sound and the creaking motion of the rocking chair. None of her children had fought sleep as her grandbaby did. None had walked or talked as early. And none at the tender age of two had had the degree of confidence this little mite did.

She feared nothing and was curious about everything — kittens and tadpoles, spiders and spider webs, beetles and baby chicks. Only that morning, she had eagerly helped Granny scoop up eggs out of the chicken coop into her apron and been allowed to help her place them on a soft cloth in a still-warm oven to hasten their hatching. Then, eyes bright with excitement, she had watched the miracle of the babies pecking their way out of their shells.

"Can I hold one of them in my hands, Granny?" she had asked.

Her very words. A complete sentence. While other two-year-olds only said a word or two here and there or merely pointed at things they wanted.

Nora smiled down at her.

"You Tee's grandchild all right," she murmured.

Her well-spoken husband was, she reckoned, the smartest person she knew, and this baby was going to be just like him. Nora's medical knowledge, her wisdom, and her compassion were recognized and valued by others, including her husband. But Nora never believed herself the equal of Reverend Theodore Waldron.

She carried the sleeping child to her bed, noting as always her striking resemblance to Jerusha. It had been more than a month since her daughter's death, and the reality had still not sunken in. She kept turning to say something to her, kept expecting to hear her laugh or see her walk into the room. It was the same for Tee and their three sons who still lived at home. It was hard to believe Jerusha was with Jesus now.

Before she had become ill, Jerusha had been energetic, easily keeping up with her whirlwind of a child. For Nora and Tee, it was much harder. But they both realized that Theora, whom they decided should carry their last name instead of that of her absent father, was a special gift. And this child, Nora believed, would be a healer like herself, carrying on a long family tradition.

NORA OBSERVED THEORA'S fascination with the natural world and believed she had inherited the gift: she was a born healer. Jerusha, like her brother Joshua, had preferred music to all other pursuits. Blessed with a beautiful contralto voice, she was often called upon to lead the church choir and had planned to teach music one day. Ministering to the sick and delivering babies had never interested her. But many of the women in Nora's family had been healers, at least as far back as she knew. Granny Reba, who was her maternal great-grandmother, had been a walking encyclopedia of folk medicine. She had passed all she knew down to her granddaughter Amalie, who then passed her knowledge to Nora. Whether Ivy, Reba's only daughter, was a healer was not known, because she had been sold away when she was just fifteen.

Reba, Ivy, and her sons Morris and Tillman were the property of Henri Bouchard, owner of twenty-seven slaves and a backwater cotton plantation near the Tombigbee River in Washington County, some fifty-five miles north of Mobile. Reba's husband, worn down by the brutal work and one bout of malaria after another, died before the children were half grown.

In 1850, Ivy was a willowy fourteen-year-old with large expressive eyes, a throaty laugh that lifted the spirits of those around her, and a beautiful smile. She was blessed with a soul that could rejoice in simple things — a colorful patch of wildflowers, a mockingbird's song, a cooling rain on a sweltering hot day. Her mahogany skin was flawless, and she had the slim body, long neck, small head, and delicately sculpted features of a ballerina. Her movements were fluid and graceful. Had she been born in different circumstances, in a different time and place, she would have turned heads wherever she went and might have had the world at her feet.

Her fate instead was to strengthen her young muscles through physical labor rather than at the ballet bar. But she was meant to dance, and when she danced, it was not in a highly disciplined, painstakingly choreographed fashion but with a creativity and spontaneity that would have earned her the praise of Isadora Duncan seventy years later. When celebratory fires burned in the slave quarters on certain holidays, she loved to dance in the firelight, her graceful body keeping perfect time to the singing and clapping of hands. Ivy's ankle-length cotton shift had been scrubbed clean so many times on Reba's washboard that the fabric was worn thin. In the glow of the flames, the diaphanous gown revealed her slim, taut, dancer's body.

More than once Reba had observed Bouchard watching Ivy as she danced, understood the look on his face, and feared for her daughter. When he exercised what he felt to be his prerogative, Ivy tearfully acknowledged this to Reba, who was powerless to do more than watch the girl for the inevitable signs of pregnancy.

Ivy gave birth to Amalie early on a cool April day in 1851. There was no privacy in the quarters, so she had seen babies being born and knew what to expect. But the miracle of this tiny child with her perfect little fingers and toes, her beautifully formed head and lusty cries that declared her in resounding good health, was a different experience altogether, because this child had been carried inside her. She looked at the baby with wonder and felt a deep sense of joy.

Bouchard was away on business for several days when Amalie was born, inspecting some property across the river in Clarke County which he was considering buying. Two days after the birth, his wife Lavinia was informed of the child's arrival while being assisted into her billowing gown by a house servant.

"She be a pretty child, ma'am," the servant commented, glancing up at her as Lavinia adjusted her dress in front of a mirrored-door wardrobe. "And look to be healthy." She did not comment on the baby's fair skin, nor betray her true feelings toward the man who had preyed on Ivy; but Lavinia, being neither deaf nor blind, had caught the whispers and looks these past months and was well aware of the baby's paternity.

She abruptly changed her mind about her dress and had the servant fetch her traveling clothes. She had been waiting for the child's birth to finalize her plans for a trip to Mobile.

Lavinia was a bitter woman who knew about each of the slave children her husband had fathered. She had borne him seven children, four of whom had survived, including two sons, and she had suffered in silence over these dalliances with his female property. What need had he of them when she had given him healthy children? Unknown to Bouchard, she had made a decision some time ago that if he sired one more slave child, she would act. And today her resolve did not fail her. She swept into Reba's cabin, snatched the newborn child from Ivy's arms and handed it to Reba, commanding her to "find another gal to nurse it." She ordered Ivy to dress herself and get in the waiting wagon. Taking her eldest daughter, Adelais, as her companion on what would be an overnight trip, Lavinia directed a servant to drive them to a steamboat landing, where she booked passage to Mobile.

There were no plantations close to Mobile, but it was a bustling port for cotton shipped down the Alabama and Tombigbee Rivers, which converged into the Mobile River fifty miles north of the city. It was also well known for its brisk slave trade, with several busy auction houses.

Never since she had been born had Ivy known the Bouchards to sell any of their slaves, and she did not understand what was happening to her until she had been handed over to a slave dealer at the landing in Mobile. That same day, she was put on the auction block at Royal and State Streets. She wept then, not for herself, but for her helpless baby girl.

In her fury, Lavinia did not bother to keep the bill of sale with the trader's name on it. She used the money from her business transaction to buy new gowns and an oil painting for the parlor. Then she and Adelais dined at a restaurant noted for its European cuisine and spent the night at a hotel before returning home. The wagon driver met the steamboat and drove them back to the plantation. The day before, Lavinia had seen no reason to enlighten him as to the purpose of the trip, but he now understood that he had unknowingly delivered Ivy to her fate and sat silent the entire ride home, sickened to the depths of his soul.

When Bouchard found out, he was furious. Ivy was his; she did not, by God, belong to his wife. He commanded Lavinia to give him the name of the slave trader, but she truthfully told him she did not know it. For the first time, Bouchard looked at his wife with undisguised loathing, the mask that had for so long concealed his disdain for her stripped away. He went to Reba, who was shrunken with grief, and swore he would get Ivy back. But though he searched in Mobile and for miles beyond, following several leads that petered out, he never found her.

One day less than a twelvemonth after her crazed dash to Mobile, Lavinia stood staring at an exquisite porcelain figure on the mantelpiece that was her most prized memento of her honeymoon in Europe fifteen years earlier. Henri had bought it for her in a charming little shop in Paris, discussing the price with the shop keeper in his flawless French, and deciding that even though it was ridiculously expensive his lovely bride should have it. It was a figure of a slender young woman clothed in an ankle-length Regency gown. The dress was deep rose, embellished with tiny yellow and wine-colored flowers about the neck and the edges of the short puffed sleeves. An intricate leaf design ran all the way around the hem of the dress. Her dark hair was pulled up into a pile of curls on the top of her head, bound with narrow wine- and rose-colored ribbons, and the artist had managed to give the face a sweetness of expression.

She was posed as if about to dance, with one slipper-clad foot slightly lifted, one hand on her slender hip and the other outstretched, as if reaching for a partner. The gown was slightly swirled to give the illusion of movement. It was an utterly charming figure that Lavinia had always loved because it recalled to her a happier time, when her long brown hair was not thinning and turning gray, her waist was not thickened from childbearing, and her husband had seemed to love her.

But for some time past, whenever she looked at the figure a feeling of malaise had overcome her. At this moment it dawned on her why. The face and long slender neck and graceful arms were a pearlescent white, but they might as well have been chestnut brown. She realized that she no longer cared for the figure because it reminded her of Ivy.

As soon as that realization seized her, she snatched the figure and hurled it at the marble fireplace as hard as she could, where it shattered into hundreds of brilliant bits on the hearthside. Only the perfect little head remained intact. It seemed to be staring up at her, and she shuddered. Hearing the noise, a servant came into the room, surveyed the damage, and hurried away to get a broom. She did not seem to notice the tears on mistress's face.

ONE YEAR BEFORE emancipation, Henri Bouchard died mysteriously, perhaps of food poisoning — although the doctor could neither confirm nor rule out that diagnosis. His eldest son, Maurice, sought glory in the Civil War but did not find it. He was killed during the forty-eight-day siege of Port Hudson, Louisiana, a Union victory that gave the Federals control of the Mississippi River.

The younger Bouchard son, André, an effete individual who had no interest in politics or war and had paid a substitute to fight for him, now inherited. With the fate of the plantation dependent upon him, he decided to sell the property, settled an equitable amount upon his female relations, and announced that he could not reside in a reconstructed South. Claiming that his French blood beckoned him, he left for Quebec one morning in 1866. He never returned.

IN 1864, REBA'S sons joined the United States Colored Infantry. Their regiment was one of nine black units engaged in the successful Union assault on Blakely, Alabama, a crucial factor in the fall of Mobile in April 1865. The brothers lived to a great old age, and when Amalie and her family visited them in Mobile, their uncles told them stories of slavery times and the battle in which they had fought.

Amalie explained to Nora that the family kept hoping Ivy would return to them one day. When the war ended, she would have been just twenty-nine years old, and they prayed that she would find her way back to her family. Morris and Tillman appealed to the Freedman's Bureau, which helped them search for her, but to no avail. Reba grieved for her daughter until her own death in 1876, never abandoning hope. But Ivy was forever lost. Amalie was saddened by Reba's death, but comforted herself with the thought that the Lord had taken her into his bosom and annihilated her grief and suffering with his golden light.

Amalie married a blacksmith, Burl Freedman, in 1867. Despite the establishment of the repressive Black Codes that circumscribed every aspect of black people's lives, making even one inch of progress difficult, Amalie and Burl managed to raise their children in a small but decent house in the rural community of Gator Pass, just north of Mobile. They were surprisingly unbitter. They worked hard and were never rich in material possessions, but with freedom they had choices and possibilities and hope.

Amalie was especially blessed because she had inherited Ivy's lightness of spirit, her ability to rejoice in God's world despite the injustice and oppression all around them. Reba had thoroughly schooled her in the healing arts, and she in turn passed this knowledge to Nora.

Chapter 3

JACKSON

ONE SEPTEMBER MORNING in 1927, Benjamin Tomlin, eight-year-old heir apparent to Comfortroot Farm, watched his father saunter across the yard toward a stand of poplar trees about fifty yards from the house. He knew there were graves there — a lady and a little boy. Pierce Tomlin never talked about them, and Benjamin had remained uncurious until he overheard his father and their housekeeper, Keziah, discussing Mary Alice, the name on the lady's gravestone, talking about her as if they had only just seen her. But Benjamin knew she had died a long time ago because her gravestone said so.

He ran and caught up to his father and grabbed his hand just as they arrived at the graves.

"Who is that lady?" he asked, pointing at her marker.

The love of my life, cruelly taken from me by a harsh God, went through Pierce's head.

"She was my first wife," he said. "She died when she was young."

"And who is that little boy?"

"That's George. Your brother."

"You mean I had a brother?"

"You did," Pierce said, seeing the beautiful infant boy struggling for breath, locked in the arms of his desperate mother.

"Well, if he hadn't gone to heaven, I would've took good care of him."

Pierce smiled.

"He would be a lot older than you. He'd be a grown man now."

"Oh. But anyway, he'd still be my brother?"

"Yep."

"Well — I wish I could've got to know him, Papa. You think he would've liked me?"

"Of course he would. Now help me clear away these leaves and let's find some pretty flowers to put here."

COMFORTROOT FARM ENCOMPASSED 600 acres of land bordered by two creeks and faced on the Enterprise road near the Chinkapin community five-and-a-half miles west of Dothan. Pierce Tomlin, a transplanted Virginian, had owned the property for more than twenty years and was one of the most prosperous farmers in the Wiregrass. Prosperity by Wiregrass standards did not mean Dusenberg automobiles, fur coats, and trips to Europe. Prosperity meant having a well-built, well-maintained farmhouse and outbuildings and up-to-date farm equipment. It meant that the members of your household were well-fed and suitably clothed. To achieve this, you worked alongside the farm hands and managed the concerns of the acreage rented out to several tenants, staying abreast of every farmers' bureau bulletin and attuned to every natural sign that could affect the crops.

None of Pierce's tenants could accuse him of offering harsh terms or cheating them out of their share of the profit, if any, at harvest time. But none were content with the lot of the tenant farmer. Once, before cotton became the primary crop, virtually every farmer in the Wiregrass had been independent. But with each passing year the number driven into tenancy increased, felled by their dependence on a crop vulnerable to an army of pests, particularly the ubiquitous and ineradicable boll weevil, and a fluctuating cotton market over which they had no control. Every farmer forced into tenancy sacrificed pride when he approached the large farm owner, hat in hand, and asked for a chance to farm on his land.

AT THE TIME of Jackson Knightley's death in 1924, life was good for his youngest son, Nathan, unexpectedly born to his mother when she was forty-six and Jackson fifty-three. His father always contended that because Nate was the youngest by seven years, Sophronia coddled him, and so he felt it necessary to be especially strict with Nate to prevent his being spoiled. A devout Primitive Baptist, Jackson believed in a heaven and a real, fire-and-brimstone hell and impressed upon all seven of his children the wisdom of adhering to the tenets of their faith.

In 1924, Nathan had been married to the love of his life for five years and was the father of three small children, two boys and a girl. Jackson, a successful farmer in Barbour County, had helped his youngest boy establish a farm of his own in Houston County. Nathan was proud of the 100 acres he farmed in the community of Chinkapin in Houston County. It was not a very big farm, and the work was backbreaking, and the boll weevil proved over and over again that it could not be eradicated. Calcium arsenate treatments helped but little, and Nate had hired workers to help him spray turpentine-derived toxaphene dust on the cotton plants, supposedly a more effective pesticide; but whenever it rained the dust was washed away, and the weevils resumed feasting on the bolls. Still, he always managed to harvest sufficient cotton and peanuts to provide for his family, and that income was supplemented by the sale of some of the produce they grew for their own consumption. Nate was proud of his family's independence.

Jackson died in August of that year. As befitting an old soldier, he did not die in bed. He was killed during a violent thunderstorm when his horse was spooked by lightning and threw him.

That same year, a combination of other misfortunes — torrential rains that flooded the crops and the strong resurgence of the boll weevil and a broken leg that prevented him from working for weeks — overwhelmed Nate. Even though his wife worked in the field as much as she could, it was far beyond her capacity to look after the children and the household and work the land alone. Last year's profit, on which they depended to get through the current year, had been lower than in any previous year, so they could not afford to hire the help they needed. Their meager resources shriveled to almost nothing, and Nathan was forced to sell the farm at a loss and search for a piece of land to rent. As bitter as that pill was to swallow, he counted himself lucky that Pierce Tomlin took him on as a tenant at Comfortroot Farm in March of 1925.

Nate was saddened by the death of his father, but he was glad that Jackson had not lived to see his son driven into tenancy. Nate would always believe that if Jackson had stood in his shoes he would have somehow found a way to hold on to the land. Jackson had been more than a mere farmer. He had been a fighter. He possessed a kind of strength that Nate did not. And Nate would always feel that he was walking in his father's shadow.

UNLIKE NOBLE COLTAYNE, Jackson Knightley had been an honorable man. A religious man. In the Civil War, he had served from Manassas to Appomattox. The Knightleys were yeoman farmers who worked their own land; they had never owned a slave. But when the Federals invaded Virginia at First Manassas, seventeen-year-old Jackson and his two older brothers, David and Peter, enlisted in Company H, 15th Alabama, known as the Glennville Guards. By the grace of God or through incredible luck, Jackson survived battle after battle engaged in by the 15th. He was at Winchester, Second Manassas, Chickamauga, Dandridge, Second Cold Harbor, and Petersburg. Except for a flesh wound inflicted by a sniper's bullet at Second Manassas, he had come through unharmed. Only 170 of the 1,958 men who had joined the 15th were among that bedraggled company of Confederates who were rounded up and gathered in the fields near Appomattox Courthouse to hear the announcement that General Lee had surrendered. They were begrimed, unshaven, ill-clothed, and poorly shod. Their malnourished bodies evidenced the skimpy diet they had subsisted on for weeks, months, or even years.

When the surrender was confirmed on April 9, Palm Sunday, General Lee himself riding among the troops and telling this soldier or that one, Yes, we are surrendered, many battle-hardened veterans fell to the ground in tears.

IN THE EARLY morning hours of April 12, Union Brigadier General Joshua Chamberlain watched the Confederates form into column on a distant hill, then march through the valley up the Richmond-Lynchburg stage road toward Appomattox. The Union line was so positioned that the armies could see each other. To the surprise of the Confederates, as they approached the Union officers overseeing the surrender, General Chamberlain ordered the bugle blown, and the entire Union line came to attention and gave the "carry arms" or marching salute — the rifle held by the right hand and perpendicular to the shoulder. The Confederate command then sent back word to the rear for each division of Confederate troops to reciprocate with the marching salute in mutual salutation and farewell.

Nearly an entire day was necessary for the more than 25,000 defeated soldiers to pass by General Chamberlain and his men, who watched the humiliated Rebels in silence, with not one drum roll, not one triumphant cheer. The Confederates then, in an orderly fashion, surrendered their battle flags and weapons. Cartridge boxes were emptied in the street, and at dusk the Federals set them ablaze.

The following morning, many of the foot soldiers, who over the years had been commanded to march hundreds of miles, for whom marching was as natural as any bodily function, hung about for a bit, trained to wait for orders, until finally a few muttered words to the effect, "Well, boys, let's get a-goin, then." Their prisoner parole passes were carefully tucked away in a pocket or a hat where they would not lose them.

Like many of the soldiers now starting the long journey home on foot, Jackson Knightley faced the problem of disintegrating boots. The solution was to use strands of wire to tie pieces of bark to the feet to protect them. He counted himself fortunate to have the wire. Some soldiers had to tie on the bark with vines they found in the woods.

As they tramped down wagon trails and through fields, Jackson was still on the alert, looking over his shoulder, scanning a stand of trees, listening for enemy fire. War had been a portable thing, he had always found; wherever he and his comrades went, war was there. And if you were not being deafened by cannon and artillery fire close at hand, there was frequently the faint, distant rumble of big guns over a faraway ridge towards which you were headed, and you could see little puffs of smoke and sputtering fire from exploding shells away off on the horizon, you could hear the faint pop-pop-pop of rifle fire, so you knew that whatever hell you had experienced on the battlefield just quitted, there was the guarantee of more of the same up ahead.

Now the guns had stopped. But Jackson still heard the boom of the cannon and the whistle of artillery shells. He still started at the slightest sound and reached for his rifle and cartridge box that were not there, ready in an instant to bite off a cartridge, dump the powder into the muzzle, ram in a Minie ball, cap the weapon, fire, and repeat the whole process no fewer than three times a minute.

The quietude of the woods he wandered through was unnatural to him. Birds flitted through the trees as if they had never risen in great startled flocks at the sound of thunderous explosions; screeching carrion birds did not hover over fields strewn with the dead and dying; no terrified horses desperately whinnied, attempting to wheel away from the dreadful death that so often befell both the rider and his mount. This quietude was strange to him. But he concentrated on putting one weary foot in front of the other, as did his fellow parolees. Although a soldier's mentality had been ingrained in him through four long years of fighting, he was now expected to go on home as if the war had never happened. And that was what he was trying to do.

He had set out from Virginia in the company of several others, but within days their paths began to diverge, and only he and another Barbour County, Alabama, fellow, his good friend Jimmy Bridger, were left. Jimmy had been shot through the calf of his leg at Petersburg, but the Minie ball missed the bone, so he had had no need of a sawbones; his leg was still attached to his body. But every step hurt him, and the discomfort worsened with each passing day. He could only limp along, and after several days of this slow progress he insisted that Jackson go on without him.

"I ain't in no hurry," Jackson lied. "We'll get there all right. We'll just slow down a bit, that's all."

In early spring no wild berries had yet appeared, the apple and pear trees they came across were bare of fruit, and what little hardtack they had come away with was soon gone. Game had to sustain them, and killing game without a rifle was a challenge. But both were handy with the bowie knives they'd been permitted to keep, so they managed. They could not bring down a deer, but small prey were no match for hungry men who had learned how to throw a knife with deadly accuracy before they had learned how to shoot. They were no nearer to starvation than they had been throughout the war and hoped that on their journey home they would not ever be reduced to begging for food.

Because of Jimmy's wound, they had not traversed more than twenty-five miles in five days. They were in Charlotte County, near the Roanoke River, when sleet penetrated the lean-to of brush and branches they had constructed the night before, leaving them cold to the bone. Jackson's forebears had lived in North Carolina for generations before venturing south, but he had always lived in southeast Alabama, and he was sick to death of the frigid springs in the upper South.

"Down home it'll be warm by now," he muttered through chattering teeth.

Jimmy succumbed to a coughing spell and then said, "Down home I'd be under a sound roof. Minnie'd be a-settin a plate of biscuits and molasses in front of me. And a cup of real coffee, not that sorry substitute."

Minnie was his wife.

For a moment they thought on all the comforts of home.

"Well," Jackson said, standing up and trying to shake off the damp, "let's get on down the road."

But Jimmy could not get to his feet. He tried several times and sat back down. He began coughing hard.

"Now just a minute, here, Jackson," he rasped.

And he began coughing again.

Jackson reached for his hand and yanked him to his feet and pounded on his back, which did not alleviate the cough. He'd had much experience of sick comrades and put his hand to Jimmy's forehead.

"You're fevered," he said.

"Naw, I ain't."

Jackson put his arm around his shoulders and pulled him along.

"Let's go. Ain't nothing we can do for you here. There's sure to be a farm hereabouts. Come on."

And so they staggered along, Jackson allowing Jimmy to sit and rest every mile or so. Finally they saw a farmhouse up ahead with smoke coming out of the chimney. As they wandered into the yard, a woman was hanging up clothes in the chilly April wind. She reminded Jackson of his mother, with the same white-blond hair, but a bit younger.

"You boys lost? Ain't no regiments around here."

A girl of about twelve was helping her, and twin boys of six or seven ran up to stare at the ragged soldiers.

"No, ma'am. War's over, you know. My name's Jackson Knightley, and this here's Jimmy Bridger. We're heading home."

She keenly eyed them both, with particular attention to Jimmy. He had started coughing again.

"You're sick. You come on in the house."

She glanced at Jackson, who was waiting for an invitation.

"You, too."

She led them into a large room with a fireplace that extended nearly the width of a wall. A spinning wheel and a loom stood on the other side of the room. The woman indicated a chair, and Jimmy, further weakened by their three-mile trek that day, fell into it.

She directed the girl to fetch well water, threw some more wood into the fireplace, then poured water into the kettle suspended on the crane above the fire.

"Tea and honey," she said to Jimmy. "Always works."

The fragrant smells of recent cooking wafted through the room, and Jackson found it hard to keep his hands by his sides at the sight of a pan of cornbread set on the hob inside the fireplace and a jar of what appeared to be fruit preserves on the table. His mouth watered, and it was hard to stifle the urge to beg this woman for some of her food.

"I'm Mary Branson," she offered. "And this is Laura and Dick and Joe."

She fussed an interminable time over the tea making until she finally set a mug in front of Jimmy, liberally spooned honey into it, and expectantly watched as he took the first few sips.

"Better?"

"Yes, ma'am."

Jackson still stood, used to waiting for the wounded and ill to be tended to first.

"Now, then," Mary finally addressed him. "My grown son Zackery went into town today for supplies, and he'll be back just any minute now. He's overworked, with both my husband and his older brother gone off to the war. You could help us out by chopping up them logs out in the yard."

The logs were piled waist high to a tall man, and Jackson's belly grumbled with hunger as he contemplated how long it would take him to chop them up.

"I'll get to it right away," he said.

Mary heard the loud stomach noises and decided, "It can wait a bit. Seems like you could do with a good meal."

He felt like hugging her but restrained himself. If he had ever wondered what a ministering angel looked like, he wondered no more.

An ample helping of cornbread and canned corn and tomatoes was set before Jackson and devoured, washed down with coffee. The children marveled at this skinny person's appetite. Where did he put all that food?

Jimmy managed to swallow a piece of cornbread and drank more tea for his sore throat. Mary rubbed a warming salve on his leg wound. Then he lay gratefully on a corn shuck mattress pulled close to the hearth and snuggled under a warm quilt. He was soon asleep.

"Best thing for him," Mary said.

After the meal, she and her daughter finished hanging out the clothes, which Jackson doubted would dry before nightfall in the harsh wind, and he chopped up most of the wood and brought a good supply into the house. He walked out in the neglected fields with her and agreed to start work on clearing the rotting stubble from last year's crops the next day.

As the sun was setting, Mary began preparing supper. A pot of savory bean and onion soup flavored with pork had been simmering on the fire all day, occasionally stirred by Laura, whose job that was. Mary started mixing up flour, lard, baking powder, and buttermilk, and Jackson inwardly rejoiced at the sight of a woman wielding a rolling pin on a slab of biscuit dough. To distract himself from his appetite, he asked, "And so Zackery — he's due back this evening?"

Mary paused and wiped her hands on her apron. This man was a stranger, and she had intended keeping to the fiction that an adult male family member was on the near horizon. But there was something in Jackson's steady gaze, his compliant manner, the compassion he showed his friend, that made her trust him. It might turn out to be her undoing, but she decided to tell him the truth.

"I don't reckon my boy'll be home just yet. He ain't in town, Jackson. He went off to the war. My husband was kilt at Gettysburg. Then my eldest joined up, and he died, they tell me, of dysentery at a prison up north. Last fall when that letter come from the war office, Zack said by God he had to go, too, because the damn Yanks was killing too many of us and had to be stopped."

Mary turned back to her rolling pin and pounded the dough as if trying to pound sense into her boy.

"He weren't but fifteen, and I begged him not to go. Who's going to do the planting in the spring, I asked him. Who's going to take care of me and the other younguns? But my words fell on deaf ears. We've been barely hanging on here. It was all me and the younguns could do to plant half an acre of vegetables this year. But Zack was hell bent and determined to go, and he went. He was with the 18th Virginia Infantry."

She turned again to Jackson.

"You ever come upon any of those men?

Jimmy, who had been supine all day, stirred and raised himself up on an elbow.

"Why a course we did, didn't we, Jackson? Wasn't there some of them at Appomattox?"

The words "at Appomattox" were synonymous with "survived," and Jackson could see hope flicker in Mary's eyes. He frowned at Jimmy for giving this poor woman false hope.

"Maybe so. Don't rightly recall."

"But I'd swear I heard a roll call on that very regiment," Jimmy insisted. "We was all prisoners of war that day, ma'am," he added in a bragging way, taking some pride in their POW status. "But General Grant didn't hold us. We was all issued parole passes and told to go."

"Then why ain't he here by now?" Mary asked in an anxious tone. "*You're* here. So why ain't Zack – why ain't *he*? He should've been here by now!"

She brushed her sleeve across wet cheeks and went back to work.

Jackson shot Jimmy a look that said, *Now see what you went and done?* Toughened by war though they were, a woman's tears could still fell them. Glib, empty phrases of comfort were not in their vocabulary, so they simply remained respectfully silent.

Mary began forming the perfectly rolled dough into biscuits. A jar of butter the girl had dipped out of the large jug kept on a shelf of the well was set next to blackberry and strawberry preserves. Jackson felt ashamed of himself for focusing more attention on the prospect of a delectable meal than on the plight of this lone woman.

"Ma'am," he offered, "I'm a right poor cook, but I'll be glad to help out any way I can. Is there anything I can do?"

Mary sniffed.

"Well, you can start by brushing away them embers and ashes."

Jackson immediately cleared the fireplace floor. Mary set biscuits into an iron spider, then pushed the three-legged pot well into the fireplace.

"They should brown up pretty fast," she said.

They'll disappear pretty fast, too, Jackson thought, as he offered to make the coffee and Laura set the table.

After the men enjoyed the most satisfying meal they had eaten in longer than they could remember, Mary commented, "Maybe you fellas need to stay on till Jimmy's well enough to go."

Jackson was itching to be on the road to his own family's hearthside, but he acknowledged the truth of her words with a nod. In the wild rush of war he had had to leave far too many wounded and sick fellows behind, their moans and fevered looks tearing at his soul, even as he shouldered his rifle and shot other folks' friends and sons and brothers to pieces, as he had been trained and ordered to do. But now he could stay with Jimmy and see him safely home.

"That's mighty kind of you. I promise I'll help out as much as I can here, and so will Jimmy before we leave."

He had no doubt she would find plenty for them to do.

JIMMY'S COUGH WAS gone in a few days, and his fever was vanquished by drafts of Mary's gingerroot tea. For a couple of weeks while he regained strength and became better able to walk, he and Jackson enjoyed being bossed by a woman as they always were at home. Jackson's mother was not happy unless ordering her children about, and Minnie could make Jimmy toe the line with no trouble at all. So Mary provided them with a touch of home while they performed every chore they were assigned.

A bath in a tin tub was a rare luxury for the men, but from Mary's standpoint bathing was a prerequisite to their remaining in her house. As Dick commented soon after they arrived, "Them fellas stink worse than the hogs, Ma." She also allowed them the use of two of her most precious possessions, her husband's shaving brush and razor. For the duration of their stay, Jackson's silken-textured, pale brown hair was clean and combed, his face clean shaven, and Jimmy's untidy dark beard was exchanged for the neatly trimmed one he sported at home.

Mary could not replace their worn boots because her menfolk had gone off to war wearing the only ones they owned. But she did supply each of the men with a set of sturdy work shirts and jean-pants.

It was early May, and they knew every day their families' faces were turned eastward for the sight of a returning soldier who for once was one of their own. Jackson's brother Peter had been killed at Sharpsburg, and his brother David had died of typhoid at Elmira prison in New York. Jimmy's younger brother had perished at Gettysburg. As comfortable as Mary's home was and as much as they wanted to help her, it was not right to keep their own families waiting for the return of their surviving sons.

They had cleared two fields for Mary, planted more corn and some potatoes, repaired her barn roof, and cleaned out both chimneys in her house. They had daily fed and watered her livestock, including the sheep she kept for producing her own wool. They had sat with bowed heads as she prayed for her deceased loved ones and Zackery's return. There was nothing more they could do.

They had planned to leave early one morning, but a prized cow was giving birth, and Jimmy volunteered to be the midwife. The calf took its time making an entrance, but at last the men joined in the excitement as the children welcomed the new heifer. By the time Jimmy had washed up it was almost noon, and Mary insisted they stay to eat.

"Lord, but I'm a-gonna miss your cooking!" Jackson said over a plate of corn bread, grits, and pork.

"Well, at least now it ain't as cold as it's been a-bein'," Jimmy said consolingly. "So we can get on down the road without any of them freezing rains holding us up."

Laura began clearing away the dishes, and Mary set aside portions of food for the men to put in their haversacks.

"I want you boys to pack up as much food as you can," she said.

There weren't any restaurants for miles, and none anywhere that would feed them for free.

Suddenly Joe came running into the house, shouting, "Ma, here comes another one!"

"Another what?"

"Another one of them soldiers. See — he's almost to the gate!"

Laura ran out onto the porch before Mary and the men could get to the door and was screaming, "Oh, Mama! Mama! It's him! It's him!"

Mary's hand was to her heart as she stood in the doorway and stared unbelievingly at the towheaded young fellow who was running towards her. Her brain recorded that he had all of his limbs and was not limping as she began to scream his name.

Zackery enfolded his mother in his arms while the children clamored around them. Jackson and Jimmy teared up.

When she could speak, Mary said scoldingly, "Where have you been, boy? War's been over nearly a month. We thought — we thought — "

Zack nodded as they all filed into the house. He caught a whiff of the food, and his mother immediately fixed him a plate.

"I know, Ma. And I tried to get home right after Appomattox, I truly did."

"Told you so," Jimmy said to Jackson. "Told you they was there."

"But I got sick on the road and like to died. And then some folks took me in. An old man and his wife — older than you, Ma. My friends hauled me into their house, and those folks tended me till I got well. And that's why it took me so blessed long to get home."

"Angels," Mary said through tears. "Them folks're angels."

"Sure are," Zack agreed. "But that lady cain't cook near as good as you."

He began wolfing down food in Jackson style as his brothers stared at the beginnings of a scraggly beard on the face of this battle-tried veteran.

BY MID-JULY JACKSON was reunited with his parents and his sisters, Ellie and Maudie, and Micah, his youngest brother. His return helped his family cope with the loss of David and Peter. Two years after his homecoming, he married sixteen-year old Sophronia Goodman, a pretty strawberry blonde who had been a scrawny ten-year-old child when he went away. He looked to the future, establishing a farm and settling into married life.

But the carnage and suffering he had witnessed, the stench and horror of every battlefield he had miraculously walked away from, whether on the winning or losing side that day, would always haunt him. Only his stern Primitive Baptist God, who offered salvation to the chosen, even murderous sinners who repented, could give him any peace of mind. He would not know until the Judgment if he were one of the chosen. But when thoughts of men his true aim had sent to eternity disturbed his mind, he surely did repent.

Chapter 4

JULIA

A DEVOUT MAN, Jackson Knightley would have been regular in church attendance even if his grandfather, John Knightley, had not been one of the founders of Galilee Primitive Baptist Church more than forty years before. Within the walls of this simple, unadorned sanctuary, where people expressed their humility through the washing of one another's feet, where God, not money or power, was worshipped, he was able to repent in peace and quietly pray for salvation in a place far removed from the horrors he had witnessed. Although seven years had passed since he had killed a man, he still struggled with disturbing memories of war. In church, it had always been easier to put those memories aside. But that changed the day he met the Yankee schoolteacher.

JULIA TENPENNY, A Freedman's Bureau schoolteacher in the farming community of Crossvine in Barbour County, resided with Dr. Caleb Royal and his wife, Ilsa. The Royals shared a household with Ilsa's father, Dr. Gerhardt Nordhoff, in Eufaula, a small town set on a high bluff above the Chattahoochee River. Named after a band of Creeks that had once inhabited the area, Eufaula boasted magnificent homes and had become a major port.

 Julia made a habit of visiting different churches in the area, and on a Sunday in August 1872 she drove one of the Royals' buggies to Galilee Primitive Baptist Church located not far from New Road School where she taught. Because she was accustomed to handling the reins since she was a young girl, Caleb allowed her to use one of his buggies in traveling to and from Crossvine and to get about in town. His only requirement was that she always take one of his gentler horses.

She had attended other Primitive Baptist churches and was familiar with the austere atmosphere: no musical instruments, no cushioned seats, no embroidered altar cloths, no fancy vestments. The song leader used a tuning fork to sound out the first note of each song for the alto, soprano, tenor, and bass lead singers in turn, then beat time with one arm as the congregation joined in, reading the shaped notes in their hymnals. She knew that Primitive Baptist ministers were referred to as "elders," and Elder Reuben Faraday's sermon was predictably fiery, leaving Julia with the feeling that she should search the depths of her soul and beg forgiveness for any sins she had unknowingly committed at the earliest possible moment.

On the day she visited the church it was veteran recognition day, and several congregants came forward to share their regimental information and praise God for their deliverance and safe return home. She listened with the full attention and respect due to each one of them, but was struck by something Jackson Knightley said. He was not more than five-foot-eight, but his slender build made him appear taller. He had an ascetic, clean-shaven face, and his carefully brushed light brown hair reached almost to his shoulders. He murmured in a low voice, and she had to strain to hear. He was at Winchester, she heard, and Second Manassas and Dandridge and someplace else her ear could not distinguish. And then she heard, "And I was at the Battle of Cold Harbor in June 1864." Suddenly her blood ran cold, and she found herself staring at him, her heart pounding.

Certainly she knew that every man standing there had probably shot and killed at least one, and perhaps dozens, of Union soldiers. At any similar event in the North, she would be looking at men who had killed an equal number of Rebels. What unraveled her was that for the first time she was encountering a man who had fought at the battle where her fiancé, Jeremy Gaither, had died. Jackson had occupied that same space, had been on that particular battleground at the exact same time as Jeremy. He was present when the bullet struck him, when he fell to the earth in his death struggle, when his last breath escaped his body.

Jeremy was one of thousands, and to Jackson he would have been just another of the faceless enemy coming at him and his comrades with deadly weapons, intent on killing them. She realized all that. Still she could not take her eyes from Jackson's face as he walked back down the aisle, past the pew where she was sitting. She found herself turning to watch him as he took a seat a few rows behind her.

She was impatient for the service to be over. When the a capella-sung notes of the last hymn had finally sounded, she bounded up in an unladylike fashion, almost losing her hat, which was pinned onto her abundant, impossible-to-tame hair, and hurried out of the church. Jackson was untying his mare's reins from the hitching post when she approached him.

"Mr. Knightley," she said, extending her gloved hand. "My name is Julia Tenpenny. I'm a teacher at New Road School."

"The colored school."

There was no rancor in his voice, only confirmation.

"Yes. And I — well, I think I heard you say you fought at Cold Harbor."

Jackson's eyes narrowed.

"I fought at a lot of places."

"Well, yes, I heard you say that. But — "

"War's over, Miss Tenpenny. No sense in talking about it now. People always want us to talk about it. Honest to God, the best thing to do is to forget it."

If Julia were the typical young woman of her generation she would have blushed deeply at this rebuff, apologized, and walked away. But Victorian constraints did not shackle her. She was an educator, a torch bearer of knowledge, and she had the courage and tenacity to perform her duties among a conquered people — many of whom, she knew, must hate her and all she stood for. So instead of turning away, she looked directly into the eyes of this somber veteran and said what she had to say.

"Mr. Knightley," she said firmly. "I don't mean to intrude on your privacy. I cannot even imagine what experiences you had in the war, and I am deeply sorry you had to endure them. I only wanted to say — my fiancé, Jeremy Gaither, died at Cold Harbor. He was with the 20th Massachusetts Infantry. We know nothing of the details of his death, only that the Union losses were very great, and he was among the fallen. I — so often, I have tried to imagine his death. If he suffered. Or if it were mercifully sudden. Can you tell me anything at all about the battle — anything I might share with his parents?"

Jackson scratched the back of his neck where a hornet sting suffered in the field was beginning to heal. Then he leaned his head back a bit and looked down at this short, plump Yankee gal from underneath his broad-brimmed hat. Of all the battles he'd been in, Cold Harbor had been the worst. And she wanted details! But war had not calcified his heart. He saw the supplication in her face and could not simply turn away.

"Jeremy was so proud to be going to war," Julia went on. "He was carrying his father's old sword from the Mexican-American War. It was truly beautiful. The hilt was engraved with an eagle's head, with a blued blade, etched with scrollwork."

Jackson chewed on his lip for a second before he spoke. An emotion that might have been pity darkened his face.

"Swords wasn't much use at Cold Harbor. We got down in trenches and just mowed them down."

"Mowed — "

"That's what I said. Nigh on to 7,000 Union casualties to our 1,500 within a few hours."

Julia blanched, her strong backbone suddenly weak. Jackson reached out and grabbed her elbow, afraid she was going to keel over.

"But — how could that have happened? Did they not defend themselves? I don't understand."

"You cain't defend yourself against what you cain't see. They didn't know we was down in them trenches. They didn't even know about the trenches."

"But I still don't see how — "

Jackson released her arm, having determined she was going to remain upright. He had said enough about Cold Harbor. He did not want to say anymore. He set one foot in a stirrup and mounted his horse.

"Maybe the folks you should be asking about how that coulda happened ain't us Rebel soldiers. Maybe you should be asking the Union generals."

He touched the brim of his hat courteously.

"Good day, Miss Tenpenny."

THE BATTLE OF Cold Harbor took place in central Virginia from May 31 to June 12, 1864, over the same ground as the 1862 Battle of Gaines Mill, sometimes referred to as the First Battle of Cold Harbor. But it is the bloodbath that occurred on the morning of June 3, 1864, that is remembered as one of the most horrific and lopsided battles of the Civil War.

The mismanagement of Generals Grant and Meade, whose corps commanders failed to reconnoiter the Confederate position; the skillful maneuvering of General Lee, whose engineers and troops frenziedly constructed a complex labyrinth of trenches while the Federals repeatedly delayed the main attack; the inexperience of Grant's 108,000-strong army, many of whom were new recruits, versus the well-honed fighting skills of the 59,000 seasoned Confederate veterans resulted in a staggering number of Federal losses in a shockingly brief time. Compounding the debacle, the Union leaders refused to concede defeat for days, while scores of Federal wounded who might have been saved lay between the lines without medical attention, food, or water. Most were corpses by the time Grant capitulated and hostilities were halted on June 7.

JACKSON KNIGHTLEY DID not mention his conversation with Julia Tenpenny to his wife Sophronia. He never discussed the war before his wife or their children. Their newborn, Rebecca, was but two days old and Sophronia was still recovering strength, but thanks to her sisters, who had brought abundant dishes of food for dinner and supper that day, a meal was on the table when he got home. Rebecca and two-year-old Lee were napping. Sophronia took his coat and hat and hung them up. Then they held hands while Jackson said grace.

"So who all got up?" Sophronia asked as she passed the spoon bread.

"Pike Sherman. Seth Garner. Jimmy Bridger."

"And you?"

She was not sure. Some years he had remained seated, close-mouthed even about sharing regimental information.

"And me."

He delved into the liberally seasoned rabbit stew, savoring every bite. He was a man who never took plentiful food for granted.

"Yankee schoolteacher was there."

"That Miss Tenpenny?"

He nodded.

Sophronia sipped her buttermilk, sorry she had missed meeting the teacher. She had encountered her on a few occasions in Eufaula, but only to nod to. She would like to have met her, but Sophronia was a retiring sort of person, unused to approaching strangers.

"She's been here a while," Sophronia commented. "You reckon she plans to stay on?"

"Doubt it. I hear tell she's moving back up north pretty soon."

Sophronia was disappointed. So now she would likely never meet the Yankee teacher.

JACKSON STAYED UP late that night, smoking his corncob pipe out on the porch. Even though a few short hours hence the rooster would stridently announce the dawn, he did not want to sleep and surrender to God knows what nightmares. Scenes he had thought buried beyond retrieval had been resurrected that morning in the churchyard, and they relentlessly played out in his mind. Despite his efforts to focus on the manifold blessings he enjoyed in the here and now, rogue thoughts intruded, casting him back.

He found himself reliving a June morning in Virginia. A heavy ground fog hampered sight. Despite the date, at that early hour there was a chill in the air. His tattered butternut jacket provided little warmth. His filthy, frayed, and torn jean-cloth pants had long since replaced the military trousers he had been issued in '61. His boots, taken off the body of a Yank in '63, and thus of better quality than Confederate-issued ones, had served him well through many a long march, but were beginning to fall apart.

Despite his attire, his aim was as true as it had ever been, his eyes as sharp as the days when he had shot rabbits as a boy. The contents of his battered cartridge box were newly manufactured at the Richmond Arsenal, and his Pattern 1853 Enfield rifle-musket was in excellent condition.

Breakfast had been a scalding tin cupful of coffee substitute and a piece of hoe cake. Now his belly rumbled as he positioned himself better against the earth-and-log barricade. Hunger had been his companion down all the days of the war. He had disciplined himself to disregard it.

He lay securely entrenched behind the breastwork, feeling less vulnerable than he had on any other battlefield. Unless he were foolhardy enough to stand up, no Yankee bullet could find him.

Before the fog cleared enough for him to see, he heard the command to fire. Shouts and screams were nearly drowned out by cannon and artillery fire, and the acrid, sulfuric smell of gunpowder clogged the air as gradually the fog cleared away. He wished to God it had not. He did not want to witness this, let alone be a part of it. Because this was not battle: this was murder.

There was no hand-to-hand fighting, no exchange of volleys. Even though some of the Federals were equipped with seven-shot Spencer repeating carbines, they could not overcome the disadvantage of being easy targets for the entrenched Confederates. As line after line of Union soldiers charged, the Confederate fire dropped most of them before they could even aim their weapons. In minutes, thousands lay dead or wounded.

Jackson was reloading his weapon when he looked up and saw a soldier drop his gun, perhaps realizing it was of little use, and begin waving a sword with a polished blue blade that caught the first gleam of sunlight. In his new blue uniform, unsoiled and unbloodied, every shiny brass button in place, and gripping the finely crafted sword that in a different kind of battle might have saved his life, he was a striking figure. And a pathetically easy target.

"Get down, fool!" Jackson yelled, even as he shouldered his rifle and aimed.

Perhaps seized by hysteria, the sword-brandishing soldier ran on, miraculously crossing considerable ground before Jackson's rifle took him down. He was not dead. He dropped the sword and grasped his bloody left side, his hands frantically clawing at his body, trying to tell if he were gut shot; then he lay writhing on the ground.

By noon, the Battle of Cold Harbor was finished. It was several days before Jackson's company moved on. The screams and moans of the wounded Federals left to suffer in the field as their leaders dithered over the terms of a ceasefire troubled even the most callous of the men. And for Jackson, the image of the maddened young fellow with the blued sword, the sound of his groans as he lay suffering on the bloody field, would never be cleansed from his memory. Most especially since now, thanks to Julia Tenpenny, he knew his name.

JULIA TENPENNY WAS eighteen in the spring of 1864 when scholarly, twenty-one-year-old Jeremy Gaither, who aspired to be a history teacher, proposed. A Harvard student who had joined the 20th Massachusetts Regiment, known as the Harvard Regiment, in August 1861, Jeremy was a rangy, lantern-jawed young man with a ready smile. He had been Julia's friend since childhood. Unlike other boys of their acquaintance, he recognized that her keen mind, strong principles, and kind heart more than compensated for her somewhat dowdy appearance. He was delighted when she agreed to become his wife.

With brilliant strategist and tactician Ulysses S. Grant now in charge of the Union forces, many northerners believed the war was nearing its end, and Jeremy was confident he would come back to her. But on June 3, 1864, he died at Cold Harbor.

The war took the lives of hundreds of thousands of men, and thus, with Jeremy gone, Julia — like so many women of her generation — had no one to marry. But although she was fated never to have children of her own, she nurtured and educated scores of children, first in Alabama and then back home in Little Turnbridge, a village on the outskirts of Boston where her family had lived for generations.

Julia's father, Thaddeus, was an Episcopal clergyman who at forty-five had married an attractive, childless, forty-three-year-old widow. Through twenty-two years of marriage, Anne had experienced the feelings of inadequacy common to barren women. Her late husband, a lumberjack of a man who owned and operated a grain mill, had expected to sire many sons and would have welcomed a daughter or two as well. But year after year the cradle Anne had inherited from her mother remained empty. While the miller loved his wife and did not blame her, his disappointment and that of his family, who *did* blame her, had been a continual trial for Anne. Thus it was with not only joy, but utter amazement, that she realized she was pregnant just six months into her new marriage. Thaddeus was likewise astonished and overjoyed.

And for Anne, there was vindication as well. Her late husband, then — not she — had been the reason for the empty cradle. At times during her pregnancy, gazing at the gentle, physically uncommanding vicar and reflecting upon the robust, athletic miller, Anne laid a hand on her rounded belly and smiled at God's mysterious ways.

Julia proved to be a plain, exceptionally bright child with enormous blue eyes who was fiercely protective of her pretty, brown-eyed baby sister, Louisa, born three years after her own much celebrated arrival. Julia learned to read by the time she was four, and Thaddeus was hard pressed to keep her supplied with books. She also loved to dig in the dirt with her mother, an avid gardener, and by the age of six was cultivating a small flower garden of her own. Louisa preferred dolls to dirt and was only interested in a book if her sister were willing to read it to her. Despite the fact that Julia inherited Thaddeus's plain looks and keen mind, while Louisa was beautiful and as indifferent to scholarship as her mother, the girls bonded as deeply as twins.

The family was still grieving over the loss of Julia's fiancé when in 1866 she announced her intention to become a Freedman's Bureau teacher — as she was sure Jeremy would have done.

"You will melt in that dreadful heat!" Louisa cried. "And how will you be treated? Those are the very people who killed Jeremy."

"Now Louisa," Thaddeus intervened. "The war is over. It's time for the country to heal. And it's not Confederate soldiers Julia will be teaching, but ex-slaves. How can you not support her in this?"

"But if she meets with an accident — or becomes ill — she'll be so far away from everyone she knows. Papa, you cannot let her go!"

Anne put her arms around Louisa's shoulders.

"Julia will be doing God's work. She will be in God's care."

Louisa tearfully shook her head.

"But I don't see why she must go so far away to do God's work. There are plenty of needy people right here in Massachusetts."

"And there are plenty of charities already assisting those folks," Julia pointed out. "And in any event, I won't be leaving for quite some time. I have to finish my training first."

Thaddeus smiled at his eldest daughter with evident pride. He lacked the missionary spirit, preferring the quiet, steady path of vicar in a small church. But he admired a questing soul and encouraged Julia in her desire to go where she felt she was most needed.

Louisa could not grasp such an attitude and was exasperated with both of her parents for encouraging her sister to go and live among people she regarded as hateful and backward. She searched for another argument and found one.

"Perhaps Julia won't come to any harm down there. But what about you and Mama, Papa? You're not young folks anymore. You need Julia and me. I know that *I* would never leave you. Didn't I turn down the proposal of that haberdasher who wanted me to go and live in Ohio?"

Julia laughed, and her parents could not help smiling.

"He bored you to tears, darling. And as you pointed out, he was not half as handsome as John."

Louisa and John Atwater, a clerk in his father's mercantile business, were engaged to be married the following year, when she would turn eighteen. John had mercifully escaped combat, serving in the Ordnance Department of the Union Army during the war.

"Well, still — I would never — "

"I am not leaving for good, Louisa. Freedman's Bureau teachers are only assigned for two or three years. And Hubert and Clemmie have solemnly promised to help you keep an eye on our parents."

Hubert was Thaddeus's favorite nephew, who was like a son to him and had always been close to both girls. Clemmie was his devoted wife, Clementine.

Julia took her petulant sister's hands, resisting the pleading look that so often resulted in her doing whatever Louisa asked.

"I must go, Louisa. I must. From everything I have heard, from everything I have read, the freed people have a desperate need for education. And I feel it will be not only a duty, but a privilege, to help them all I can."

Her voice nearly failed her as she added, "Jeremy gave his life to end slavery. How can I not give a small part of my life, a mere two or three years, when Jeremy gave everything he had?"

For once bested by her sister, Louisa put on a brave smile and murmured, "You are right, Julia. You must go."

JULIA ARRIVED IN Barbour County, Alabama, in 1868, alight with the desire to help educate those who had been denied an education for hundreds of years. At New Road School in the farming community of Crossvine, she would be teaching as many adults as children. Freed people of all ages flocked to the schools. During the decade following the war, approximately 3,000 schools were established across the South by Freedman's Bureaus, missionary societies, and black people themselves, evidencing the unquenchable thirst for knowledge among those who were so long denied an education.

Julia was grateful for the assistance of Dr. Caleb Royal and his family, who provided her a home during her stay. When Ft. Sumter was fired upon in April 1861, Caleb was a medical student at Harvard University. He was also engaged to Miss Ilsa Nordhoff of Eufaula, Alabama. They had met through his sister at the finishing school both girls attended. Of but medium height, stockily built, with an unremarkable face made only slightly more interesting by a well-tended blond mustache, Caleb's wit and gracious manners were what attracted Ilsa. And while she was something of a beauty, her hazel-green eyes and fair skin contrasting with her dark hair, it was her compassion for others, which matched his own, and her strong anti-slavery beliefs, which soon created a bond between them. Within weeks after their meeting, they were engaged.

Ilsa had been sent north by her father, who saw war coming and privately believed the South would be defeated. Gerhardt Nordhoff, a physician, was a Swiss immigrant whose friends had coaxed him across the ocean to Boston after he lost his wife to Bright's disease when Ilsa was six years old. He had planned to set up a practice there, but during a reckless period borne of grief he had won a piece of property in Barbour County in a poker game. Deciding to travel to Eufaula to look at his property before selling it, he arrived at the tail end of winter, when Bostonians still huddled before fires or trudged through ice and snow. He had been unprepared for the beauty of an early spring and the mild climate, so like a Swiss summer. The property was comprised of several acres of land situated on a rise, with a striking view of the Chattahoochee River, where he could envision a house one day. It seemed a good place to raise a little girl, and he decided to put out his shingle in the town and bring his daughter south.

He prospered, and on the land where the unlucky poker player had planned to establish a farm he built a two-story home with fourteen-foot tall windows across the front and a wide, wraparound veranda, its roof supported by square, elaborately carved Italian columns. Two rooms were reserved for his medical practice.

A freethinker, Gerhardt was annoyed by Bible thumpers and disapproved of slaveholders, but refused treatment to no one, white or black. Few slaves received professional medical treatment, but when one of them was brought to him he provided the same competent, compassionate care he gave to everyone. Confounded by the notion that it was legally and morally acceptable for one human being to own another, he impressed upon Ilsa that in the country of their birth there had never been a single slave. "Then why do we not go and live there, Papa?" she had sensibly asked at the age of thirteen. This stumped him. He was a good man. He was a compassionate man. And if his conviction that slavery was evil was so strong, why did he remain here? The majority of his patients were yeoman farmers or trades people, but it was true that the prosperity he enjoyed was partly gained through affluent patients who were slave owners. He finally admitted to himself that his anti-slavery sentiments were not strong enough to outweigh his love for his southern home. His conscience was salved by the belief that the anti-slavery movement was gaining strength and that slavery would inevitably be abolished.

Gerhardt spoke out against secession, but while he was a respected doctor he would always remain a foreigner, who most believed should keep his nose out of their business. And even if he were a native Alabamian, his voice would have been drowned out by the powerful Eufaula Regency, a group of wealthy lawyers and plantation owners who used their substantial political influence to promote secession and secure the election of secessionist candidates, notably Governor John Gill Shorter.

When Alabama seceded, Gerhardt entreated his daughter to remain in the North and gave his blessing for her marriage to Caleb. Caleb was pressed into service at a field hospital during the war, while Ilsa lived with his family. In 1867, the Royals came south so that Caleb could join Gerhardt in his medical practice, and at Gerhardt's invitation they took up residence in his commodious home.

Since the end of the war, Gerhardt had witnessed the plight of many freed slaves who left the plantations but had no place to go. Some simply wandered from place to place until, defeated by lack of opportunity and the threat of starvation, they returned to their former owners, who were desperately in need of workers. Although the freed people were now paid wages, they were little better off than they had been before.

The Freedman's Bureau, established by an act of Congress in March 1865, provided not only schooling but food relief and medical care to many ex-slaves, as well as impoverished whites; Gerhardt donated his services in a clinic established by the Bureau for this purpose. But he shared with the Royals his belief that the greatest need was for education. Caleb and Ilsa enthusiastically agreed that the best way for them to help the freed people was to provide room and board for a Freedman's Bureau teacher.

When Miss Julia Tenpenny stepped across their threshold in August of 1868, Ilsa observed that her traveling clothes were rumpled by long hours in the stagecoach and that her abundant, flyaway hair, the color of taffy, was in dire need of a brushing and a great many more hair pins. As Julia set down her reticule, Caleb, who had met the stagecoach, retrieved her luggage from the buggy, and Ilsa and Gerhardt stepped forward to greet her.

Gerhardt shook her hand, while the two women exchanged hugs.

"Come, come," he said, taking her arm, "we have tea and some of Ilsa's pound cake waiting for you in the parlor."

"So kind of you," she responded.

Noting his corpulent build, she suspected his fondness for cake equaled hers.

"We have been looking forward to your arrival for months," Ilsa said.

She was struck by Julia's large, lavender-blue eyes, which were the only attractive feature in her plain, round face.

"I just finished my training two weeks ago," Julia said. "I have been longing to come south for the past two years."

"Well, now you are here, Miss Tenpenny," Caleb said with a smile as he entered the room. "And we are very glad to have you."

Within an hour the little group were on a first-name basis, and it was soon apparent that mutual interests and beliefs augured well for friendship. Ilsa showed Julia to her comfortable room, with a large window overlooking the back lawn.

Julia had packed more books than clothing, warned beforehand of the scarcity of school materials. As she helped her unpack, Ilsa found this willingness to share her books admirable, but doubted that her pupils would be reading *A Journal of the Plague Year* or *Vanity Fair* or *A Discourse on the Book of Ecclesiastes* anytime soon.

Neatness was ingrained in Ilsa, and so it was with difficulty she resisted an urge to brush strands of Julia's hair back from her face and help her tuck her blouse more neatly into the waistband of her wrinkled skirt as she said, "You know that most of your students are illiterate, don't you? Did you bring any simple books — picture books, perhaps?"

Julia paused in the midst of her haphazard stacking of books on the floor, as the two shelves in the one small cabinet were already full.

"Oh yes, I do have some primers from a Boston school."

She set the remainder of the books on top of a teetering pile and began unpacking her few clothes, which Ilsa placed in the wardrobe for her.

"I quite understand that the children will require a lot of help," Julia said.

"The children? But surely you know adults attend the school as well."

Julia gazed at her calmly through her extraordinary eyes.

"I do indeed. I have a detailed letter from my predecessor describing the classroom and many of the students to me. He wrote that he was leaving because in his opinion it is impossible to teach young children and grown people at the same time in a one-room school with inadequate materials. He was wrong. It is not impossible. But it will undeniably be a challenge. And Ilsa," she said with a twinkle in her eye, "I love a challenge!"

She pulled the last items out of her trunk, a large world map and an abacus. She unfolded the beautifully illustrated map and spread it across the bed for Ilsa to see.

"This is my father's favorite map — he wanted my students to be able to learn from it. Father is a dedicated armchair traveler. We've spent many an hour planning trips to this or that country, to all of the great cities across the seven seas."

"And have you ever visited other countries?"

Julia smiled affectionately at the memory of her father poring over the map.

"Oh, no. Father is a vicar of a very small church, and while I was growing up, after making sure my little sister and I were properly cared for, my parents applied every extra penny to their charitable works."

This statement was made with obvious pride.

"We did travel to Philadelphia once, and we've been to Washington twice. My father loves our nation's capital. But we've never been abroad, no."

She picked up the map, carefully folded it, and set it on top of the wardrobe.

"We have always traveled in our imaginations, through the map and through the books we read. When we planned a trip to Spain, we read Cervantes. When we decided to visit Rome, we read up on Michelangelo and spent an afternoon strolling through the Italian masters section of the Museum of Art in Boston. And of course we read the *Adventures of Marco Polo* when we mapped out our trip to the Forbidden City."

"And you want to teach your students about all of that, don't you," Ilsa said.

Julia reflected a moment.

"I don't expect any of them to love the same things I do. I only want to instill a love of reading. With that, there is no limit to what they can learn or where their imaginations may take them. But I am practical minded, Ilsa. We will begin at the beginning, with our ABCs."

The following morning Julia was installed as the new teacher at New Road School in the Crossvine community. There were seventeen pupils, ranging in age from six to forty-seven. Not in the least doubting that this classroom would be the greatest challenge of her life, she mentally rolled up her sleeves and took charge. The first order of business was to learn everyone's name. She informed them that children up to the age of eighteen would be addressed by their first names. Students eighteen and over would be called by their last names, with the title of "Mrs.," "Miss," or "Mr." She correctly surmised that this was the first time anyone in the room had been addressed by a title and last name. This set the tone for the mutual respect that would prevail in the classroom.

Julia realized that she and her colleagues in similar schools throughout the South were often held in little higher regard than carpetbaggers, and some teachers were branded troublemakers for urging their students to demand their rights. But attacking illiteracy occupied most of her time, and she also tried to teach a smattering of history, geography, and mathematics to her students — equally eager but diverse in their ability to grasp the subject matter. It took every ounce of her time and energy to perform the job she was sent to do: teach. Through education, she firmly believed, would come opportunity, more certainly than through any other means.

And in teaching, Julia found fulfillment. When forty-one-year-old Joe Hargrove wrote his name for the first time in his life, beaming with pride, and eleven-year-old Rose Grimes finished every lesson in the primer and eagerly looked to her for a more challenging book, Julia experienced a deep sense of purpose. Her fiancé had been training to be a teacher when he joined the Union army, and it was partly in the spirit of lifting the fallen torch that she had followed in his footsteps;

but in Crossvine she discovered that she had truly found her calling.

While always regarded as an outsider, Julia was not ostracized in Eufaula or Crossvine or other surrounding communities because it was apparent that she did not view the defeated southerners as enemies. She saw them as people struggling to recover from the devastation of war — struggling, sometimes in vain, to overcome the poverty into which war had plunged them.

AFTER MEETING JACKSON Knightley that August morning in 1872, Julia found herself hoping that his family was among those who had not merely survived the war but were prospering. She was afraid she had offended him with her probing questions, and on the Sunday following their conversation she decided to try to make amends. Through Caleb, who served rural families as well as those in town, she learned that Jackson owned a farm on the outskirts of Crossvine, and he gave her directions. He mentioned that Jackson had a two-year-old son and a newborn daughter. He offered to take her there, but she felt it would be inconsiderate to tie up the doctor's Sunday afternoon when he had little enough time with his family as it was. Ilsa urged her to leave the Knightley place well before dark, and Julia assured her she would.

Julia chose not to arrive empty handed. Louisa, married now five years and the mother of two, knitted exquisite, finely-detailed garments. Once a year, she and her knitting circle produced a boxful of clothing and toys for the New Road families. Leaving Louisa, her dearest companion in the world, had been hard, but frequent letters kept them close, and Julia would soon return home for good.

Before she set out for the Knightly homestead, Julia searched through the box and found a delicate pink cap and sweater with a matching receiving blanket and a small yarn horse, brown with a bright red mane.

The aroma of Sophronia's cooking still flavored the air when she welcomed Julia into the cooking and dining cabin. The home consisted of two log cabins connected by a breezeway, or dogtrot, under a common roof. Sophronia had changed out of her dark blue Sunday dress into her workaday calico. Her black poke bonnet with the satin ribbon was hanging on a peg on the wall, and her everyday bonnet with the wider bill to shade her face in the field hung beside it. Her strawberry blond hair was worn in two simple braids fastened on top of her head. She had just cleared the table when Julia arrived.

Sophronia put the toy horse in Lee's eager hands and then admired Louisa's intricately patterned handiwork.

"I'm sorry it's still too warm for her to wear them. But first frost — "

"It'll come soon enough," Jackson said.

The family had been to church together for the first time since Sophronia's lying-in. Julia had been careful to arrive well past dinner time and not too close to supper to avoid interfering with cooking and to spare them the necessary courtesy of asking her to share either meal. She felt her visit was something of an intrusion. She had no intention of asking Jackson any more questions; in fact, she felt she had been unkind at their first meeting in dredging up dreadful memories. The small gifts were not much, but she hoped he might consider them a form of apology.

Today, she felt sure his native taciturnity would not be breached, and she accepted that.

As soon as she had handed the gifts to Sophronia and taken a seat in a cane-bottom chair, toddler Lee trained his devastatingly charming gaze on her and lifted his hands in her direction.

"Up!" he commanded.

She obeyed, pulling him onto her lap, and treated him to a game of "Ride a little horsey up to town," bouncing him on her lap, then pretend-dropping him through her knees at "hurry back, hurry back, don't you fall down!" After several repetitions of this, she took his pudgy fingers and pulled on each in an old finger-naming game, beginning with the thumb — "Tom Thumpkins, Betty Watkins, Long Daniel, Bill Wiggins," and ending with the smallest finger — "Little Dick!" Lee promptly offered his other hand. After they finished the game, he yanked her bonnet off her head.

"Lee!" Sophronia scolded.

Julia smilingly set the bonnet on his head and tied it under his chin.

Jackson watched this Yankee girl playing with his child, his smiling wife enjoying the novelty of a newcomer in the house, and reflected as he often did on the absolute stupidity of war that had divided Julia's people from his people and caused them to slaughter one another.

Sophronia was engaged in a lively conversation with Julia. As they talked, she rocked Rebecca in a cradle by her chair.

Julia enlightened her on the latest Boston fashions, while explaining that the folks in her hometown of Little Turnbridge were not always fashionably clad. Then she described bustling Boston Harbor, with its majestic ships, and some of the imposing homes on Beacon Hill.

"Well, I declare," Sophronia murmured more than once.

Jackson was enjoying his after-dinner pipe, relaxed in his cotton work shirt, jean-pants and suspenders. He knew how much Sophronia enjoyed female conversation and considerately waited until it seemed his wife had gleaned every possible bit of information about Boston and its environs that she could. Then, to Julia's surprise, he invited her to see his scuppernong arbor.

Julia glanced at Sophronia, who indicated with a smile and a wave of her hand that she should go on without her. The sun was still high. Jackson slapped on his hat, and Julia retrieved her bonnet from Lee.

The arbor was located about thirty yards behind the house, near a shallow creek that ran through the property. Clusters of the plump, round green fruit, some burnished with gold, hung from every vine. The sweetness of the grapes was intensified by the thick, tart skin one had to bite through to reach the delectable center. Eating scuppernongs required effort, but it was worth it.

"Started harvesting them yesterday," Jackson explained.

"I never heard of these before I came here," Julia said. "But now I believe they are my favorite fruit."

"Got a couple of baskets full in the house. I'll give you some to take with you."

Julia was delighted not only at the thought of a bowl of scuppernongs for dessert that evening, but also because it appeared Jackson was not as upset about her questioning him at the church as she had feared he was.

"How long have you been growing grapes?"

"My father has been growing them for twenty-five years. He planted this arbor in '61. It was here a-waitin for me when I come home in '65. July it was."

She glanced up at him quizzically.

"But I understood you to say you were paroled at Appomattox a day or so after the surrender in April."

"Yes, ma'am, I was. Walked home. It's a pretty far piece. Took more than two months to get here."

"Oh."

They walked up and down the rows together as he explained how the plants were trained upon the arbor poles.

"I suppose Mrs. Knightley will preserve a lot of these."

"She will. But most of them go into the wine."

Julia had heard of Jackson's avocation and knew he reputedly made some of the best wine in the county. He invited her to pick a few grapes to get a feel for the harvesting of them, and she did so.

"Don't reckon school teachers do much planting and picking," he commented.

"Now, there's where you are wrong!"

Her fervid response surprised him.

"I have always, from the time I was a young girl, kept a garden, Mr. Knightley. Mostly flowers — but I have grown some very fine squash and tomatoes, as well."

Jackson grinned.

"Why, Miss Tenpenny, I do believe you are a farmer!"

"Well, if being a farmer means knowing how to properly plant seeds, nurture the seedlings, and harvest the plants at just the right moment, then I certainly am."

Jackson was silent for some moments, then put one hand on an arbor post as if he needed support. He had been troubled by his first encounter with Julia and regretted the rudeness with which he had treated her. It had occurred to him that he would welcome an opportunity to speak with her further, never imagining that he would ever have the chance. But now Providence had sent her to him.

To Julia, Jackson appeared to be thinking deep thoughts and having difficulty putting them into words. It was now clear to her that the arbor tour was not the only reason he had asked her outside.

"Miss Tenpenny, I wanted to speak with you alone. I don't never talk about the war in front of my family. Now, I know you — it was hard for you to come up to me and ask about the battle where your sweetheart died. And I was short with you."

"Oh, but Mr. Knightley — that was all right, really. I understood."

"No, ma'am, you didn't. Nobody that wasn't there could ever understand what it was like. And how hard it is to forget."

Julia again felt uncomfortable that in questioning him she had opened old wounds.

He read her expression and wished he could explain himself better.

"I don't mean to say there's not ary a reason folks should ask questions, especially where loved ones they lost is concerned. All I'm a-sayin is, it's hard to talk about."

"Mr. Knightley, I promise I won't ever — "

Jackson held up his palm to shush her.

"It's all right, Miss Tenpenny — "

"Julia. Please."

"All right then, Julia. And as you're a farmer, too, I guess you can call me Jackson."

She smiled and nodded.

The heat was becoming less bearable by the minute, but mercifully a late afternoon breeze found them. Julia enjoyed the soughing of the pines and the rustle of the grapevines as the wind brushed her face. Just then Sophronia stood at the back door and beckoned them in, holding up a jug of cider which had been cooled in the well.

Jackson nodded to her and shouted, "In a minute," then turned back to the schoolteacher.

"I just want to say that I — well, I'm afraid to say this for fear of upsetting you. Julia, the reason I wanted to talk to you was because — "

She was appalled to see tears in his eyes.

"Julia, I've thought and thought since I seen you last, and I do believe I seen Jeremy at Cold Harbor."

Julia clutched her hand to her heart.

"Alive?" she asked.

He nodded and whispered.

"Yes."

She struggled to speak, her voice tear stained.

"But how could you possibly know it was him? There were so many soldiers — "

Jackson wiped the dampness off his face. It was ridiculous to shed tears for a Union soldier who had killed who knew how many Rebels before he got to Cold Harbor. But his sadness was as much for the young woman before him as it was for the one she had lost. She would probably never have what he and Sophronia had — what they now, five years into their marriage, took for granted: shared joy and grief, the pleasures of the marriage bed, children. Julia would more than likely never have these things and certainly would never have them with her Jeremy. It was several moments before he could master his emotions and answer her question.

"You're right a course. There was thousands there. Maybe it weren't Jeremy. But I have to tell you I did see a Yankee waving a blued sword, and I hadn't never seen another one like it afore and ain't never seen another such since. I was on a lot of battlefields. I seen lots of bayonets and small swords and come up against them in combat. But I never seen the like of that blued sword anywhere else."

"And so — this soldier — Jeremy? He didn't use his gun?"

"You got to understand, guns was no more use than swords against the Rebel fire down in the trenches. He must have decided it was just no use. Maybe he felt the sword would somehow protect him. I do not know. But he come on a-runnin toward the trench where I was holed up. He was shouting something and waving that sword. He wasn't but a few yards away, and I seen the sword shining in the sun, and I thought, you shouldn't oughta do that, you shouldn't oughta wave that bright color around, you should lay low — they all shoulda laid low."

Julia saw in Jackson's face the pain and horror of murdering men by the score who had no means of defending themselves.

"And so you saw Jeremy fall, Jackson?"

He nodded and looked her dead in the eye.

"There was a lot of men shooting, and I don't know for sure, but I think maybe I was the one kilt him, Julia."

A shock went through her. She stared at him wordlessly.

Pain scored Jackson's face. He was remembering the confusion, the deafening noise of the cannons and artillery, the need that always drove him to aim and shoot, reload and aim and shoot again, relentlessly firing until the ceasefire was ordered and he could walk away, having dropped or killed every Yank coming at him.

Julia reached out and touched his arm.

"And so — did he die quickly, Jackson? Did he suffer? Do you know?"

Jackson let go of the arbor post and pushed his hands into his pockets and looked at the ground.

At this question he was finding it hard to look into her eyes. He knew this woman was counting on him to tell the truth, and he was by nature an honest man. But it was only by lying that he could be merciful. There was no chapter on Mercy in the soldier's guidebook. He had shown none to Jeremy or dozens of others he had killed or wounded. Like his father the Indian fighter, he had been a soldier, and he had done what he was trained to do. And God knew the Federals had shown no mercy to him or his fallen comrades. He had been wounded at Second Manassas, himself.

But now, at last, here was an opportunity to be merciful. And so, accruing yet another black mark on his soul, he told Julia a lie.

He took a sharp inward breath and forced himself to look at her.

"He died quick, Julia. I saw him go down. He dropped the sword as he fell. He did not move. I'm sure he was dead."

Julia held her palms together at her lips for a moment as if in prayer.

"Thank God for that," she murmured. "And thank you for telling me. I know it was hard for you. I will write to his family and tell them what you said. They have always been afraid he suffered a lingering death, as so many soldiers did."

Burdened further by a lie now extended to Jeremy's family, Jackson said nothing as they walked back to the house.

Sophronia was dismayed by Julia's sad expression. Jackson explained.

"Been telling her a little bit about the war. Seems her sweetheart and me both fought at Cold Harbor."

The name meant nothing to Sophronia, only that it was yet another battlefield her husband had managed to survive.

"Well, I'll be. The two of you in the same place. If that don't beat all."

She led Julia to a seat.

"You rest here, Miss Tenpenny. Jackson ought not to of kept you out in that heat."

"Well, first of all," he said, pouring a spicy drink for himself and the teacher, "it weren't all that hot. We had a good breeze. And second, this here's Julia, not Miss Tenpenny. She's a farmer like us, Phrony."

Sophronia unbelievingly shook her head.

"Oh yes," confirmed Julia, rousing herself after a few refreshing sips, "I truly have a green thumb."

"Then maybe you can teach me how to make roses grow in this here clay."

"I've had some success with roses. I helped Ilsa Royal establish a rose garden, which is thriving. I'll be glad to help you start a rose garden as well."

AT SOPHRONIA'S INVITATION, Julia returned the following week. She wore her gardening dress, faded and worn from much use, with a floppy old straw hat. Once again, she did not arrive empty handed, but brought two three-foot-high camellia bushes donated by Ilsa. She and Sophronia chatted companionably as they planted them. The glossy-leaved plants were bare of buds, but, as Julia noted, they were the perfect choice for planting in late summer.

"Camellias love cold weather. You'll have pink and white blossoms all through the winter months."

"I've seen those blooming in town in frosty weather and wondered what they was. They're truly beautiful."

"They are. And they blossom up a storm — although it may take a couple of seasons before you see them in their full glory."

She had not forgotten Sophronia's desire for a rose garden and commented, "You'll want to set out your roses in early spring. Ilsa will bring some plants to you then and help you pick a good spot for them."

She patted the earth around the bushes with a spade Ilsa had also donated to Sophronia. Handing it over to her she said, "Indispensable tool for the gardener."

Sophronia smiled.

"I'll put it to good use."

Jackson and his brother Micah had been repairing some fencing near the cabin when Julia arrived. Jackson strode over and with some amusement watched the women's gardening efforts for a while.

"That's a lot of work for a bunch of flowers. They grow wild all over the place," he observed.

"But not in winter," Sophronia responded. "And in the spring we'll have us some roses, too."

"Roses ain't edible."

Realizing he was teasing her, Sophronia only shook her head and assigned him a chore.

"Get us a bucket of water so these plants have a fighting chance in this heat."

Jackson obeyed, taking care that the roots were thoroughly soaked, then turned to go back to work. He could not long be absent if he wanted Micah to continue helping him, as there was plenty of work to do on the home place down the road. Twenty-two-year-old Micah and their father, Josiah Knightley, ran the farm that had been in the family more than thirty years.

"Best I get on back to work, ladies," he said.

But then, a remark Julia had made about her imminent departure to the North caused him to pause.

"So when are you headed home, Julia?"

She took off her dirt-caked gardening gloves and swiped at some dirt on her face, only making it worse, and blew at a strand of hair that had fallen across her nose.

"The new teacher will arrive in a couple of weeks."

"Well, I was just a-wonderin if you might like to come out to the home place Sairdy and enjoy a meal with us."

"Sairdy? Oh – you mean Saturday."

"That's right," Jackson said. "Sairdy. We generally have a get-together once a month. My sisters and their families will be there so you'll meet them, too. And when I mentioned you to my father, he said as how he'd sure by God like to meet a Yankee face to face for once."

Julia knew Jackson had lost two brothers in the war, and her startled expression at the manner in which he delivered his father's remark prompted Jackson to say, "Oh, but not to shoot at, a course. He'd just like to meet you and hear about where you come from."

Deeply pleased by the invitation and amused at herself for her first reaction to Josiah's words, Julia responded, "Well, of course, Jackson. I'd be honored to meet your father and the rest of your family."

THE JOSIAH KNIGHTLEY farm sprawled over more than 275 acres, with a well-maintained farmhouse, a cavernous barn containing not only hay and farm implements of all kinds but several large wine casks, a wagon shed, numerous less imposing out buildings, and long stretches of split rail fencing. When Julia arrived, a mule was plodding in a circle, pulling a pole attached to a small mill for grinding sugar cane. Several gallons of the sweet juice were already boiling in a cauldron in the cane shed. A teen-aged boy in charge of the operation, one of the Knightleys' hired hands, stopped the mule in its monotonous round so Julia could pet it.

"May I feed him?" she asked.

The boy grinned and handed her a carrot. She knew to offer it in her open hand, not on the tips of her fingers, to avoid being nipped. She briefly stroked the mule's withers, not wishing to keep the boy from his job.

"How's the syrup coming along?" she asked.

"There's four gallons of cane juice already a-boilin. We'll have plenty of syrup in two or three hours."

Jackson spotted her from the porch and came to collect her.

"Hard workers, aren't they?" she commented.

"Oh, he works right enough. But I have to watch him. Caught him smoking one of Josiah's pipes behind the barn last week."

Julia was startled for a moment.

"Oh. You mean the young man. I was referring to the mule."

Jackson did not comment. He had long since lost the child's fondness for the mule as a mount and a wagon puller. To him, a mule was simply a work animal. As they strolled to the house, Julia noticed a grape arbor considerably larger than Jackson's and several baskets of just-harvested fruit.

She was ushered into a large front room, scrupulously swept clean with the fennel brush broom that stood in the corner, with an enormous fireplace and several chairs, some of which appeared to be hand crafted.

Jackson's mother, Sally Ann, greeted her with a hug. Her hair at first glance appeared white but was actually tow colored. Slightly plump, like Julia, her barely lined face made her appear younger than her fifty-two years. She introduced Julia to her two daughters as Sophronia gestured for her to take a seat in a cushioned pinewood chair. As Julia glanced about the room, she was struck by an antique musket mounted on the wall and a long bow that hung beneath it.

"My husband's out back a-helpin Micah scale some fish they caught down at the creek this morning. So we'll be having catfish and trout with the venison. Josiah'll be in right soon."

Ellie and Maudie kept Julia occupied with their questions about her school and her Massachusetts home. While Rebecca was passed around from one adoring aunt to the next and toddler Lee practiced his climbing skills on the furniture,

Ellie and Maudie's children, who ranged in age from three to sixteen, wandered in and out of the house.

Josiah appeared after scrubbing the fish scales off his hands. At fifty-five he was still fit, a reward for his years of farm labor, with pale blue eyes that seemed to be faded by the sun. He still had a full head of hair, although it was gray, and looked surprisingly stylish for a farmer, with sideburns and a clean-shaven face.

The cooking and dining operations were carried out in a spacious back room. Gradually the front room cleared out as the womenfolk stepped away to attend to the meal preparations. Sally Ann hated to miss a word of what Julia had to say, but she was clearly the matriarch, always in charge of the domestic activities in her own home, and was continually drawn to the other room to make sure the preparations were coming along as they should.

Into a quiet pause in the flow of conversation Josiah commented,

"My son says your fiancé was kilt in the war."

Julia nodded

"Two of my sons was, too."

"I know. I am so sorry. It was a dreadful time for all of us."

Josiah dabbed at his faded eyes. Any mention of Peter or David caused tears to well up.

"They was good boys. David was planning on marrying that gal — who was it, now?" he asked Sally Ann, who had just re-entered the room after demonstrating for one of her granddaughters the correct way to crimp a pie crust and scolding Maudie for nearly scorching the biscuits.

"You know — the skinny one with the brown eyes that can sing so pretty. He was always over at her house."

"You're talking about Libby. Libby Madison."

"Her. He was a-gonna ask her to marry him. Told me so afore he left."

He looked at Julia in what she hoped was not an accusing way.

"She's a spinster now and likely will remain one."

Josiah sighed and pulled out his pipe. Sally Ann quickly filled it and lit it for him as she commented, "So many young women who ought to of been married by now ain't, because they lost their — "

A glance at Julia's pensive face reminded her why Julia, too, was single. A change of subject, she felt, would not be unwelcome.

"Jackson tells us you're something of a farmer, Julia."

"I do enjoy gardening. But you know, rather than talking about me, I'd really like to hear about that bow hanging on the wall and that old musket."

Josiah readily complied.

"That's my old smoothbore, the very gun I used in the Creek War. And that there bow was give to me by a warrior I once knew."

Julia was fascinated.

"You knew them? You knew some of the Creeks?"

"I knew one of them. His name was Harjo, and he give me that bow afore the war. Afore we took to fighting."

"I would love to hear about that — if you don't mind telling me."

Sally Ann laughed.

"Why, he'll talk your ears off about them days if you let him!"

"I am all ears," Julia smilingly said.

Josiah leaned back in his chair and took a few contemplative puffs on his pipe.

"Well now, I did fight some Indians. It's been — let me think. It's been thirty-five years ago. Me and my brothers fought in the 42nd Alabama Militia. And we did rout them Creeks."

It was clear as he began telling the story of the Battles of Hobdy's Creek and the Pea River Swamp that, while he was not given to braggadocio, Josiah took pleasure in describing his exploits. He did not slight the Creeks, but gave them their full due for bravery and fierce fighting. Julia was raptly attentive to his stories of the events of 1836 and 1837, but as he wound down she was left with the odd feeling that she had been entertained, not edified; that she had been led down one path when other paths to the same destination lay untrod. As she thanked him for his tale, her steady gaze seemed to unsettle him for a moment, and he looked away before commenting, "It was a long time ago, Julia. But that is how I remember it."

Elder Reuben Faraday arrived just then, and it was obvious to Julia from the informal way he was greeted and the ease with which he made himself at home that his presence at Knightley get-togethers was customary. It was a source of some embarrassment to her that on the one occasion she had visited Galilee Primitive Baptist Church she had been so focused on talking with Jackson that she had failed to exercise common courtesy and shake hands with the elder and thank him for his sermon. Now Jackson introduced her to him as "the Yankee schoolteacher" — a manner of introduction she had become accustomed to over the years — and Elder Faraday firmly shook her hand as if to assure her that he harbored no ill will toward her or her kinsmen.

As Sally Ann summoned them all to the great, heavily laden table for what turned out to be not just a meal, but a feast, Josiah offered Julia his arm. "Now this, young lady, is what we call southern hospitality."

Julia was led to her seat as honored guest at the foot of the table, opposite Josiah, and following the recital of a long and fervent grace by Jackson, every adult in the room raised a glass of golden wine in a toast. "To peace," Elder Faraday intoned. "And let us cease dwelling upon the late unpleasantness, which only engenders wrath." He included them all in his flinty gaze as he added, "For wrath, brethren, is a sin."

THE FREEDMAN'S BUREAU halted operations in Alabama in 1870, but the New Road School survived through the efforts of a missionary society. Julia's replacement, a young black woman who was a graduate of Fisk University, arrived early in September of 1872. Julia was soon convinced that the new teacher was as dedicated as she was competent; it was a great relief to leave her pupils in such capable hands.

On the afternoon she took her leave, there were misty-eyed goodbyes, with many warm hugs and heartfelt handshakes. As a parting gift, the class delighted her by singing several of her favorite hymns. She found herself wishing that Jeremy

Gaither could be standing there next to her that day, his strong arm around her, his face illumined by his sweet smile, reliving with her the joy of helping these determined people lift themselves out of ignorance.

Chapter 5

PIERCE AND KEZIAH

TWICE WIDOWED, PIERCE Tomlin was raising his three children with the help of Keziah Cates, a capable black woman of whom his mother-in-law, Delta Crandall, thoroughly disapproved. Before the passing of Pierce's second wife three years earlier, in 1924, Delta had only rarely ventured south from Montgomery to visit Comfortroot Farm. But after Rowena's death from heart failure, a result of the rheumatic fever she suffered as a child, Delta made periodic trips to the Wiregrass in her capacity of dutiful grandmother.

Delta Crandall was no stranger to rural life; she had been reared on a small farm in Lowndes County west of Montgomery. But she despised all things agrarian — the sights, the sounds, the smells — especially the smells. She married well and for many years had enjoyed a comfortable city life as the wife of a prominent attorney. Her marriage to the scion of a Montgomery family awash in old money had been the major achievement of her life. The Crandall family occasionally dined at the Governor's mansion. Her father-in-law sat on the screening board of their exclusive country club and reveled in his power to exclude. Delta and her husband had been entertained at the home of Judge Anthony Sayre, whose daughter Zelda was married to F. Scott Fitzgerald. So Delta's disdain for the farm scene was understandable.

Rowena, on the other hand, had been unfortunate enough to become enamored of "that farmer" (as Delta usually referred to Pierce Tomlin) during one of her summer visits to a cousin's home in Dothan. While he owned a large property, and his neatly trimmed Vandyke beard and close-cropped, salt-and-pepper hair lent him an air of distinction, Pierce was not in the same class as the professional, moneyed young men who moved with ease in their social circle, almost any one of whom Delta would have preferred as a son-in-law. Rowena met him at her cousin's church, Poplar Leaf Baptist, when she was seventeen years old. The following summer she determined to ensnare Pierce Tomlin, and with her Mary Pickford prettiness and unabashed admiration of him, she succeeded. They married in 1912, soon after her nineteenth birthday.

Rowena had not settled easily into the role of farmer's wife and took every opportunity to travel to Montgomery, which over the years she had come to miss more and more. She had insisted on "going home" for the birth of each of the Tomlin children, leaving Pierce to wonder when Comfortroot would ever be home to her. He was present for the birth of each of his children, but farm duties required him to leave his wife and children with their grandparents during Rowena's several weeks of recuperation after each birth.

Keziah Cates and her husband Daniel, one of Pierce's most trusted farm hands, had moved into one of the small houses on the farm upon their arrival from Columbus, Georgia, in 1904. She had always worked in the Tomlin household, and after Daniel's death from pleurisy in 1915, accepted Pierce and Rowena's invitation to move in with them as a live-in cook and housekeeper. A petite woman who barely weighed ninety pounds, her duties did not extend to the rough work of laundry and floor scrubbing, which was performed by part-time hired help. Disappointed that she and Daniel never had children, she was fond of the Tomlin children and helped Rowena care for them.

Rowena's hands had never touched a mop, broom, scrub board, or dust cloth in her life, and she could not properly boil an egg, facts Pierce was aware of when they married. She did play the piano, and he provided one for her; and she was an avid pinochle and cribbage player, games he enjoyed. She was also an excellent hostess. Pierce was not an outgoing person, but his wife loved entertaining, and he did not object as long as she kept to the budget and gave him the freedom, in return, to host an occasional poker game. Although he anticipated that the care of their children would be turned over to a nursemaid, he was pleasantly surprised to find, with the birth of their first child, that Rowena was a devoted, hands-on mother, willing to undertake any chore concerning the children, not even objecting to cleaning up after them.

While not made in heaven, the Tomlin marriage was on the whole a successful one, even though Pierce realized that Rowena unfavorably compared her household to that of her parents. He had never been in love with her, but after her untimely death he keenly missed her. However, in time he came to feel a sense of relief that now, at least, he no longer had to compete with the Crandalls. A sentiment Delta Crandall did not happen to share.

Delta held sway in a two-story Georgian brick home in a fashionable Montgomery neighborhood. She had full authority for running the household, and she ably performed her duties, which largely consisted of supervising their staff: a cook, a laundress, two maids, and a gardener. There had also been a procession of nursemaids over the years until her son and daughter outgrew the need for them. The servants knew their place (anyone who did not was summarily dismissed), just as she knew hers. Thus it deeply troubled her that the person in whom Pierce had entrusted the daily care of her grandchildren was one of those coloreds who gave herself airs. There was nothing Delta could put her finger on, to complain to Pierce about — no rude language, no eye rolling, no smart remarks. Yet in quite a few encounters with Keziah she had felt — oh, what was the word? *Sassed*. The woman sassed her. Not verbally — at least, not in anything she said. It was her *manner* of speaking. A cockiness. A complete lack of — of *deference*. That was it. No deference at all. No matter how many yes ma'ams or no ma'ams she uttered, Keziah's direct gaze and unsmiling face, her composed, non-subservient response to Delta's comments, revealed the disrespect at the woman's core. And her just a maid. A *colored* maid. The woman was insufferable.

Delta intended to strongly suggest two possible remedies for this situation to her son-in-law: fire Keziah Cates and hire a suitable replacement, selected by Delta herself; or, inasmuch as Pierce's parents were deceased, turn over the rearing of eight-year-old Benjamin and his older sisters — Amelia, twelve, and Lorraine, ten — to their maternal grandparents. In the latter case, not only would they be appropriately raised, but they would reap all the benefits of living in a beautiful, civilized city with every social and educational advantage.

For Rowena's sake, Pierce had always been tolerant of his meddling mother-in-law, who was so unlike his first wife's sweet mother, and thus even though he knew Delta probably had something unpleasant to convey, he agreed to a front parlor tête à tête. With her permission, he lit his pipe. He believed he would need its soothing effect to weather this meeting.

By the light of the oil lamp, one could still see, in the rouged cheekbones and Cupid's bow lips, the upswept, still abundant, silver-streaked dark hair, and the large brown eyes a hint of the pretty girl who had captivated the Yale graduate she married. But the moment she was able to put the physical exertion of the farm behind her she had done so, and she had never taken up any physically demanding leisure activity to replace it. The sedentary life and a fondness for sweets had taken their toll. Her skin was no longer firm, and she was forty pounds overweight. Still, with a generous wardrobe and beauty parlor allowance, Delta was an attractive dowager who could be imposing. She took for granted her power to manipulate. She was quite good at it.

Settling into a comfortable chair, completely confident and at ease, Delta politely, in the gentlest of tones, laid out her arguments for removing the children to Montgomery — for Pierce's benefit as well as theirs. He clearly had his hands full with not only managing the farm but also working the farm (the latter something else she disapproved of, preferring a gentleman farmer for a son-in-law). Surely his life would be easier and he would have greater peace of mind knowing that his children were being raised in a charming city with opportunities not available to them in — well, Dothan. This last word was uttered with the contempt of the sophisticated city dweller for a provincial small town where the making of turpentine and the extraction of cotton oil were considered praiseworthy pursuits.

Not the most patient of men, Pierce nonetheless patiently listened. When she finally fell silent, gazing expectantly at him, he tapped out his pipe, laid it aside, and unhurriedly, in his slow Virginia drawl, disabused her.

"Delta, your concern for me and my family is appreciated. But I have all the help around the farm I need, and the absence of my children would not make my life any easier. On the contrary, it would make it unbearably hard, because it would take the meaning out of my life. It's true I love this farm, and I know that's hard for you to understand. But I love my children more. And as for them being better off in the city, let me remind you that I was raised in Richmond. Not on a farm near Richmond, not on the outskirts, but in the very heart of the city. And so from personal experience I know all about the noise, the congestion, the pollution, the restrictions, and the endless rules and regulations that city folk have to endure. And the dangers. As you know, my father was killed when he was jostled in a crowd of people and fell under the wheels of one of the newfangled trolley cars the city had just put into use. So life in the city is not all that grand, not all that safe, and certainly not something I would permit my children to experience, unless I myself were there to protect them. And Delta, that is not going to happen. Until they are grown, at least, my children are staying right here with me."

Taken aback, Delta was quiet for a few moments. She had believed she could fairly easily persuade him to let her take over the raising of the children, which is why she broached that argument first. The other solution to what she perceived as a serious problem in the household would be more difficult, because it called into question his judgment in employing Keziah Cates, who had been with the Tomlin family for a number of years.

Thinking they were done, Pierce started to get up from his chair.

"Well, Pierce, I can understand your feelings."

He nodded, once again starting to leave the room.

"But — "

"But?"

"And I can't argue that there are possibly some advantages to country living. But — "

Pierce sighed, tired of this discussion, wanting to say "Spit it out!" But he restrained himself and sat back down.

"Yes, Delta. What's on your mind now?"

"Well, Pierce, do you really think it's wise to have that — that colored woman in charge of your children? I mean, she seems to be the, the main person in their lives — I mean besides you. And — "

"All of your servants are colored, Delta."

"Well yes, they are. But they are all — They're respectful. And they do exactly what I tell them to do."

"Has Keziah ever said anything insulting to you?"

"Oh, no. Not in — well, not in words. But sometimes — it's the look on her face. I just know she does not respect me. And she's just so — full of herself. So — like she doesn't need me to tell her anything, like I'm not in charge. She's just not the kind of person you should have raising your children. And I think you should let her go and let me help you find someone more suitable."

Pierce found himself biting his lower lip in the attempt to remain polite. Finally he stood up again, making clear the discussion was over, as he said, "I've known Keziah for more than twenty years, Delta. And she has helped look after my children not only since we lost Rowena, but during all the years since they were born. Your daughter never once indicated that Keziah Cates was anything but a godsend. I'm sorry you feel the way you do, but Keziah stays."

He refrained from adding, *And you, thank the Lord, are leaving on the first train tomorrow,* as he grabbed his pipe and exited the room.

A FEW DAYS after Grandmother Crandall's visit, Benjamin accosted Keziah after his father smiled and referred to her as a spring chicken while rushing out the kitchen door. This was in response to her comment that she was feeling her age that day.

"You ain't a chicken," Benjamin said.

"Your papa just meant I was young, like a chick born in the spring time."

Benjamin looked at her appraisingly, and in a factual, non-derisive tone said, "You ain't young, either."

Keziah tried not to smile.

"And you're not an ignorant, uneducated boy. How many times have I told you not to say ain't?"

Benjamin sat down at the kitchen table watching Keziah set out the ingredients for a cake. He was satisfied with her explanation of "spring chicken," but another expression was puzzling him.

"Keziah, Amelia says you're high up."

She did not pause in sifting flour. She was busy preparing the batter for a chocolate cake for Amelia's birthday. It was going to be real fancy, with white icing drizzled artistically over the chocolate.

"Why'd she say you're high up, Keziah?"

She began to fold in the eggs and other ingredients, throwing all of her ninety pounds into beating the batter smooth.

"What's high up, Ben? You're not making any sense."

"But Amelia said — " he concentrated for a moment. "Oh, I remember now. She said you're uppity."

Keziah abruptly stopped beating.

"Uppity? Amelia said that?"

"Uh huh. What's that mean, Keziah? You ain't up in the air."

She wiped her hands on her apron and used a poker to stoke up the fire in the wood-burning stove. The oven was almost hot enough.

Benjamin sat quietly watching her. He could be very patient waiting for answers to his unending questions.

Keziah sat down next to him. She brushed his lank, dark blond hair off his forehead. An easy lie flitted through her head. It would be so easy to smile and say it was just a silly word that didn't mean a thing. But Keziah could not lie to this child.

"Uppity is a word white people call colored people they think are trying to act smart."

"But you *are* smart."

Keziah tried again.

"A lot of white people believe colored people are dumb, and they get mad if a colored person doesn't act dumb. Then they call the person uppity."

"Amelia's white."

Keziah nodded.

"And you're colored."

She nodded again.

"But she's the one who's dumb."

"No, she's not. She's young and ignorant about some things. And she got mad because I told her she had to finish her school work and help with supper before she could sit down and read that foolish romance magazine. I know that's why she disrespected me. I got on to her and Lorraine both yesterday evening. Sitting around when their papa told them to help out."

She stood up and poured the cake batter into two pans, then set them in the oven and started on the icing. But not before she handed Ben a wooden spoon coated in chocolate batter. He licked it greedily.

"Well, Lorraine didn't say you're uppity."

"No?"

"Uh uh. She said you're biggity."

Keziah shook her head.

"Lord, these younguns are a mess. Reckon I need to straighten them out."

"Papa told them not to say those words."

"You mean he was there when they lit into me?"

Benjamin nodded.

"He told them, you girls are getting too biggity for your britches. But girls don't wear britches, do they? Only boys do."

"Well now, Benjamin, don't be so narrow in your thinking. I've seen plenty of girls in overalls out in the fields, and overalls are a kind of britches, too."

Benjamin absorbed this.

"I reckon you're right about that." He held up his spoon hopefully. "Can I have some more?"

COMFORTROOT FARM WAS home to the usual array of bovines, equines, and canines, but the animal closest to Benjamin Tomlin's heart was none of these. In the same summer that he was enthralled by Tennyson's *Idylls of the King*, she was born in the hay loft one morning, a short-haired, green-eyed cat he named Guinevere, not realizing that her true feline name was Rodent Slayer.

In mostly nocturnal forays, she stalked and killed large insects, small birds, and the occasional frog, but her specialty was *Rodentia*. A blended tortoiseshell whose coat provided excellent camouflage in the leafy brush she prowled, Rodent Slayer could capture prey with greater ease than could her strikingly marked cousins. No mouse, rat, mole, chipmunk or shrew was safe in her presence. For this reason, she never responded to the name Guinevere, and in fact would turn and walk away at the sound of it.

Her days were largely given over to slumber — a harmless pursuit, one would think. Yet what action of Rodent Slayer's was ever uncalculated? Before drifting off into the somnolence so beloved of cats, and at which they are so expert, she would shamelessly arrange her fluid, glossy-furred frame in a fetching manner — head tucked under a paw, with two or three feet in the air in feigned submissiveness — for the intended purpose of further charming and captivating humans, especially Benjamin. She had chosen Benjamin as her own almost the moment her shuttered eyes first opened.

There he was, an eight-year-old boy, stroking her multi-colored fur and telling Keziah, "This is the one I want," little knowing that *he* was the one being chosen by this tiny predator destined to be one of the finest ratters ever born. Rodent Slayer could not have expressed why she chose him and not one of Benjamin's siblings. Squinting and blinking her unfocused eyes, she could not really see him. Was it the gentle way he stroked her, the sound of his voice, the pleasing scent of peppermint on his breath? Was it because she sensed his vulnerability to her adorableness? Or was it because her mother purred her approval of Rodent Slayer's choice? In all the long years of her life, Rodent Slayer would never know why, but it went unquestioned by everyone, including the humans, that Benjamin was hers.

Why Benjamin could not surmise her true name never ceased to confound Rodent Slayer. Although like all those of his species he was handicapped — nighttime blindness, feeble legs that could not jump higher than two or three feet, clawless paws, and dull-edged teeth that could tear almost nothing apart — still, he seemed bright enough. He had readily learned all of her commands and immediately fetched water, food, or provided a lap whenever she demanded it. He was exceptionally well trained. Yet the matter of the name always stood between them. It was a pity. How she would have loved to hear him call, with even just an attempt at catlike pronunciation, "Rodent Slayer." At that sound she would have been willing to relate to him as an equal and come to him at his bidding — just as he always came to her when she called him. She was careful to use the only cat word he could understand, "meow" — which in feline language means, "Do my bidding."

But it was not to be. And so their relationship remained one-sided, she successfully summoning him whenever she had the least need of him, he being ignored when he called her that ridiculous human name. She consoled herself with the knowledge that many other cats experienced the same frustration in trying to relate to their human devotees.

IN LATE SEPTEMBER, much of the cotton had been harvested, so school was in session. Green Sedge Elementary usually opened later than the schools in Dothan because so many rural children labored in the fields. Benjamin and his sisters had never had to pick cotton, but they were always assigned enough chores to keep them busy.

Benjamin was eager to return to school after the summer break. But on the first day of school his father asked Keziah's opinion as to whether he should stay home for a couple of days because of the injury he had received the day before. He could not wear a shoe on his left foot, only a sock, and he would have to use crutches to keep him off that foot for a week or so.

"He'll be fine," Keziah said. "He seems to be able to get about all right. And he really wants to go."

So Pierce had driven him to school, deciding he should not ride the bus that morning, and had also spared him a bus ride that afternoon. As soon as Benjamin came in the door, Keziah changed the bandage and applied more iodine according to the doctor's instructions.

The day before, Lorraine had come into the kitchen where Keziah was plucking a chicken, reached for a pitcher of tea, and suddenly shrieked as a mouse ran across the floor, with Guinevere streaking by in hot pursuit. Lorraine dropped the glass pitcher, where it broke into several large pieces, just as Benjamin came running into the room to see what all the commotion was about. Barefooted, he stepped down hard on a shard of broken glass, splitting the arch of his foot wide open. Blood gushed forth in an amazing quantity. Lorraine screamed again, wide eyed at the sight of the injury, and Keziah reached for a towel, told Benjamin to sit, and pressed it hard against the gash. She expected him to cry like any eight-year-old, but he only grimaced in pain and said, "I'm so sorry Keziah, I'm so sorry. I've messed up your clean floor. I'm so sorry!"

"That's all right, Ben. Just you let me stop this bleeding." But the bleeding would not stop. She glanced up. "Lorraine, phone for the doctor. I think Ben's going to need some stitches."

Pierce was present when the doctor sewed up the deep wound and was proud of his son's behavior throughout the ordeal. There was much squirming and wincing, but no tears. This was a relief to Pierce, who sometimes feared his son might be sissified. There was his affection for that cat, when most boys not only despised cats but loved to tease them, preferring for company some malodorous hound dog; and the way he still submitted to Keziah's motherly hugs at an age when boys were usually embarrassed by a show of feminine affection and scornfully shrugged it off; or the way he spent hours, if you would let him, holed up with a book — a habit

Keziah encouraged. And so Benjamin's endurance in the face of a painful wound was, to Pierce, a very good sign.

As Keziah sat supervising his homework, listening to him read his weekly writing assignment and nodding her approval as he finished with not one grammatical error, Benjamin inquisitively touched the small but quite visible scar on her upper lip. He had often wondered about it, and today, perhaps because of his own injury, his curiosity found voice.

"Keziah, where'd you get that scar from?"

Benjamin had had the usual number of childhood mishaps, although not as severe as his present injury, and Keziah knew the history of every one of his scars, so he saw nothing intrusive or improper in his question.

Keziah sighed and pursed her lips.

"You are the most noticing child in the world, Benjamin."

"Well, I was just wondering — "

She smiled.

"You're always wondering about something, son."

"So then — what happened?"

"It was a long time ago — when I was about Amelia's age. Someone hit me on the mouth. It left a scar."

She started to get up. It was time to start supper.

"Who on earth would hit you? Why? You always say — Papa says — it's wrong to hit people. Especially girls. Who did that? Because if I knew who it was, I'd fix him good."

"It happened long before you were born, Ben. And I have forgotten all about it. Now get busy and put those books away and set the table."

As she set the potatoes to boil and floured the chicken, Keziah reflected that Benjamin was a caring, sensitive boy — perhaps too sensitive. She did not feel it was appropriate to load him down with all of her hurts; he would have enough of his own along the way.

And so she chose not to share the history of her scar and the slap she so vividly remembered.

IN THE FALL of 1898, sixteen-year-old Keziah Tolliver was presented with an unexpected opportunity. Her mother had a friend who worked as a cook in a big house in Columbus, Georgia, near the small community of Dollarleaf where the Tolliver family lived. Mary Gibbons told Lena Tolliver that one of the maids had just quit and that she would recommend Keziah for the position. With Keziah's younger sisters now half-grown, Lena had all the help she needed for her laundry business and could think of no reason why her eldest daughter should not take this opportunity to earn some money working in a big fancy house.

On a brisk yet sunny October morning, John Tolliver drove her to town, proud to be taking his grown-up daughter to work at one of the finest houses in Columbus. When they arrived at the address Mary had given them, they both stared in awe. Situated on a rise with an expanse of lawn extending more than a hundred yards down to the tree-lined street, the two-story brick house had a broad veranda that swept across the front and around two sides. A tower with a steepled roof ascended over the entry foyer. It was surrounded by scalloped shingle dormers on all four sides.

John drove the wagon up the long driveway around to the back, where Mary was waiting for them at the kitchen door. He helped Keziah down, admonishing her to do her best before he left. Then Mary led her into the house and told her Mrs. VanStyer was already in the drawing room waiting for her, so they had best hurry.

Keziah caught sight of crown moldings with a leaf pattern and deep burgundy walls. As they came to the large foyer, sunlight streamed down from the stained glass windows of the tower.

In the drawing room just off the foyer, Verbena VanStyer was seated in a brocaded chair. Deep green velvet swag curtains hung from windows on either side of the room, and French doors opened onto red-tiled, semi-circular steps which led into a garden. Asters and late roses vibrantly bloomed, even as oak, poplar and beech leaves were dying in golden and scarlet splendor.

Mrs. VanStyer was dressed in a lilac gown with leg-of-mutton sleeves. It was decorated with multiple small pleats down each side of the bodice and corded black velvet trim around the collar. Her dark, graying hair was swept up, and her face was framed with ringlets painstakingly created with a hot iron by her personal maid.

Mrs. VanStyer was severe with all of her servants because one had to be. Otherwise, they would perform their work in a slipshod manner and be up to God knew what foolishness behind her back. Each of her servants was convinced that she had superhuman hearing and eyes in the back of her head.

The young woman before her was polite, respectful, and, according to Cook, well trained in the rough housework she would be performing.

Keziah stood at attention, like a lowly private before a five-star general, and only opened her mouth to answer Mrs. VanStyer's questions, hoping to acquit herself well during the catechism to determine whether she were fit for the position. She tried not to let her eyes wander around the elegant room with its rich furnishings or outside to the garden, but that was difficult. At one point in her glancing about, Mrs. VanStyer sharply directed her to answer the question she had already asked her once — *and girl, do not require me to ask it again!*

"Yes, ma'am."

Keziah was dressed in her best outfit, a white blouse and light blue skirt, and her long, braided hair was coiled into a neat chignon. Apparently Mrs. VanStyer felt she was gaudily attired, because she looked her up and down and informed her that she had two work dresses that would fit her, both dark gray, and she expected her to take those home and wear only that clothing when she came to work.

"Yes, ma'am."

Mrs. VanStyer explained that the household consisted of her husband and herself and five children, the youngest a boy of thirteen. Two personal maids lived in, occupying dormer rooms in the finished attic. In addition to the position Keziah would be filling, there were four other servants, including a gardener and his assistant.

During the interview, twenty-four-year-old Priscilla VanStyer entered the room and sat on the sofa opposite her mother. A tall, large-boned young woman, she would never, even with the most constricting of corsets, achieve a hand-span waist. Unlike Mrs. VanStyer, she did not sit perfectly erect but reclined against a cushion and regarded Keziah with a half smile on her face. Her ornate Gibson girl blouse had a stain on the crosscut ruffle jabot and was haphazardly tucked into the waistband of her gored skirt. Her maid's efforts to twist her straight, fair hair into sausage curls had failed. Occasionally she pushed the limp hair back off her face, but she seemed unconcerned about her appearance. After a bit, she leaned forward and seemed about to say something, but Mrs. VanStyer frowned, curtailing her comment with a chilly look.

Keziah was afraid the displeased expression was meant for her, but then Mrs. VanStyer continued questioning her in a polite, if strict, manner. When at last the interrogation was finished, she directed Keziah to follow her upstairs into one of the seven bedrooms, where a maid was making up the bed.

"Evie, this is Keziah. She will be doing much of the heavy cleaning and assisting with the laundry. You may put her to work immediately."

Evie nodded as she smoothed out the top sheet. "Gots plenty for her to do, Miz VanStyer."

Apparently confident Keziah was in good hands, Mrs. VanStyer left, first commanding her new employee to arrive promptly at six o'clock the following morning.

Evie, a woman of substantial girth in her forties, shook her head at the sight of the petite girl who was now assigned the rough work — scrubbing floors, beating rugs, washing windows, cleaning fireplaces, and helping with the laundry. But when Evie led her into the laundry room, Keziah was relieved to see the household was equipped with a mangle to wring the clothes and a wench to haul the clothing up to the drying racks near the ceiling, which would be much easier than wringing out clothes by hand and then lifting the heavy, sodden garments up on to clotheslines, as she and her mother were accustomed to doing. All in all, she had been shown nothing she did not know how to do, and she would prove to Evie and the other staff that she was much stronger than she looked. She could do this job.

By the end of the day she was exhausted, but believed she had performed every task satisfactorily. She had caught several glimpses of Priscilla's siblings, but they were absorbed in their own pursuits and ignored her, to Keziah's relief. Mrs. VanStyer's scrutiny had made her nervous, and she wished to remain inconspicuous.

She reported upstairs to Evie to collect the brown paper package containing the two dresses she had been instructed to wear beginning the following day. On the stair landing, she gaped at the hand-painted compass rose on the ceiling. As she descended the curved mahogany staircase imported from England, she admired the polished wood, then stepped into the foyer. She was about to walk out the front door when Mrs. VanStyer spotted her.

"Keziah! Where on earth do you think you're going? Servants do not use the front door!"

Keziah stopped in her tracks.

"I'm sorry, ma'am. I'll just go — which way should I go?"

Priscilla, in a bedroom just off the landing at the top of the stairs, overheard the exchange. Holding onto the banister all the way down, she joined her mother and Keziah at the front door. Once again she had a slight smile on her lips. Keziah noticed that she seemed to stumble slightly, as if she had tripped on a rug. But there was no rug; there was only the intricately patterned parquet floor.

"Is somebody lost? Come here, girl — I'll point the way."

"I'll handle this, Priscilla. You go on back to your room, now. Cook will bring you a cup of coffee."

"So sweet of you, Mother," Priscilla said. But there was something in her tone that suggested she did not think her mother was being sweet at all.

She was wearing a blue dressing gown over fancy lace garments the like of which Keziah had never seen. She seemed unconscious of any embarrassment her *dishabille* produced, and as she and her mother sparred, Keziah noticed that she was holding a long-stemmed glass in one hand.

In a singsong voice she said, "Go to your room, Priscilla. Sober up, Priscilla. Get out of my sight, Priscilla."

She took a sip from the beautiful, multi-faceted glass.

"I'm implying that's what you are really saying to me, Mother dear — or, or — wait a minute — I mean, that's what I'm inferring — "

She cocked her head to one side with an exaggeratedly puzzled air.

"Or then, maybe I *am* implying — "

Trying to be helpful, Keziah said, in the English her teacher, dear Miss Williams, would have been so proud of, "You mean you are inferring, Miss Priscilla. The rule is, 'The first speaker implies, and the second speaker infers the meaning from what is implied.' So Miz VanStyer implied, and you inferred the meaning from what she implied."

This elucidation was greeted with subterranean silence.

"That's what the rule says," Keziah said in a quiet little voice. Then as she saw the amazed look on Priscilla's face, quickly supplanted by fury, she understood what a ghastly mistake she had made. For the space of three sentences, she had dropped her ignorant-colored-girl mask. Worse than that, she had corrected a white person.

Hardly had this knowledge registered than Priscilla hurled the glass, red wine splattering the gleaming floor and her mother's pale gown as it shattered. Then with the back of her hand she struck Keziah across the mouth with all the force she could muster. Knocked to the floor, Keziah landed on her right side, skinning her arm and bruising her knee. Blood spurted from her lip.

"Priscilla!" shouted her mother. "I will not tolerate such common behavior in this house!"

Keziah made several attempts to get up but was too dazed. Hearing the commotion, Evie came and helped her to her feet.

"Take Keziah into the kitchen and ask Cook to give her a cold cloth for her face."

As Mrs. VanStyer spoke these words, she was looking not at Evie but at her daughter, who had collapsed on a stair step, legs askew, and was staring at her hand, smeared with Keziah's blood and stinging from the blow she had struck.

Evie put her strong arm around Keziah's waist. As they left the foyer, they could hear Mrs. VanStyer lecturing Priscilla, in a high-pitched, angry voice, on the proper treatment of one's inferiors.

Mary sat Keziah down while she staunched the blood with a cloth. She and Evie both fussed over her, but Keziah was oblivious to their efforts to comfort her.

Mary shook her head in mystification.

"I ain't never knowed Miss Priscilla to do such a thing," she said.

Both she and Evie tried to coax what happened out of her, but Keziah shrugged as if she did not know. It made no difference what had caused that evil woman to knock her to the floor, because she had decided she was leaving and never coming back.

Evie offered to retrieve the package of clothing from the foyer floor.

Keziah shook her head and muttered, "Never mind." Her lip was swollen, and there was a cut so deep it would leave a permanent scar, so it was difficult to talk.

Both women hugged her, and then she walked out through the servants' door to where her father was waiting to take her home. As soon as she saw him she began to cry — not only from pain, but also from disappointment and shame. Disappointment that now her folks could not brag about having a daughter who worked in one of the biggest, fanciest houses in Columbus; and shame because she feared she had brought this on herself by showing off.

John was alarmed at the sight of her swollen lip and the blood stains on the white blouse Lena had so carefully laundered and ironed. He helped her into the wagon and put his arm around her as they started off.

After describing what had happened, holding her painful lip as she spoke, Keziah raised her head from John's shoulder and declared, "I will never set foot in another white person's house as long as I live, Papa. *Never.*"

"Ain't no reason to, Baby."

He hugged her and kissed her forehead, then clicked his tongue at the plodding mule and shook the reins.

"Get along now, Jack. Us needs to get this little gal back home to her mama."

JOHN AND LENA Tolliver were newly married teenagers when freedom came. The plantation on which they had been born and where they and their family members, as far back as they knew, had labored, was on the eastern edge of the Black Belt, in Russell County, Alabama. Some freed men and women stayed on as poorly paid laborers, but the Tollivers chose to get as far away from cotton as they could. For a while, John worked as a stevedore on the banks of the Chattahoochee River at Columbus, Georgia. But the backbreaking work of loading and unloading bales of cotton was not suitable for a man with his slight build, and he was not often chosen for a day's work. He began to seek odd jobs — shoeing horses for a farrier, delivering packages, yard work — and after a year or so found a regular job as a porter at the train station. The family rented a shotgun house not far from the river in the community of Dollarleaf, and Lena took in washing and ironing to help support them. In their all-black neighborhood, the only white people Lena and the children dealt with were the peddlers of all sorts of things, from household products to medicines to gardening supplies, or those who dropped off their washing — although even then it was often black servants who delivered and picked up the white folks' laundry.

John and Lena had both bent to the earth from dawn to dusk picking cotton for many years before they married, and they were determined their children would not. Nor were they willing to sacrifice their children's chance at an education for the paltry sums they could earn as full-time workers in the Columbus textile mills, which ground up the youth of many children laboring there twelve hours a day, six days a week. And even if John or Lena considered mill work, black people were mostly hired as cleaners and for the dirtiest jobs in the mills and were not allowed to move up to the better paying positions. So the Tollivers survived on John's pay and the laundry business. Their house was situated on a patch of land large enough for them to keep chickens and grow their own fruits and vegetables.

Keziah and her siblings benefited from the efforts of the Freedman's Bureau and other organizations which had established schools for black children throughout the South after the Civil War. Keziah loved school. She did not merely attend school; she actually attended to everything her instructor had to teach her.

One of her teachers was a young black woman who had been educated in New York. Despite the drabness of the two-room wooden schoolhouse, Miss Adella Williams dressed as if she were teaching in a New York City school. She wore crisp white Gibson girl blouses with leg-of-mutton sleeves, fashionably embroidered, with high necklines reaching almost to her chin. Her dark blue or gray serge skirts fitted snugly at the waist and hips, then flowed to a wide hem so that only the toes of her high-top, button-up shoes showed. Her skirt swished when she walked. Every female child in her classroom wanted a skirt like that, but their plain cotton dresses just reached to mid-calf. Miss Williams' hair was straightened and pulled up into a fashionable pompadour, which was also envied by the pigtailed or corn-rowed little girls.

Miss Williams strove mightily to iron the southern black dialect out of her pupils' speech. Perhaps as deeply as did the great playwright Shaw, she understood the relevance of correct speech to social progress. She was gratified every time a child grasped the concept of subject-verb agreement or used "aren't" or "isn't" instead of "ain't," or correctly pronounced any of the vocabulary words with which she constantly challenged them.

Keziah was a particularly apt pupil, and by the time she was fourteen Miss Williams had pegged her as teacher material. Perhaps if she had remained on the scene her influence would have resulted in Keziah's going on to normal school to become a teacher. But in 1896 Miss Williams relinquished her teaching career at the insistence of her fiancé, a dentist who traveled all the way from the Bronx to propose. Her pupils were doubly impressed: that this well-dressed, obviously well-to-do young man had proposed to their Miss Williams and that a black man could be a dentist.

No one was sadder to see her go than Keziah. Her schooling ended at the seventh grade, but she had developed a passion for reading and spent any money the family could spare for her on books. She intended to marry an educated man. And Daniel Cates did not fall into that category.

Daniel Cates was a twenty-nine-year-old childless widower when he met Keziah while visiting with friends in Columbus the summer of 1902. Daniel had been a farm laborer down in the Alabama Wiregrass since he was six years old. Son of a sharecropper, he had by dint of hard work become a tenant farmer in Henry County, owning all of his tools and able to buy his own seed and fertilizer, thus reaping a greater profit than the average sharecropper, who rented everything from the farm owner.

Daniel's first wife, Matilda, was a plain, rather thin young woman from a neighboring farm who was sweet tempered and easy to talk to. More than a few young women had been attracted to Daniel and let him know it. But early in his search for a wife, Matilda's sweet ways put her near the top of his list — just below pretty, sloe-eyed Jane.

What steered him in Matilda's direction was not his eyes but his stomach, for Matilda was an excellent — no, a magical, cook. Her comestible concoctions — whether feather-light pie crust filled with buttery, sugared, cinnamon-dusted apple slices that bubbled enticingly as they baked; or black-eyed peas and okra flavored with exactly the right amount of ham and boiled to the precise tenderness most pleasing to the palate; or chicken fried to crisp, golden-brown perfection — sent forth tantalizing aromas that teased his taste buds and unleashed an overpowering appetite, driving him to Matilda's kitchen table time and again, each meal raising her in his estimation. Meanwhile, Jane's sour looks in Matilda's direction at church steadily diminished that young woman's appeal.

And so Daniel and Matilda were married. And although they were childless, it was a good marriage. Daniel knew that he had made the right choice, for this wife suited him.

But one summer, in the seventh year of their marriage, kind-natured, obliging Matilda agreed to keep two of her nieces in her home, both of them ill with chickenpox, in the hope that their younger siblings would not be infected.

Neither her sister nor her husband understood that the greater danger was to Matilda, who had not had chickenpox as a child. She caught the disease and died in less than a week.

Although Daniel's grief for Matilda was deep and long lasting, he managed to carry on. But when the crops he had put his mind, body, and soul into were destroyed by hail, it seemed to him, staring at the ruined fields, that God must be angry with him. His sweet, loving wife was gone. His farm was gone. He had to sell all of his farm equipment to pay his debts. If he had been a drinking man, he might have drowned his sorrows in whiskey and let the world go by. But he was too earnest and hardworking, too hardwired to wake up at dawn and wrestle with the earth until sundown, to vegetate. While he was considering searching for a job as a farm hand, his cousin Grover Cates, visiting from Columbus and seeing his stone-broke, grief-stricken condition, invited him to return with him for a nice long visit in the Dollarleaf community where he lived.

Daniel fell for Keziah Tolliver at first sight while visiting her church with Grover. He was struck by her petite size, erect bearing, and long braided hair. She had large eyes for such a small face and a bee-stung mouth with naturally deep-rose lips. Her long hair and cinnamon-toned skin were courtesy of one of her grandfathers, a Choctaw Indian.

Keziah was not equally impressed. When she was introduced to Daniel that day, she did not even note his name. Her mother was suffering from a sick headache, and she was worried about her and mentally planning the family's dinner meal.

Daniel's church attendance at home was erratic, but now he became a regular churchgoer. He began traveling to the Dollarleaf community via the Chattahoochee River almost every weekend. A Sunday came when he was able to seat himself right beside Keziah. He helped her hold her hymnal. He picked up her cardboard fan when she dropped it. When they stood up at the end of the service, she realized that he towered over her, almost six feet tall to her five feet. His height, broad shoulders, and attractive smile were somewhat appealing, but she lost interest at the first words out of his mouth.

"Is you ready to go, Miss Keziah?" he asked quietly. "Us can ride home in Grover's wagon, if you likes."

When she just stared at him without responding, he said, "Or us can walk. I'd be right proud to walk you home." And he offered his arm.

Trained to be polite, and knowing from Daniel's cousin, whom she had known all her life, that he could be trusted, she took his arm and permitted him to lift her up on the wagon seat while her amused father, brothers and sisters watched. Keziah frowned at them as the wagon started off, thinking, *I am just being polite to this fellow. That's all.*

It took many trips up to Columbus, but finally Daniel won her heart. He had only a fourth-grade education, but he could read well enough, otherwise he would not have had a hope with Keziah. They found they could converse on many subjects. And she came to appreciate his farming background. She not only helped with the family's vegetable plot, so important to their subsistence, but kept a flower garden as well. Daniel helped her improve her gardening techniques so that the roses and asters and begonias bloomed as never before. Time and again, in the way he quickly took a laundry load from Lena and carried it himself, or showed one of her younger brothers how to win at a card game, or brought her father a special brand of pipe tobacco he knew John would enjoy, Daniel demonstrated his consideration for others and his strong capacity to give of himself.

At first Daniel's uneducated speech jarred on her. But so deeply did she come to love this gentle man that when they talked of their future and she said "children" and he said "chillun," or when she said "we will" and he said "us will," she would think of his kind ways and his great leap from sharecropper to tenant farmer, purchased by so many long, hard years of toil, and his dialect would fall like music on her ears.

In May 1904, on the day before their marriage, Daniel fondly watched Keziah packing for the trip to southeast Alabama. Her family had given her a traveling trunk as a wedding gift.

It was packed with household items such as skillets, candle molds, and smoothing irons, linens, and dishes, as well as the dozen books she owned. Croker sacks full of cotton and feathers had been thrown into the wagon to be used for bedding. Keziah believed herself well provisioned to set up housekeeping. But on her wedding day, she discovered something special had been missing.

She and her sisters and friends had worked on a half dozen artistically designed quilts for more than a year, with the goal of selling them and donating the money to the small church in Dollarleaf. The friends exchanged secret smiles throughout the many hours of quilting. It was difficult to keep a secret, because in addition to the gossip and amusing stories spun out of their daily lives, concerns and confidences were routinely shared. But following the wedding, Keziah was genuinely surprised when she was gifted with one of the quilts. When she protested that it belonged to the church, the reverend's wife, who had been in on the deception, let her know that one of the quilts had been earmarked for her from the beginning, as something to remember them by. This brought home to her that she was leaving them all, and she indulged in a few tears and submitted to many hugs before agreeing with Daniel that it was time to start out for their new home.

They were traveling by wagon, and they had a long way to go. As they started out on their journey south, Daniel knew he had to own up to the truth about their future home. In all of their conversations about the farming life they would share in the Wiregrass, he had tried to be honest about his situation. But he had struggled with telling her the truth, letting Keziah assume he was still a tenant farmer, not just a farmhand. He simply could not admit that he had been unable to accumulate enough money to rent another farm and purchase all of the necessary equipment and supplies he needed. And sharecropping was a state he was unwilling to re-enter. Instead, he was working as a hired hand for Pierce Tomlin at Comfortroot farm in Houston County.

Daniel was aware of Keziah's deep desire to be independent and understood her mistrust of white folks. But he also knew that Pierce Tomlin was a fair boss who was giving him increasing responsibilities, for which he was fairly compensated. In addition, Pierce had agreed to let Daniel and his bride live in one of the well-maintained cottages on the property as long as Daniel worked for him, with the understanding that Keziah would help with some of the chores, particularly the cooking, in the bachelor's household. Thus Daniel had decided that he and Keziah could marry without waiting the months or even years it might take for him to rent another farm.

Fortunately, he had rightly judged that his new wife was a sensible young woman, and after reprimanding him with a frown or two during his guilt-ridden disclosure, she kissed him on the cheek and declared that she had no intention of jumping out of the wagon and running back home, so they might as well continue on their journey to their new home, no matter what kind of place it turned out to be.

KEZIAH WAS NOT so sure living on the Tomlin property was a good idea. Slavery times were over. Being so near to the boss man, at his beck and call, was too much like occupying somebody's slave quarters. Her parents had strong memories of those miserable times. Maybe it would be better for them to find their own place off the Tomlin property where they could live more independently.

But then she saw the snug little cottage. It had a variety of fruit trees in the yard — fig, peach, persimmon, and apple, as well as a couple of pecan trees — and red and yellow rosebushes by the porch which a previous tenant had carefully tended; a clothesline stretched taut between two pines right close to the house so you wouldn't have to carry a wash load but a few feet; and even a well a stone's throw from the back steps. Daniel had planted a flower garden at the rear of the cottage, and already multi-colored blossoms brightened the yard. When she saw all this, she could not resist the temptation to settle in and make a home there. The cottage was furnished, and she added some cozy personal touches, like her treasured quilt and curtains she fashioned out of a bright blue print fabric.

But Keziah remained wary of Pierce Tomlin. Although he was a fair employer who worked as hard as any of his hands, black or white, he had done nothing to prove he was different from any other white, privileged male. He might deceive her husband, who was unfailingly loyal to the man, but not her.

Soon after Daniel and Keziah arrived, Pierce confided to Daniel that he was courting a young lady and expected to marry before the year was out. At this Keziah sighed, thinking that even though they had found a tolerable boss, he might well select a Verbena VanStyer for a wife.

TWENTY-TWO-YEAR-OLD Pierce Tomlin had purchased Comfortroot Farm in 1903, the same year Houston County was carved out of Henry, Dale, and Geneva Counties to become Alabama's 67th, and last, county. The previous owners, delighted with the cash sale and eager to retire from a lifetime of farming, left him with a hired hand list, wished him luck, and settled in Birmingham near their only child, a daughter, who was married to a doctor.

Pierce had no family in Houston County; in fact, he was rumored to be a Virginian. There was no call to apologize for that. After, all, Virginia was the birthplace of Robert E. Lee. What raised eyebrows was that a man so young had somehow acquired the wherewithal to buy Comfortroot Farm lock, stock and barrel. Pierce not only owned the land, but a ten-room farmhouse with a wraparound porch, decorated with gingerbread trim and fish-scale siding and containing four fireplaces; a smoke house and a cane shed; an enormous barn; a chicken hatchery with 200 setting hens and ten roosters; a dozen fat cows and fifteen hogs; every necessary farm implement, all in good repair; a wagon; six mules; a smart, shiny black buggy; and three quarter horses.

As far as anyone had heard — and they didn't hear it from Pierce Tomlin, because he was as tightlipped in Alabama as he had been in Virginia — he was from a moderately successful family. And even if they had been well-to-do, he was the youngest of four sons and so would not have inherited. So if he were not an heir, nor old enough to accumulate the small fortune needed to buy Comfortroot, where in the name of heaven had the money come from?

Some speculated that his fortune consisted of ill-gotten gains. Maybe he had robbed a bank in some northern city and then lit out for Alabama. Why, any day now a posse might show up with a Wanted poster for young Pierce Tomlin. Another faction argued that, no, it wasn't no bank. He most likely robbed a train, like Jesse James or Sam Bass, and it wouldn't be surprising if he swung for it. These ghoulish speculations were voiced by the younger men, who did not appreciate the way Mary Alice or Jocelyn or Eloise looked at this stranger. Quite a few of them also resented the fact that Pierce was not only rich but, they had to admit, not bad looking. He was average in height but well-muscled, dark haired and dark eyed, with a neat Vandyke beard. He had even, very white teeth — for he neither dipped nor chewed — a fact deeply appreciated by the ladies. And he spoke in that cultured Virginia drawl, with never an "ain't" or "ary" or "by durn it" falling from his lips.

More than one young lady came to Pierce's defense, insisting that he was obviously an honest young man. He went to church and politely tipped his hat to her whenever they met. But that didn't cut any ice with the men.

In the late summer of Pierce's arrival, these spirited discussions were carried on at peanut boilings, picnics, and, in the case of the Primitive Baptist folk, all-day sings. He was invited to most of these events but was so caught up in getting the farm established that he seldom attended. Thus he could be discussed quite openly.

It was Jocelyn Fielding who suggested the true source of Pierce's fortune. Her brother Arthur had played poker all over the South, was in fact a habitual gambler. He had just returned home after an absence of six months. One Sunday afternoon a group of young people were enjoying dinner on the ground, seated on quilts spread beneath the trees at Poplar Leaf Baptist Church, when Jocelyn informed them she had learned the source of Pierce's fortune. They were sated with fried chicken, watermelon, biscuits, potato salad, chocolate cake, and lemonade and ready for a good story.

Without dwelling too much on Arthur's gambling habit, Jocelyn regaled an attentive audience with Pierce's exploits on the Chattahoochee River.

It seems the previous winter Arthur had been on a steamboat and seen a fellow the spitting image of Pierce Tomlin playing for high stakes. Arthur did not see the outcome of the game because of an unfortunate misunderstanding with another card player that resulted in a fight, and he had had to retire from the gaming room to attend to his bloodied nose.

Jocelyn rolled her eyes over this "boys-will-be-boys" episode, but reveled in making her point: Pierce Tomlin, the most eligible bachelor in Houston County, was not a robber, which would certainly have diminished his eligibility, at least in the eyes of the parents of some of the assembled group. He was in actual fact a gambler, or more accurately, a reformed gambler. Instead of continuing in sin and losing his fortune in the next poker game, as Arthur was forever doing, Pierce had sensibly invested his money in Comfortroot.

When the rumors about the source of his fortune got back to Pierce, he smiled the quiet smile that lightened his usually serious expression, a smile that raised the heart rate of more than one unmarried lady when it was directed at her. My, my, what a reputation he had acquired in such a short time. Train robber, bank robber, or riverboat gambler — which was it? Some men might have felt compelled to satisfy everyone's curiosity at this point. But Pierce preferred to keep his own counsel, and as far as he was concerned even the wildest of rumors could go untamed. All that concerned him was Comfortroot Farm. And, of course, the matter of acquiring a wife. He smiled again as his thoughts turned to certain attractive young women who had caught his eye.

ON A MILD April morning in 1904, Pierce Tomlin drove his shiny black buggy into Dothan and pulled up in front of the site for the new courthouse scheduled for completion the following year. He had been present for the groundbreaking and often stopped by to watch the progress being made in the construction of what was to be an impressive stone building, with a dome and a two-storied front entrance framed by

Corinthian columns. To him, the building symbolized the strides Dothan was making in evolving from a village into a real city. After chatting with a couple of the laborers for a bit and commending them on their work, he drove over to the hardware store on East Main Street, where he had some business to conduct.

Mary Alice Whitby was standing outside, and two young boys were running about. She called one of them back just before he crashed into Pierce Tomlin's buggy as he was reining up his horse. She and Pierce had crossed paths at church on a couple of occasions, and each time he had noted that she was one of the most beautiful women he had ever seen. Although he was glad of this opportunity to talk with her, he was surprised to see her with children and wondered if she were married. That would be a disappointment.

Pierce had not gone unnoticed by Mary Alice, either, and when he politely inquired as to her little boys' names, she promptly assured him that they were her brothers, not her sons. She was accustomed to admiring glances, which she usually ignored, but Pierce's pleased expression over her single state affected her so deeply that she did not notice when the youngest boy decided to climb into the buggy, which was much fancier than the Whitby wagon, to investigate.

"Oh, I'm so sorry, Pierce. Buddy! Come back here! Papa's in the store buying supplies, and we're just waiting for him, but these boys won't be still for a single minute."

"He's fine," Pierce said with a smile. "In fact, why don't I take the three of you for a spin around town while you're waiting for your father? I'm in no rush to take care of my business."

"Oh yes, Mary Alice! Please!" the boys begged.

"Well, all right. But I'd better go inside and ask Papa first."

Gabe Whitby insisted on being introduced to Pierce before allowing his children to go anywhere, even around the block, with this newcomer to their town. The father of eight, including five daughters, he was not opposed to his eldest girl socializing with Pierce, whose reputation as a prosperous bachelor had preceded him; but he nonetheless required the young man to return his children within the half hour.

As Pierce handed Mary Alice up into the buggy, he was delighted to finally have the chance to talk with this lady, who had caught his eye the first time he saw her, doubting she would ever give him a glance. Aphrodite had not omitted a single touch in bestowing beauty on this woman. She had an oval face with a wide brow and large, dark blue eyes; eyebrows so even and perfectly arched they might have been drawn. She had magnolia skin unmarred by a spray of freckles across her nose. She was also gifted with an abundance of dark, naturally wavy hair and a smooth hairline accented by a widow's peak. She was tall for a woman, just a couple of inches shorter than he was, with a generous bosom and a small waist.

After that day, having obtained her parents' permission to call on her, Pierce learned that Mary Alice's beauty was not merely skin deep. She was neither frivolous nor self-centered as might be expected of one so well endowed. She was intelligent, much better read than he was, and a loyal sister to a houseful of younger siblings. She had never had to work in the fields, but as the eldest girl in a large family she had early learned how to cook, clean, sew, and care for children. In a matter of weeks, Pierce proposed marriage and was accepted.

Although it was true that Pierce was considered a supremely eligible bachelor, the focus of much feminine attention, most of which caused him embarrassment, he had been amazed that one of the prettiest girls in the county had fallen as deeply in love with him as he had with her. The real question, he felt, was what on earth she saw in him. What had he done to deserve her?

When their engagement was announced, an equal number of bachelors and spinsters breathed sighs of disappointment.

PIERCE TOMLIN AND Mary Alice Whitby were married in November 1904 at the Poplar Leaf Baptist Church on the outskirts of Dothan, with three of her sisters as bridesmaids. Her parents and younger siblings, as well as numerous other relations, almost filled the church. Pierce's parents were both deceased, but his eldest brother, Eustace, came all the way from Richmond to serve as best man, bringing the other

Tomlin brothers, Clarence and Lawrence, with him. Pierce's favorite uncle and aunt, Jared and Peggy Milson, who owned a farm near Petersburg, also made the long trip from Virginia for this occasion. After a honeymoon on a riverboat on the Chattahoochee, the newlyweds settled down to make a life at Comfortroot.

When Keziah Cates was introduced to Mary Alice, her first impression was that this was a woman who would expect to be waited on hand and foot. But she quickly realized that nothing could be further from the truth. As they performed chores together, she learned that Mary Alice was inured to hard work and skilled in all the arts and crafts of housewifery: making soap and candles, canning and preserving, making her own cleaning products, baking, sewing, knitting, cooking, and growing herbs to season food. She was busy all the day long and seemed to appreciate Keziah's help. In Mary Alice's large family they could not afford hired help, and she was accustomed to coaxing and nagging younger children to perform their chores. It was nice to have someone helping out who did not have to be nagged.

Both Pierce and Mary Alice were healthy, vital young people and looked forward to a long life together. They expected to have many children. But thirteen months after they married, their full-term, perfectly formed son died within minutes of his birth. Mary Alice could not be consoled, and Pierce would awaken in the middle of the night, panicked to find her gone, only to catch sight of her by moonlight wandering across the yard, barefooted, wearing nothing but her nightgown. He knew she was hoping the cold would numb her grief. Each time he dragged her inside he would stoke up the fire, wrap her in a blanket, and make her drink something warm while she stared dully at him. The third time this happened, she became ill, and by the next day was fevered, her lungs beginning to fill with fluid. The doctor could do nothing against pneumonia and a woman who did not want to fight it. Within three days she was dead. This was a blow from which Pierce never entirely recovered.

Heartbroken and bitter, in the twilight hours he developed a close acquaintance with Johnny Walker and Jim Beam. On a frigid December night on the anniversary of Mary Alice's passing, he climbed up on the tin roof of his barn with boozy thoughts of jumping to his death, only to learn when he accidentally slid off while getting ready to jump that, although the roof was not high enough for successful suicide, it was sure as hell high enough for a body to hurt himself. With a broken collarbone and a fractured tibia, it would have been difficult to move even sober. Drunk, movement was not possible. He lay shivering on the cold hard ground, in excruciating pain, for three hours before Daniel Cates found him just as the sun was coming up.

Against his wife's wishes, Daniel had come by to check on Pierce, a habit he had developed ever since Pierce had started drinking himself senseless most evenings. It was that fallow time of year when farmers and farmhands can rest a while, and although Pierce had been giving him increasing responsibilities about the place, there were no chores that required his presence that morning. But his concern for Pierce summoned him there. When he could not find him in the house, he searched the yard and almost stumbled over his inert form in front of the barn.

"Good God, Mr. Pierce! What you done to yourself?"

Pierce gestured weakly toward the barn roof and mumbled something that sounded like, "Jumped," and then changed it to "fell."

"From up there on the roof? What you was on the roof for?"

While he was talking, Daniel was kneeling beside Pierce trying to figure out what was wrong.

"Where you be hurt?"

"Shoulder, I think," he rasped through chattering teeth. "Maybe leg, too. You got any whiskey, Dan'l?"

"You needs a doctor, Mr. Pierce. Let me help you into the house, then I'll take one of them fast horses and go."

Pierce's fractured bones screamed at him, and he could not stop shaking, but somehow Daniel got him into bed and covered him with a couple of quilts. There was a fireplace in the spacious bedroom, and Daniel started a roaring fire and brought Pierce a shot of whiskey. Before he left, he fetched

Keziah from their cabin, asking her to stay with Pierce until the doctor arrived.

She came unhesitatingly in the face of this emergency, but she did not come willingly. In the two-and-a-half years she and Daniel had been living at Comfortroot, she and Pierce had spoken few words to one another. Before her death, Mary Alice had facilitated most of their communication — "Keziah, Mr. Pierce wants to know if you and Daniel can pick up three more bags of grain at Satterwirth's when y'all go into town tomorrow;" or "Pierce, Keziah says Daniel keeps forgetting to ask you if they can have some of that spare rope in the barn so she can add another clothesline." After her passing, Pierce and Keziah exchanged information as needed, but she was not comfortable at the thought of holding conversation with the man and assumed he felt the same way. She had found that if he ever had two words to say, he didn't say them to her.

Nonetheless, she came up to the house to sit with Pierce in his time of need. She had not seen him in more than a week and was shocked at his appearance. His clothes were filthy, his hair overlong and unkempt, and the neat beard he took such pride in had not been trimmed in days. She pulled a chair close to the bed and sat down, heartily wishing she were anywhere but here. He fretfully reached for the whiskey glass, and she found she would have to hold it to his lips in order for him to drink it. He was still shivering from spending hours on the cold earth and did not seem able to speak.

"Just you try to rest, Mr. Tomlin. I know you're in pain. The doctor'll be here soon."

He moved slightly, which caused him to groan. She instinctively stroked his forehead and held his hand, which he squeezed so hard from the pain that she cried out. Then he let go and pitifully sighed, and she grabbed his hand again.

"Don't you go dying on me, Mr. Tomlin," she said.

The broken bones were probably not fatal, but he had lain out in the cold, in pain, for a long time, and she knew about shock and how people could die from it.

After a time, Pierce's teeth had stopped chattering sufficiently that he could speak, albeit in a hoarse voice that she had to lean close to hear.

"You know it's been a year since she — since Mary Alice — " He could not verbalize the thought.

"A year ago yesterday since Miz Mary Alice passed. Yes. Daniel and I remarked on it — on her passing — yesterday."

"Tell me something, Keziah," he almost whispered. "Why'd God have to take 'em both?"

She was silent. There was no answer to that question. Pierce's voice was becoming shakier, and she felt her composure slip a bit. Were those tears in his eyes? He had not cried, even at the funerals. She straightened his quilt and averted her eyes from his face.

"Best you don't dwell on it, Mr. Tomlin."

"Why'd he have to take 'em both, goddammit!" he managed to shout, banging a fist on the bed. He started trying to get up.

"Now you calm down before you hurt yourself."

Keziah put her small but strong hands on his shoulders and pushed him back down as hard as she could.

Pierce fell back on the pillows. The effort further injured his collarbone and caused him to grimace in pain. Tears streamed down his face. Keziah found a cloth and wiped his face. She wished Daniel and the doctor were there, but at present there was no one to help this man but herself. He sniffed loudly and then glared at her, looking as if he thought this were all her fault. She stiffened defensively, then realized that wasn't it. He wasn't blaming her. He was staring at her in desperation, with haunted, pleading eyes. He was looking to her for answers, but she didn't have any.

The sight of Mary Alice hugging that baby boy, dead after his first few ragged breaths, clutching him to her breast, rocking him, and screaming when her mother and the doctor insisted it was time to take him away for burial, had deeply saddened her. Pierce had mutely, powerlessly, stood by. And Keziah could scarcely believe it when this vital young woman was dead within a few weeks.

"Mr. Tomlin," she said softly. "You know your dear wife and your little baby are with Jesus now."

He responded with a fierce look that threw her words of comfort back in her face.

"No, they're not. They're in the cold ground. I know, because until I jumped — fell — off the roof, I visited their graves every single morning. And I never saw either of their graves open up or any grave stone roll away with an angel shouting 'they're alive!' God, no. All I saw was just red clay. You know, I always put pine boughs on their graves in the winter and wildflowers in summer. And I talk to them." Tears blurred his vision again, and he weakly swiped at his eyes. "Every morning, Keziah. But now I can't do that. And nobody will bring them flowers or pine boughs, and I can't talk to them."

Keziah sat on the chair beside the bed only because she had to, because there was no other soul to watch over this injured man until help came. It was not easy for her. She had always iced up in the presence of Mr. Tomlin the white boss man. He represented so much she hated. Not only was he white, but privileged — although he worked hard, it was well known he had not gained Comfortroot by the sweat of his brow. But watching this not unkind man dissolve before her eyes, touched by his pain and his need, she felt her heart thawing. She found she could no longer view him with the cool detachment that insulated her from the arrogance and mean-spiritedness of so many white people. She felt an ice-melting rush of compassion for this pitiful fellow. She reached for his limp hand and held it tightly.

"Now you listen to me, Mr. Tomlin." She stared directly into his reddened eyes. "You just listen. I don't know what your beliefs are. I thought you were a Christian, but I guess I was wrong. Christian folks grieve, of course they do. But they can carry on because they know they'll see their loved ones again."

She reached over and brushed Pierce's unkempt hair off his forehead.

"Now I knew Miz Mary Alice — what a good person she was. And your baby boy was as sweet and pure as it's possible to be. And if they aren't in heaven, then there must not be any heaven. But I don't believe that. I believe they're looking down on you right now, sorrowful because you're sorrowful, when God wants them to be joyful in the light. So you got to try to get over this here grieving, Mr. Tomlin. And you got to get over trying to do away with yourself. Daniel and I both know you wanted to die last night — whether you slipped or you jumped. And I believe God's plan is not for you to be sorrowful and in pain. He wants you to heal and get back to this here farm you love so much. It's going to be planting time soon. You want to still be laid up when it's planting time?"

Pierce shook his head. He held tight to her hand.

"And I'll tell you what else. There's some holly bushes near the house just bursting with red berries. After Daniel and the doctor get here to take care of you, I'm going to cut some holly branches, the prettiest ones I can find, and I'm going to put them on the graves for you. And I'm going to have a nice long talk with Miz Mary Alice and tell her how you're getting along. I'm going to give her all the details. Will there be anything special you want me to say to her?"

"You just tell her I'm getting better. You tell her I'm gonna be up and around real soon. And then I'll come visit again."

Keziah pried his fingers from her hand and, for the first time since they'd met, graced him with a smile.

"That's just what I'll tell her," she said.

Chapter 6

NOBLE

IN NOVEMBER 1927, Nathan Knightley pulled his jacket more snugly about him as he stood staring at the leveled fields he rented from Pierce Tomlin and briefly enjoyed the realization that it had been a good year. But he was seldom worry free for long. He soon reflected on the money he owed for seed and supplies, including the all-important chemicals to diminish the damage from boll weevils and the labor of the pickers he'd had to hire — nine of them this year. After paying Tomlin the annual land rental which would be applied toward the purchase of the property he had agreed to sell, the Knightleys would clear several hundred dollars. True, this was in addition to the sale of food crops over the summer and the milk and eggs Abby sold — the milk company sent the truck around every two weeks, and each time they got a check for $10. Even so, they would be just getting by, with nothing extra for emergencies. Nate staved off his worry by lighting up a Camel cigarette as he started on the long trek up to the house.

Bryce and Letty were picking the last of the pecans from the two large trees by the porch. Toby was trying to help but did not have a basket, and he could not hold more than four pecans at a time in his small hands. Nate noticed the boy was not wearing a jacket and motioned for him to go on inside. Toby looked disappointed but obeyed and dropped his pecans into Letty's basket.

Nate put out the cigarette, which Abby did not allow him to smoke in the house. He also observed her rule about reserving indulgence in corn whiskey to the evening hours after the children were in bed. The source of the whiskey was a still operated by a Coltayne cousin, one of Uncle Grayson's sons, who believed that in a democracy a man was entitled to his liquor. He declared he would dismantle the dang contraption (as his disapproving wife termed it) the day Prohibition was repealed. Nate's drinking was moderate and Abby knew drink did not control his life, but still there were times when in her opinion he drank too much, especially when anxiety about the crops and holding on to their hard-worn possessions and regret over the farm they had lost overwhelmed him.

Now he glanced at the pecan collection and asked, "Pecan pie?"

Bryce grinned and nodded.

Nate found Abby rolling dough at the kitchen table. The baby was sucking her fingers and watching her mother's every move from where she lay in the cradle. Nate pecked Abby on the cheek, who as usual issued an order.

"Well, if you want some pie, why don't you start shelling them pecans."

She gestured with her head to a half-full bowl, just as Letty came in with a basket containing what looked like enough to make a pie.

"Mama, Bryce says he's going on over to the Satterwirths."

Willoughby Satterwirth was one of Bryce's friends, the son of Millicent Tanner Satterwirth, Abby's close friend from childhood. Bryce was allowed to go to their place as long as he had no unfinished chores and so had not asked permission.

"Well, you set down and help Papa shell the nuts."

Letty plunked down on a chair with the basket on her lap. Before she started to work, she reached over and patted the baby.

"Can I hold Nobella?"

"When you're done shelling."

Nate would not be making the same request. He was still not comfortable with the thought of picking up and holding the newest member of the family. And he was still not comfortable with calling her Nobella, and in fact simply referred to her as "the baby." For now Abby let him get away with that, but when the child was past infancy that would not work. Once again, he mightily wished Abby had chosen any other name for the child. Noble Coltayne was not worthy of having one of Nate's children named after him — as anyone who knew the facts of that scoundrel's life would have to agree.

IN 1890, FORTY-THREE-YEAR-OLD Noble Coltayne was a prosperous cotton agent in Apalachicola, the third largest cotton port on the Gulf after New Orleans and Mobile. Tall and slim, with graying dark hair and a luxuriant handlebar mustache, he wore custom-made suits and a finely woven straw hat from Ecuador to shield his fair skin from the scorching Florida sun. He smoked expensive Cuban cigars hand rolled in Ybor City near Tampa.

The rich aroma of the cigar sometimes made him smile with pleasure, as did the green lawn stretching before them down to the Gulf and the sight of his wife and four healthy children. He had known hardship and loss in the past, and no aspect of the good life he now led went unappreciated.

It was not surprising that a man of Noble's intelligence and acumen should be successful. But it was just short of miraculous that he had survived the events of his youth and lived to tell the tale. He told it often to assembled relatives and friends, usually after supper while sitting on the veranda of his charming, spacious home, with one booted foot propped on the railing as he leaned back in a comfortable wicker chair and enjoyed another one of those fine cigars.

While Noble believed that storytelling was an aid to the digestion, he preferred not to bore his audience and so only regaled them with one part or another of this tale at a time. But here is the entire story in his own words, written down by one of his children, and set forth for those with leisure to read it:

AS I THINK you know, the Coltaynes and the Knightleys go way back together to the old colonial days in North Carolina. In '29, when the Government opened up new Creek lands, John Knightley and Gabriel Coltayne brought their families down the old Federal Road to Alabama. My pa, Ross Coltayne, wasn't but twelve years old when they made that rough journey on a road that was hardly more than a cattle path, always on the lookout for hostiles. Papa's sister, Aunt Sally Ann, married old John Knightley's son Josiah, and that's how our families hooked up. We settled in Barbour County and kept on a-doin what we'd been a-doin in Carolina, but because land was so cheap we had a lot more room to do it in. So we prospered.

John Knightley helped found Galilee Primitive Baptist Church near Crossvine. The Knightleys stuck to that faith, but us Coltaynes felt more akin to John Wesley, so we become practicing Methodists.

Well now, I was fourteen the year the Civil War started. There'd been all this talk of war for months — years, really. But nothing ever come of it. And there was all the talk about ending slavery, which didn't matter a hill of beans to any of us Coltaynes because we never did own the first slave. We cleared every inch of our own land, plowed it and planted it and harvested it ourselves up there in Barbour County.

Anyway, one July afternoon I was a-hoein beans or some such when my seven-year-old brother Tobias come running lickety split acrost the field, yelling at me and Papa and Grayson to come on to the house right away because our cousin Peter Knightley had come to tell us about a war going on in some funny-sounding place. Toby was red faced and sweating and all out of breath. He was supposed to be working in the fields with us, but at breakfast Ma had told my sister Susannah to churn some butter, and of course that meant a fresh supply of buttermilk, Toby's favorite drink. He had sneaked up to the house just as Susannah was separating the milk from the butter and pouring it into jugs, and like she always did she spoiled him, giving him a cup even though he was supposed to be elsewhere, hard at work.

Toby was yelling that we had to come on to the house right now. Papa Ross and Grayson had been down on their knees weeding around the beans and the tomatoes, cussing like they generally did after a few hours in the hot sun, and Pa stood up and muttered, "What foolishness is this here? I ain't got time for such." And I think more because we was thirsty for some of the buttermilk than because we believed a thing Peter Knightley said, we all stopped in our tracks and went up to the house, though not at a run like Toby.

When we got there, Ma was looking mighty upset. Susannah put her arm around her waist. Millard had been digging a stone out of his mare's hoof when he heard all the ruckus and come up from the barn.

Peter Knightley was wore out because he'd been riding from one farm to the next in the brutal heat, telling everyone about the news he'd heard at Blue Springs. Alabama had seceded in January, and when the Confederates fired on Fort Sumter in April, war was declared. Nothing much of note had happened since then. But according to Peter, the Yankees had attacked the Confederates at a place called Manassas in Virginia. The Confederates had beaten them back and easily won. The Union soldiers had tucked tail and skedaddled back home

"Alabama's really at war now," Peter said. "We're going to war. All of us boys."

Well, I about jumped out of my skin for joy. You do not know how much I wanted to go to war. I knew how to use a rifle, and I knew for sure I'd make a good soldier.

Millard and Grayson seemed excited, too, but Papa looked madder'n a wet hen.

"War! When the hell do we have time for a war? I got near a hundred acres of crops to tend to. We got livestock that needs looking after. Peter, you don't own ary a slave and neither does your pa. Let the slave owners go fight the damn war!"

Peter looked around at each of us and said, "The Yankees attacked the South. We're southern. We got to send them back up north where they belong, or else they'll just take our land. All of it. I'm riding over to Glennville in the morning to enlist, and so's David and Jackson. Micah wants to come along, too, but he's too young to fight."

"Well, you and your brothers can do whatever you want, I reckon. But I ain't a-gonna fight, and neither is any of my boys."

Grayson and Millard contradicted Papa with a look that said, "We're grown. We're gonna fight."

But they didn't say nothing. They knew they couldn't change Papa's mind. At daybreak the following day, they rode over to Glennville. I tried to tag along, but they each grabbed one of my arms and carried me back into the house, talking about how Toby and me had to stay and help Papa and Mama. About how important that was. And that turned out to be an understatement, believe me.

Well, so, they was gone, having joined up with the 15th Alabama infantry. That was 1861. Of course, the work on the farm doubled for me and Tobias and Susannah. At first Papa was able to hire some help, mostly fellows like me too young for the war, so it wasn't so bad. We was all used to hard labor anyway. Not just hoeing and plowing, but toting buckets of water from the well to the fields so many times in a dry spell that it felt like our arms would drop off.

The war was being fought mostly in the upper South, and we figured it would stay that way. In Barbour County, there weren't no factories, no railroads for the Yanks to blow up, so we didn't have to worry about Yankees showing up on our doorstep. But then one day the war become horrible real for us.

At Second Manassas, in August of '62, Millard was blown to pieces by a cannonball explosion. We learned about it a few days later when they posted the casualty list at the county courthouse. We was all stunned, and of course it like to kilt Mama and Papa.

Now I still wanted more than ever to be a soldier. Only now I didn't just want to shoot off a gun. I wanted to kill a Yankee with one. I wanted to kill the very man that fired the cannonball that kilt my brother, if possible. But any Yankee would do.

Well, as the war wore on, the slaughter got worse and worse, and the blood of the Knightleys and the Coltaynes was spilt all over the South and up north, too. Between them, John Knightley and Gabriel Coltayne had more than fifty Confederate descendants. Thirty-two of those men died in battle or of disease. Which disease don't matter — there was lots to choose from: typhoid, dysentery, pneumonia. And all of them soldiers was my cousins or uncles, one of them my brother.

Remember Peter Knightley, who got us so fired up about going to war? He died at Sharpsburg in September 1862. The following year his brother David died at Elmira Prison in New York.

Grayson and Millard was right when they dragged me back into the house and told me it was more important for me to stay and help on the farm than to go to war. Nothing was ever truer. Because the fact that I stayed on the farm till near the end of the war didn't only help our family, but dang near every family around us. Down in the Wiregrass we was luckier than folks in a lot of places — Richmond was leveled by retreating Confederates, burning and blowing up anything that might help the invading Yanks; Atlanta was burned to the ground, and on and on.

But the war didn't just level cities. It took near all of the men folk from every nook and cranny of the South. And farm after farm went to ruin because there wasn't no able-bodied person to tend it. And this went on for years. And for every farm that failed, the hungry people multiplied. But we was able to keep our farm going, and wives and widows and sisters and younger brothers from surrounding farms come to help us, and we shared every crop with them, down to the last potato and bean and ear of corn. And we fed people too feeble to do any farm work, too.

Of course, shortages of the things we used to buy in town was common because of the Union blockades, particularly in inland towns like Eufaula. Like everyone else, we learned to make do with whatever was at hand. There was dozens of substitutes for medicines. I remember us growing our own castor oil beans, crushing them, boiling them, and skimming off the oil. We used goose grease and sorghum molasses, backed up with turpentine and brown sugar, for croup. Real coffee was a thing of the past, too. We drunk concoctions of parched okra seeds, parched sweet potatoes, or parched corn hominy. Southerners might have been lacking in a lot of things during the war, but resourcefulness was not one of them.

In September of '63, we knew Grayson had been at Chickamauga, and we knew that the Confederates won, but there was a huge number of casualties on both sides. Thankfully his name had not appeared on the casualty list.

One chilly morning in October, Pa rubbed his skinny arms at the breakfast table and commented on how this was almost hog-killing weather. Susannah made a face because it always upset her to hear the hogs squealing when we slaughtered them. She claimed they always sounded as if they knew what was going to happen to them. Of course they didn't, and we killed them quick, and I noticed she always ate her share of bacon and pork. And she loved cracklings, especially when Ma baked them into the cornbread.

I went on out to chop some more firewood, and I was just fixing to raise the ax when one of our neighbors come riding up with some mail. I threw down the ax and grabbed the letter from him. I could see right away it was from Grayson. Funny thing was, it wasn't addressed to Pa, as usual. It was addressed to me. Now I don't remember word for word what the kind volunteer at the hospital wrote down for him, but it was something like this:

Dear Noble,
I hope this letter finds you all well. I am sorry you have not heard from me, but of late I was in some pretty heavy fighting.
Maybe you know we beat the Yanks at Chickamauga, but I was wounded pretty bad. A Minie ball hit my right leg and shattered it. The doctors had to take it off below the knee.
The reason I am sending you this letter is that I need you to do me a favor. I need for you to go see Eugenia. Now, I don't know if she will want a man with just one leg. I don't rightly know how much good I will be

around the farm. I will understand if she says maybe she can't marry no one-legged man.

But I surely would like to know how she feels about it before I go calling on her when I get home. I will be home as soon as I am healed up. So please go and talk to her, and tell me what she said when I get home.

      Your brother, Grayson Coltayne

Then he added,

And please tell the folks about my leg for me.

That letter hit me several ways. Shock at Grayson losing his leg. Relief that he was coming home. And then aggravation with him for fearing Eugenia would not want him. That girl believed the sun rose and set in Grayson — and still does, after more than twenty years of marriage and six children.

I couldn't get inside the house fast enough to tell the family the news, and of course they all shouted and carried on, and right away Ma started making homecoming plans. I know they heard the part about the amputated leg, but you wouldn't know it from the way they was all grinning and talking at once.

That evening I took the letter to Eugenia and let her read it, and naturally she bawled, and then she kept saying, "Thank God!" over and over. And I did not hear her say word one about how she would miss the part of him he had to leave in Georgia. Grayson was home in less than a month, and him and Tobias run that farm to this day.

Now, by 1864, with people all around us grieving, with my friends and relatives dying or being maimed nearly every day, I had about lost my soldiering itch.

My friend Fraser McFarland found this interesting and even somewhat amusing. Fraser's father Peyton was a Scotsman who settled in Barbour County in 1849. Fraser and me was about the same age and had knowed each other since we wasn't nothing but tadpoles. His sister, Maisie — a good-looking, sweet-tempered gal — was Susannah's best friend.

None of the McFarlands wanted any part of secession. Mr. McFarland was a close-mouthed fellow, but his wife Gwennie was a real tartar. Raised in a rocky clime where she claimed farming was about a hundred times harder than it was the Wiregrass, she was scornful of slaveholders, who forced others to do their work for them. She tongue lashed anyone who defended secession or the war. But she was always kind to me, especially after Millard was kilt.

Fraser and me went everywhere together. And got into all kinds of fixes together. One day we decided we was man enough to sample Papa Ross's corn liquor and drank so much we was sick for three days. Nobody whipped us because they figured the liquor had punished us enough. And sometimes we tried to race each other on the family mules, but they just plodded along and every now and then looked back to see what had happened to the plow. Anyhow, we did just about everything together. But because of his family's views, we never did talk about going to war together.

In February of '65, ready or not, it was my turn to pick up a gun and shoot some Yanks. I had just had my eighteenth birthday, and I was in a real fix. When I was a-rarin to be a soldier, I was too young. But now that soldiering was the last thing on earth I wanted to do, I was a prime target for conscription.

All along, I'd been pondering what this war was all about. If it really was about freeing the slaves, well, we never owned any to begin with, number one. And number two, Mr. Lincoln had already freed the slaves. So why should I fight? The Yankees had killed a lot of us. We had killed a lot of them. Both sides had proved to each other thousands of times over that they was capable of merciless slaughter. We treated them Union boys like animals at Andersonville prison. They treated Johnny Reb like garbage at Elmira.

Wasn't it kind of a draw?

Anyways, I'd had enough of the war, and I wasn't even in it yet. But a healthy eighteen-year-old out of uniform was not to be borne. I was required to report for service to the Confederacy, and the low-ranking, full-of-himself officer who came out to our place to inform me of this, in case I had forgotten, was downright hostile. When I reluctantly confirmed my birth date, this fellow sneered, "Eighteen? By God, lots of fourteen- and fifteen-year-olds are on the front lines, man. What are you sitting around for, letting younger men do your fighting? Do your duty, sir!"

Well, I had not been sitting around, as my callused hands and sore muscles could attest. I had been feeding my family and assorted widows, orphans, and old folks. I might also have pointed out that Barbour County was not the front lines, so if he was so fired up about going to battle, what was he doing here? And furthermore, anybody younger than eighteen was not a man but a boy, and shame on the folks who allowed children to go to war. However, I knew better than to pick a fight with a military man, and so I agreed to start doing my duty right away.

Of course, everyone at home was carrying on, trying to accept the inevitable but fighting tears as I saddled up to leave. I reassured them as best I could, but I knew in my heart that I was doomed. Doomed. There was a cannon ball or a bayonet or a Minie ball with my name on it, like there'd been for Millard and Peter Knightley and the dozens of others I knew of who was dead or mutilated — worse than dead. I knew a local man, a survivor of Sharpsburg, with no arms. Someone had to feed him every mouthful of food he ate and pour every shot of corn liquor he asked for down his throat — and he drank a lot of corn liquor. A neighbor had been blinded in an explosion and had to be led around everywhere. A seventeen-year-old boy, a gentle, shy fella who used to play the sweetest fiddle music you ever heard, sat on his mother's porch and rocked and whimpered all day long, having lost his reason in the heavy shelling of Atlanta the previous July.

I rode my last mile to the enlistment post feeling as if I was going to my execution. As I tied up my horse at the livery stable, a man stepped out of the shadows. He was not in uniform. He wore a wide-brimmed felt hat and a loose-fitting jacket which I assumed concealed at least one weapon. Before I could draw my pistol, he reached for my hand and shook it.

"Well, hello there, young fellow. How are you doing this fine afternoon?"

I knew by the first few words out of his mouth he was no southerner.

"Fine. You?"

"Oh, fair to middling I'd say. Are you here to enlist?"

I removed the saddle, took a brush out of the saddlebag, and begun rubbing my horse down.

"I don't reckon that's any of your business."

"Easy now, neighbor. I don't mean any harm. I merely wanted to impart some information to you."

"*Impart*?" I knew what the word meant, but had never heard anybody use it. "Impart just what, exactly?"

The stranger looked around in every direction before he pulled out a piece of paper from his jacket. We was alone, but he still seemed a little nervous as he handed it to me. It was a Union recruitment flyer. This fellow was clearly a Yankee, right here in Barbour County, among the very people his people was killing every day. I had to credit him for his nerve. I had heard about Confederates caught recruiting Yankees. The Union had executed them. Surely this man knew the same fate awaited him if he was caught by Rebels. I looked into his face and realized he was not much older than me. I did not see any hatred there, and strangely, I did not feel any hatred, either. As he had done, I glanced around carefully before reading the flyer.

I do not know why that flyer affected me so deeply, but it did. It took me right back to my childhood, and I remembered how exciting it used to be to see the old flag carried in a parade in Eufaula, what strong feelings Old Glory stirred in all of us. And I thought about how so many men had given their lives for our country's freedom.

And suddenly I realized I wasn't no Rebel. I was an American.

The stranger was watching me carefully, on the alert, ready to skedaddle if need be. But he read the look on my face rightly, as he must have read that same look on the faces of other men throughout the South. He did not urge me to speak, but I recognized the need to conclude this business

MEN OF THE WIREGRASS!

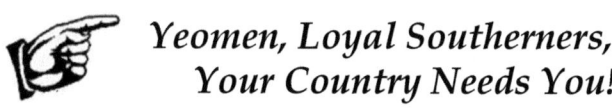 *Yeomen, Loyal Southerners, Your Country Needs You!*

UNION FOREVER

The Glorious Union was created by our forefathers and sealed with their blood.
The Union needs your help to stamp out TREASON and REBELLION.
Let us hand down to our children the legacy so hard won!

The secessionists and the rich planters whose snobbish daughters would not give you the time of day urge you to fight their RICH MAN'S WAR. But in their army it will be a POOR MAN'S FIGHT.

DO NOT JOIN THE REBELS

Farmers and the sons of farmers – loyal countrymen of good moral habits – join the FIRST FLORIDA UNION CAVALRY, UNITED STATES VOLUNTEERS today!

Fight for the OLD FLAG. Put down the rebellion and save your country, which is in dire peril! Fight for freedom and Uncle Abe.

Muster rolls are open at secret sites in Henry, Pike, Barbour, Dale, Covington, and Coffee counties.

one way or the other in a speedy manner before one or both of us was shot at.

"I'll think on it," I said.

The stranger nodded with a faint smile and then added, just in case I decided to join up, "You'll need to know where to enlist. Are you familiar with the McFarland farm?"

A shock went thought me for an instant. Then I realized it made perfect sense.

"They're friends of mine."

"A friend you may be. But just in case, I'm warning you. We have men posted around the place, and if you behave in a hostile manner, or bring others with you to do harm to that family, you will be severely dealt with. Do you understand?"

"I do."

"See you at midnight. Don't come before then. And remember, you will be watched."

I nodded, and we shook hands.

Back home, I tried to tell my folks what I was about to do, but words failed me. I truthfully said I had gone to the enlistment post but not yet signed up, that I had been directed to return that night, and that I would most likely be gone by the morrow. I said I was not sure I would see them again before I left.

That evening, we once again said our goodbyes. I started out just after sundown, because I could not explain a midnight rendezvous to my family. I was thankful for the chance to while away several hours on a peaceful creek bank in the company of a few friendly deer before I cast my lot with the Union — the enemy my people had been fighting for nearly four long, bloody years.

Yet and still, the thought of our country being whole again one day, the thought of the old flag being my flag again, was stronger than any hatred or fear of Yanks.

Thankfully, the sky was overcast as I rode over to the McFarland place. As I rode into the yard, two men stepped forward.

"I'll have your weapon," one said.

The other fellow chuckled.

"That there's just one of them clodhopper Coltaynes. It's doubtful he's ever shot anything bigger than a raccoon, so he sure ain't dangerous."

"Evening, Darby," I said as I dismounted.

Darby Jinks, a big man with a brain about the size of a chicken's, I reckon, was a wrongun if there ever was one. He'd been in one scrape or another his whole life and of late had spent a couple of months in the county lockup for drinking and brawling.

I was told to put my horse in the barn and come in the back door of the house. There was a good fire going, but lamps was turned low. Mrs. McFarland was up, but Maisie and the younger children was in bed, presumably asleep in the loft above. But if I knew Maisie, she was listening to every word through the floorboards.

Fraser and Peyton McFarland smiled a greeting, and half a dozen other men I did not know gave me the once over, seeming to accept that I wasn't going to cause no trouble.

Mrs. McFarland was pouring coffee for everyone and stopped to give me a hug.

"I always knew you had some sense, lad," she whispered in my ear.

The recruiter who'd directed me here was Captain Gilbert Parks of Springfield, Ohio.

"Let's keep this brief, gents," he began. "You all have your reasons for being here. I hope loyalty to the Union is one of them. You are joining the First Florida Cavalry Volunteers, and you will march by night under guard of several Union soldiers to Fort Barrancas at Pensacola. You leave tonight."

"You said cavalry," one fellow commented. "I come here on a mule. So where's my horse?"

"Like thousands of soldiers, blue and gray, in every part of the country, sir, you will march to your destination. When you arrive at the fort, you will be assigned a horse. You will also receive $300 and a new uniform."

None of the men, including me, objected to a bit of this.

"But first things first. Mr. McFarland, the Bible, if you please."

One by one, us new recruits placed our hands on the McFarland family Bible and swore the oath of allegiance to the United States of America.

Captain Parks explained that the man who'd relieved me of my weapon outside was a Union officer and that several men under his command was staked out around the house, ready to accompany us on the march to our first safe house, which we was scheduled to reach by dawn. Like Captain Parks, all of the Union men was dressed in plain clothes.

As we started filing out the back door, I cast a pleading look at Peyton McFarland. I did not need to put my request into words.

"I'll tell your folks where you've gone, Noble."

Tears welled up in my eyes.

"You reckon they'll ever want to see me again?"

"I can't say, son. But I do know this. I've never known Ross Coltayne to be a fire-breathing Rebel. He's just a farmer, like me. He just wants this war to be over. And when it is, I truly believe he'll want his sons to be home together, no matter what uniform they wore in the war — as will your mother."

And with that hope I had to be content.

FORT BARRANCAS WAS located on the mainland at the entrance to Pensacola Bay. It was built by the Spaniards when Florida still belonged to them. When Florida seceded in January 1861, the Confederates demanded that the Federal troops stationed there vacate the fort. Most folks don't know this, but the first shots of the Civil War wasn't fired at Fort Sumter — they was fired by the Confederates in their attempt to take Fort Barrancas from the Union. Outgunned and outmanned, the Federals moved to nearby Fort Pickens on Santa Rosa Island, where they remained throughout the war. But they got Fort Barrancas back in May 1862, when the Confederates abandoned Pensacola after the Union Army took New Orleans.

We arrived in mid-February, when the winter Florida sun was bearable, and we did the best we could to keep the sand off our clothes and out of our food. We had to build our own shebangs — huts made out of boards and branches.

My uniform was the first new, manufactured suit I'd ever owned. Ma bought our jean-pants but always sewed our shirts, and every jacket I'd ever owned was a hand-me-down.

I soon got attached to my horse. I named him Lucky, hoping that in battle he would be, and that, if so, I would benefit. However, as it turned out, I would spend most of my time in the Union army marching, not on horseback.

We got some teasing from the Yanks, such as, "Your Rebel yell's more like a squeak now, ain't it, boys?"

I ignored it. As a younger brother, I'd growed up used to insults and teasing and paid it no mind. But other Rebels, Darby among them, took issue and got into fights. As a result, the brawling Rebels and Yanks had the joy of spending several days in the brig together.

Soon after arriving, we learned why we was stationed at Fort Barrancas. The previous August, Admiral David Farragut launched the army-navy operation that destroyed Mobile's Confederate naval squadron and closed Mobile Bay to blockade runners. But even though the Port of Mobile was closed, Mobile itself could not be attacked because of how the Confederates had blocked the upper bay and fortified the city. It was only now that General Edward Canby, the Union commander in the Gulf, had enough manpower to mount an overland campaign to take Mobile.

Now, when I say overland, I mean over some of the roughest, wildest, most bug-infested land any troops was ever called upon to traverse. My unit was part of the XIII Corps under General Frederick Steele that headed out of Fort Barrancas in mid-March. We'd been told we would probably face resistance at Pollard and Stockton before we reached Spanish Fort and Blakely, where the real battle for Mobile would begin.

We trudged through swamps and run into quicksand and the occasional alligator or cottonmouth, not to mention entrenched Confederates shooting at us all along the way. We had to build our roads as we went – rough corduroy roads of pine logs that we drug our heavy guns and wagons over. The XVI Corps had it a lot easier, traveling by navy transport to

Fish River Landing, where we finally joined them after near a week of that hellacious overland journey.

At Pollard, we cut the telegraph line and busted up the railroad. We was nigh unto Spanish Fort, wore out from the rough march and subsisting on quarter rations, when the Confederates surprised us with an attack, but our forces pushed them back.

I lost track of Fraser McFarland, but at Spanish Fort I found myself close to my old friend Darby, just as he took a bead on a mounted Confederate officer. The three stars on the collar of his uniform proclaimed him to be a colonel.

If this was a rebel unit, Darby's gun would likely have been the one he brought from home, maybe even his grandpa's smoothbore musket. But our Sharps rifles was Union issue — newly manufactured, the deadliest available.

Now of course I knew I was supposed to shoot Confederates, but I had never yet done it. Nor seen another southerner do it. So I was unprepared for the speed with which Darby took aim and shot that fellow through the neck before I could say the words that was stuck in my throat: "Now, Darby, he's a southerner, he's one of us. Let's just think about this for a minute."

The fellow's boots was stuck in the stirrups, and the horse galloped off with the corpse. Darby was grinning.

"Did you see his rank? He was probably a planter. So that's one less rich boy to lord it over us."

I had never met any planters myself, but I guess Darby had and took offense at their highfalutin ways. When Darby saw the shock on my face he said, "I think you'd better remember which side you're on now, Noble. You seem confused about that."

Just then a barrage of enemy fire forcibly reminded me of which side I was on. Luckily, we was in thick, jungle-like woods, and I quickly found cover behind the broad trunk of a large cypress tree. My blood pumped wildly through my veins and sweat drenched my body as I wondered how in God's name I was still alive. My weapon was primed and ready to fire, and I thought I was safe. But then I seen a rebel to my rear spot me and take aim at me, and suddenly my concern about killing one of my own people just vanished, and I shot him. He was hit in the arm and fell down and dropped his rifle, and I rushed over to finish him off before he could retrieve it. I grabbed his gun and slung it off into the trees and then stood over him, aiming at his head.

There was a lot of blood streaming down his arm, but I could see it was probably just a flesh wound. He stared up at me. He didn't beg for his life. He stared right into my eyes as if to say, "Just go ahead and do it. I ain't afraid."

He was very young, not more than fifteen, and put me in mind of Tobias. I lowered my rifle and said, "Well, get along, then."

The boy got to his feet and staggered off. I guess he was dazed, because he didn't crouch down and try to find cover the way you're supposed to do, he just walked along like he was going for a stroll. I started to walk away, then turned back when I heard a shot and saw the boy keel over. A Yank had picked him off, shot him right through the head. Well, that just made me sick to my stomach.

That night there come a pouring rain. I hunkered down in a dug-out hole under an oak near some of the other Yanks, trying not to drown in the deluge. I kept thinking about that young Rebel. About how the rain had washed away the blood from his arm wound and his head wound by now, and he would maybe just look like he was asleep. Or maybe some Rebel boys had collected him and buried him. I could not stop thinking about the boy, and I decided I could not shoot another one. And even if it hadn't of been for the dead Rebel, I realized I was tired of being shot at and that none of it made a bit of sense to me. While it was still raining and each man was concentrating on the durn near impossible task of trying to sleep while soaked to the skin, I figured it was a good time to take my leave.

Just before sunrise, as the rain was letting up, I got to a pine scrub area near the beach where I rested. I had enough provisions in my haversack to last a couple of days, and I knew I could survive on fowl and fish, which in this area abounded.

When I reached Pensacola, I snuck into some poor fella's back yard and stole a pair of jean-pants and a shirt off his clothesline to replace my uniform. Thievery has never been in my blood, and I ain't proud of that, but there it is.

I decided to head farther east along the Gulf Coast. One of the Floridians I'd been in service with had bragged about his hometown, Apalachicola, about how it was one of the busiest ports in the country. That seemed like a good place to get away from the war and find work. But it was some 140 miles distant. At the docks, I was told I could earn my passage by working aboard ship, and within a few days I was scrubbing decks and mending nets on a three-masted sailing vessel headed east along the coast. I never found my sea legs and so was not tempted to join the crew.

When I arrived in '65, Apalachicola had been a cotton port for more than forty years. At first, the cotton was shipped downriver from Columbus on flatboats, but now twenty steamboats plied the Apalachicola River. There was more than forty warehouses in town where cotton was compressed, then shipped to any place there was cotton mills or lace manufacturing centers, like New England, England, France, and Belgium. More than 50,000 bales of cotton shipped between December and June.

Soon after my arrival there, I learned that the Federals had taken Mobile and that Lee had surrendered in Virginia. The war was over. But I also heard that the southerners in the Union Army was being held until November to allow for a cooling-off period before they went home to their defeated Confederate friends and families. This sounded like a wise idea to me, and I decided to dig in where I was for a few months before I headed out for Alabama. I wrote home and let my folks know so they would not worry. I had naturally sent them a sizable portion of my enlistment bonus, and in all of their letters they had assured me I was still considered part of the family.

When I went looking for work, it was not hard to find a job as an apprentice cotton agent, which meant I no longer had to camp in the woods, I could rent a room. After months of soldier's rations and living off what I could forage for in the woods or catch in the Gulf, I was delighted to sit down to my landlady's home-cooked meals of greens and grits, fried chicken, and cornbread.

I didn't mind being in such a beautiful place. I enjoyed walking along the Gulf shore and watching the seabirds, and I got in a lot of fishing. But I was homesick and said as much in my letters back home.

One breezy morning in late November I walked into the post office at the general store and picked up a letter from Susannah. That letter changed everything.

> Dear Brother,
> I am writing to beg you not to come home. It is not safe. As you may know the Union Army finally released the Alabama boys that served with them and they come home. A week after Darby Jinks got here he was shot and killed at his front door and someone put a piece of paper on his dead body that said Death to Traitors.
> The day after Fraser McFarland got home, him and his family went to town to get supplies and while they was gone their house and barn was burned to the ground, and all their livestock and every last chicken was stolen. So all of them, including Maisie, my best friend in the world — all of them cleared out. They just left for God knows where, and I reckon I will never see Maisie again.
> So you must not come home. Papa and Mama beg you not to come. If God wills it, we will be together again some day. But please, please do not come back to this place.
> We all send our love. We will pray for you every day.
> Your loving sister, Susannah

Upon reading that letter, I felt completely alone. And I *was* alone. Because of my dereliction of duty towards both the Confederacy and the Union, I was subject to being made an example of in some horrendous way by folks of either persuasion, and I could imagine more than one tragic ending to the tale of my unheroic life. Since arriving in Apalachicola, I had kept pretty much to myself for that very reason, but my solitary state was bearable because I intended to head home before Christmas. Now I understood that was not to be.

In late December, I walked into the general store and was startled to see a new clerk who was an old friend. The young fellow behind the counter wearing an apron and measuring out sugar for a customer was none other than Fraser McFarland. He grinned as he extended his hand.

"Well as I live and breathe, Noble! What are you doing here?"

"Surviving. Like you. Susannah wrote me about your farm. I'm sorry, Fraser."

He shook his head.

"We lost everything. But we're getting along."

"Your family – are they all well?"

"They are. We're renting a house with a yard big enough for a vegetable garden. Pa's getting the hang of catching fish for a living, but that's not for me. I'll probably remain a landlubber."

Another customer walked in, in search of some calico, and before attending to her needs Fraser invited me to dinner that evening.

If I did not truly appreciate it before, that night I realized that Maisie McFarland — with her fair hair and sea-blue eyes and gentle ways — was a gem among women, and she seemed to look favorably upon me, as well. We married the following spring.

Maisie invited Susannah to Apalachicola, and within a year she and Fraser was married, too.

In 1872, my parents turned the Barbour County farm over to Grayson and Tobias and decided to make their home with Maisie and me.

It is my good fortune to have friends and family who overlook the fact that I was a traitor to the Confederate cause and a deserter from the Union Army. Better men than me have been shot or hanged for being either of those things — and certainly I've been called a coward and worse names by quite a few individuals.

But while I do not dispute that the war had to be fought, regardless of the cost, and that maybe I should have shouldered a gun for the duration and done my share of the shooting, I have to be truthful: I ain't ever lost a minute of sleep over the fact that I did not kill ary a soul in the Civil War.

Chapter 7

A Precocious Child

AS THE SUMMER of 1890 drew to a close and Noble Coltayne was once again entertaining folks relaxed on his veranda with tales of his youthful exploits, Julia Tenpenny was contemplating another journey to Noble's birthplace, Barbour County, Alabama.

After the death of their parents in 1882, Julia's sister Louisa and her husband kindly offered Julia a home. But they had a large family consisting of numerous children — four sons and another child on the way. Julia declined becoming yet another mouth for the Atwaters to feed. While she had lived with her parents, Thaddeus and Anne Tenpenny, she had adopted their frugal ways and saved every penny she could. After her father's retirement from his position of vicar of St. Bede's Church, the family had resided in a small rented cottage in Little Turnbridge. By the time her eighty-one-year-old father died, followed within six months by her mother, Julia was able to purchase the four-room cottage, three doors down from the post office in the village. Julia considered herself fortunate to achieve the independence so seldom the lot of a spinster.

The property bore the evidence of her green thumb, with a variegated rose garden in the small front yard, the envy of her neighbors, and a sizable vegetable garden in the rear. While the cottage was a modest dwelling, it had many charming touches which Julia loved, such as a carved oak mantle over the stone fireplace and a pinewood trestle table left by the former owner which dated back to colonial times. She had inherited from her parents an adequate supply of plate, silver, and linens; a china cabinet; and a four-poster bed. Her sister had generously provided her with a slightly worn but comfortable Queen Anne sofa, green with gold cording.

Like all spinsters, Julia was aware that people sometimes pitied her. The Civil War had dramatically increased the number of spinsters. President Lincoln had urged young women not to scorn the empty sleeve, and most did not. But for thousands of women, there was simply no one to marry. This increase of single women had not raised the status of spinsterhood. The most suitable role for a woman remained that of wife and mother, and those who had safely sailed into the harbor of matrimony felt sorry for those who had not. But Julia never pitied herself. Like so many thousands of others, north and south, she would grieve for the love she had lost for as long as she lived. Jeremy Gaither's birthday and the date of his death would never go unremembered. But although she would never say it aloud, Julia did not envy her married friends and relatives locked in the protectiveness — and confinement — of domesticity.

Julia recognized that teaching suited her far more than managing a household would have. And while marital intimacy was denied her, she also escaped the continual round of child bearing that was the lot of every married woman who was not barren. Several of her friends, as well as Louisa and Clementine, the wife of their cousin, had numerous children, and again and again Julia witnessed the toll that pregnancy and childbirth took on women.

IN 1890, JULIA received a legacy from an aunt which allowed her to indulge in her desire for travel. She had just returned from a tour of New York City when she received another of many invitations from her old friends, Caleb and Ilsa Royal, to come for a visit. They had always visited her in Little Turnbridge during their occasional trips to Boston, Caleb's home town. It was not possible for Julia to entertain overnight guests since her one spare room was filled from floor to ceiling with her book collection. The Royals always stayed at a hotel, but unfailingly enjoyed a meal at her home and took her for carriage rides about the city, theatrical performances, or strolls through one of the beautiful parks. She had never had the means to accept one of their invitations until now. It had been more than six years since the Royals' last visit to Boston, and she was glad of the opportunity to see them again.

Louisa, now the mother of seven sons, was expecting yet another child, hoping to be blessed with a daughter at last, and Julia had timed her trip to be on hand for the birth in October. Louisa's husband, John Atwater, was a merchant who could comfortably support them all – and, one hoped, however many more children God might send them. But with this pregnancy, Julia experienced more anxiety than joy for Louisa. The last birth had been breech; both mother and son had nearly died. At the urging of friends and relatives, John and Louisa decided that for the first time she would give birth in the women's hospital instead of at home, which greatly relieved Julia's mind.

On a cool mid-September morning Julia boarded a southbound train, having remembered to pack for the much warmer weather in Alabama. Now there was train service all the way to Montgomery, so only the last leg of her journey had to be traveled by stagecoach.

Both Caleb and Ilsa were on hand at the station upon her arrival. Caleb was now forty-eight, portly, with thinning hair, but his genial smile was the same as always. Ilsa remained as slender as she had been at twenty-five, her dark hair streaked with more silver than the last time Julia had seen her, making her hazel-green eyes the more striking.

Julia met the Royal children for the first time — fifteen-year-old Terrence and eleven-year-old Belinda. She regretted that she had not been able to see Ilsa's father, Gerhardt Nordhoff, before his death the previous year.

Julia and Ilsa enjoyed leisurely afternoons sipping lemonade on the veranda. Caleb was busy as always with his medical practice, seeing patients in his office in one of the large rooms in their home. But he found time to join the ladies for several outings. They watched the steamboats being loaded with cotton on the Chattahoochee River from one of Eufaula's high bluffs and enthusiastically participated in an all-day sing at one of the churches. Caleb drove them out into the country one evening to witness an old harvest-time custom. Large balls of string were lit and tossed back and forth across tin-roofed houses by daring souls who did not always wear gloves. The flaming balls lit up the night sky for hours, while Terrence, Belinda, and the other children played games, and their elders caught up on all the gossip. There was always a picnic supper, so Ilsa had come prepared with a platter of fried chicken and a peach pie.

Julia could not imagine returning home without visiting New Road School. She and Caleb set out early on a Wednesday morning because the rural schools dismissed at one o'clock to enable the children to help their families with the harvest. Caleb still took an interest in New Road, but today he had a patient to see in Crossvine, a six-year-old boy recovering from diphtheria. He handed Julia down from the buggy, waved to the teacher, who was standing at the door, and drove on.

Hattie Grimes warmly welcomed her, mentioning that one of her older siblings had been among her pupils.

"You did not have to tell me that," Julia said. "You look exactly like your sister Rose."

Miss Grimes smiled.

"Everyone says that."

She called the class to attention and asked Julia to speak to the students about Massachusetts. The greatest curiosity was about what it was like to go sledding and how one walked on ice. When Julia had answered everyone's questions, Miss Grimes thanked her and directed the children to take out their slate boards for the arithmetic lesson. Just then a thin little boy stood up, walked up to Julia, and shook her hand. He looked no more than ten years old, wore large spectacles, and had a serious demeanor.

"My name is Theodore Waldron," he said. "Your talk was very interesting, ma'am."

Miss Grimes came and stood behind him, putting her hands on his slight shoulders.

"This young man is visiting relatives here for a few weeks, so his family enrolled him here. He lives down near Dothan."

Julia had no recollection of a town named Dothan.

"You might remember it as Poplar Head," Miss Grimes explained. "They changed the name a few years back. Theodore is one of our best readers, Miss Tenpenny. He can recite 'Paul Revere's Ride' by heart."

"That's quite an accomplishment. How old are you, Theodore?"

"I'm twelve."

Having assumed him to be no more than ten, Julia hid her surprise, not wanting to embarrass the child by commenting on his small size. And she noted that despite his slight build he was not all that childlike in appearance. With his spectacles, scant hair, and solemn expression, he looked mature beyond his years.

"Miss Tenpenny, I was wondering if I could ask you some questions about Massachusetts history."

"Why of course — if it's all right with Miss Grimes. Why don't we find seats at the back of the room where we won't disturb anyone. Or better yet, I noticed a bench under a tree outside. Why don't we talk there?"

She looked at Miss Grimes for permission to take the child outside, and the teacher smiled and nodded.

Under the shade of a large mimosa tree, Julia and Theodore became acquainted. She was impressed by his grasp of English grammar and the range of his vocabulary, particularly as his education consisted of six years in a rural school. Clearly he was intellectually gifted, and as she enlightened him on every point of history which interested him, she was deeply touched by this earnest little fellow. She wished she could take him under her wing and give him the benefit of her years of teaching experience. But at the end of the week she would return home.

Children began noisily making their way outside for recess, ending their discussion. Theodore seemed as reluctant to part as she was. He was not a shy child, but neither was he forward, and so he hesitatingly framed the question that had entered his mind in the midst of their discussion.

"Miss Tenpenny, I was wondering if maybe you wouldn't mind — if maybe — "

Julia smiled encouragingly.

"Yes, Theodore?"

"Well, I just thought that maybe I could write to you sometimes. I like to write, but I don't have anyone to write to."

Julia could not resist taking one of his hands and giving it a squeeze. Because he was giving her an opportunity to do the very thing she had been wishing she could do. Through correspondence, she could become his teacher, his mentor.

"I love getting letters, Theodore. And I love writing them, too. Let's see if Miss Grimes can spare some paper and ink so we can write down each other's address."

Theodore responded with his broad grin, already thinking of topics to write about.

Chapter 8

THE RIOT

JULIA HAD NOT seen the Knightley family since she left Alabama eighteen years earlier. She had never forgotten them and believed this would probably be her only opportunity to see them again. Caleb had told her that they still lived in the Crossvine community, and Julia had arranged to visit with them. Jackson was no correspondent; she was not even sure he was literate. But before coming south she had hazarded a brief letter, addressing it to Jackson Knightley, Crossvine, Alabama, not really expecting a response. She was surprised to receive a letter three weeks later penned by Jackson's daughter, Rebecca.

> Dear Miss Tenpenny,
> Papa says to tell you he remembers you well and is very glad you are in good health. Mama sends her regards and says you must come and see us. My brothers and sister are looking forward to your visit, too. We have never met anyone from Massachusetts. (Mama says Lee and I met you already, when we were babies, but we do not remember.)
> Sincerely, Rebecca Knightley

Julia smiled, recalling the two-year-old boy she had bounced on her lap in the dogtrot cabin and the newborn baby girl asleep in the cradle by Sophronia's side, who could now boast of excellent penmanship and grammar that was a credit to her teacher.

DESPITE HIS BUSY medical practice in town, Caleb remained a country doctor at heart and never neglected his rural patients. He had delivered the Knightleys' youngest child, four-year-old Bryce. He had also treated the family for various illnesses and injuries over the years — Lillian's pneumonia, Bryce's broken wrist suffered in a failed attempt to retrieve a kitten from a high tree branch, and Lee's wounded leg. Ilsa also knew the family well, because she sometimes accompanied Caleb and assisted him during his rural rounds. The Knightleys occasionally made office visits at the Royal residence, as well. Caleb had told him that his patient load would prevent his driving them out to Crossvine that morning as they had planned earlier, and Julia would be leaving the following day, so she feared she would miss seeing the Knightleys.

"We can drive out there ourselves," Ilsa offered. "Sophronia Knightley always seems to enjoy chatting," she added. "But I must confess her husband has never said more than two words to me at a time, so I cannot claim an acquaintanceship with him."

"As I recall," Julia said, "Jackson only speaks when he feels he really has something to say."

As they started out for Crossvine, Julia remarked, "Well, I don't know if Jackson will want to talk about the riot. But perhaps his son Lee will."

"Riot? My goodness, was there a riot here?"

"Oh, no. Not here. Down in Dothan. It was last fall — in October, as I recall. I don't know all the details, but there was a gunfight and people were killed. Lee was down there minding his own business, just looking for work, and he wound up in the middle of things and was shot in the leg. He was treated there, of course, but after he got back home Caleb went out to the farm to clean and dress the wound."

"Good lord! I thought that sort of thing only happened out west nowadays."

"Dothan's still a pretty wild town, I guess. The new railroad running from Brunswick over in Georgia connecting Dothan to the capital at Montgomery was finished last year, so the town's becoming more civilized, it seems. But word of the riot spread, and I hear train passengers duck when they pass through there."

They arrived at the Knightley farm mid-morning. Julia spotted red-headed Sophronia kneeling on the ground spading the earth around some rose bushes, her back to them, and she excitedly called out, "Hello there, Phrony!" as she climbed down from the buggy.

The industrious gardener stood up, wiping the dirt off her hands with a rag, and smiled a greeting as she said, "You must be Miss Tenpenny. I'm Rebecca."

She held out her hand, and Julia grasped it warmly.

"So you are. Of course. And all grown up. The last time I saw you, you were a tiny baby who considerately napped while your mother and I had a nice long talk."

"I'm very glad to meet you — again. Like I said in my letter, I'm afraid I don't remember meeting you before. And it's good to see you, too, Miz Royal. Come on in the house. Papa and Lee and William are in the fields. Mama kept me and Lillian home today so we could meet you. My little brother Bryce is here, too."

She pointed to a barefooted little boy who was jumping up and down in some mud puddles.

"You better stop that!" Rebecca yelled at him. "You're gonna get in trouble!"

Unheeding, Bryce shot around to the back of the house where there were some free-roaming chickens he liked to chase.

The dogtrot cabin had been replaced by a sizable farm house with room enough, it appeared, to accommodate all of the Knightleys. There were several outbuildings and a large fenced-in area for the livestock.

As they entered the house, Sophronia stood up from the table where she had been shelling peas, and it was apparent that she was well along in another pregnancy. Ten-year-old Lillian, light-brown haired like her father and as adept as her mother at rapidly stripping the pea pods, stood up and shyly smiled.

"Come over here and give me a big hug, Julia," Phrony demanded.

Julia obeyed, and Ilsa followed suit.

"Now, Lillian, don't just keep on a-standin there. Say hello to the ladies."

"Hello, Miss Tenpenny, Miz Royal."

"Y'all come on in the living room and let's set a spell. Ain't nothing needs doing that cain't wait."

"Are you sure?" Ilsa asked. "Julia and I can help you get dinner ready."

"This here mess of peas is for supper, Miz Royal. I already packed up dinner for Jackson and the boys, and they took it with them."

"So we won't be seeing Jackson?" Julia asked. She was disappointed.

"Of course you will! He told Rebecca to come get him around noontime if you was here. Meanwhile, he told me to be sure to offer you some of his scuppernong wine. That is, if you partake of such. I know some folks don't — "

"Oh, we do, Phrony," Julia said, as Ilsa enthusiastically nodded.

Rebecca carefully poured the golden liquid into two small glasses, and the guests appreciatively sipped it.

They adjourned to the living room, which was furnished with worn but comfortable furniture. Sophronia's and Rebecca's colorful braided rugs decorated the pine plank floor.

"When is the new baby due?" Ilsa asked.

"Right around Christmas. Jackson's hoping for another boy. He feels like he needs all the boys he can get."

"Boys!" protested Lillian. "I work just as hard as Lee and William! And so does Becky! Ain't that right, Becky?"

"Mama knows that, Lil."

"A course I do," Sophronia acknowledged. "But you ain't as strong as the boys and never will be. Papa'd rather see you all doing housework if he could spare you from the fields. Now Becky, where has Bryce got off to? I wanted you to meet him, too, Julia."

"We saw him outside," Julia said. "He seemed to be having a wonderful time in the mud — looks like you had a good rain here last night. And then he ran around to the back."

"He loves to torment them poor chickens. Just like my other boys did when they was little."

"How old are they now?" Ilsa asked.

"Lee's full growed — twenty years old last June. William's fifteen. Good strong boys, both of them."

Sophronia regaled them with tales of her sons' exploits, and Julia told her about the acquisition of her little home with its gardens.

"Well, you can see we got some roses a-growin here, too."

"They're beautiful. I have to say, they rival mine."

"Now, I don't really believe that, Julia. But I thank you anyhow. Becky, why don't you fetch Papa and the boys so they can visit for a bit."

When Rebecca left, Bryce bounded into the room, trailing mud everywhere. Sophronia directed Lillian to wash the boy off at the well and find him a dry pair of pants. Before she could haul him off, he pointed to Julia.

"Is that the Yankee lady?"

"That's Miss Tenpenny, yes," Sophronia replied.

"I'm very pleased to meet you, young man," Julia said in her most formal voice.

She often used this tone with children to establish a mutually respectful atmosphere.

"You talk funny," Bryce responded.

Lillian, embarrassed, grabbed his arm and pulled him from the room.

JACKSON HAD PUT on a few pounds but was still slim. Lee was taller than his father, and William appeared to be fast catching up with him in height. Lee's hair was darker, but still blond as she remembered, while William had the same reddish-brown hair as Bryce. They hung up their straw hats, and Jackson nodded hello to Ilsa, then heartily shook Julia's hand.

"Well, well, Miss Julia Tenpenny. It's wonderful to see you again!"

Somewhat taken about by what, for Jackson, was effusiveness, Julia smiled and said, "I would never think of traveling to Alabama without seeing my old friends. And these fellows must be Lee and William."

"Yes'm," they chorused.

"You once sat on my lap," she said to Lee.

"And yanked her bonnet off her head," Sophronia remembered.

Lee broadly grinned.

"Well, I'm sorry about that, ma'am."

"And William — why, you aren't but fifteen and already as tall as your father!"

"But not too tall to take a licking if need be," Jackson said.

"Which ain't hardly ever necessary anymore," Sophronia said. "But that Bryce, now — "

A still damp little boy, bare chested and barefooted, wearing a pair of short pants, was shoved into the room by Lillian and cast down his eyes repentantly before Jackson.

"You not been minding again, son?"

Bryce nodded his head, relieved that in the presence of company there would be no whipping.

Rebecca took pity on him, sat down in the rocking chair, pulled him into her lap, and started rocking. Bryce laid his head on her chest and closed his eyes, clearly ready for a nap.

Sophronia suggested that their guests and the menfolk adjourn to the kitchen table for blackberry pie and tea. Jackson encouraged Julia to talk about her home and family, marveling at the fact that her sister now had seven sons, while ardently hoping her new baby would be a girl.

"We could use seven boys around here, couldn't we?"

Lee nodded, but William declared, "Not if they're as big a nuisance as Bryce."

In her dealings with people, Julia had always been good at reading between the lines, and now she thought, as Jackson listened attentively to some of the details of her life, a half smile on his face, that he was pleased — and relieved — that she had a good life. On her part, she was glad her wish that this family would prosper had come true.

"And Mr. Knightley — Jackson, how is he faring these days? And your mother?"

"Fine. Papa still farms, and Mama's still the best cook in Barbour County. But my brother Micah and his family mostly run the place."

Ilsa was helping clear the dishes when she asked, "How is your leg, Lee? Has it healed properly?"

Lee nodded as Julia said, "Oh, yes — the gunfight — what on earth happened?"

"Durn town officials!" Jackson exploded. "It's always the same. Town folks want to enjoy what us farmers produce, but they want to bleed us dry with their taxes and fees and high prices for things."

"Well, it weren't none of my business," Lee said. "But the town of Dothan charged the farmers a tax on gins, so George Stringer — he was the head of the Farmers Alliance — he built a gin outside the city limits. Then Dothan decided to collect taxes on wagons that used the city streets to take their cotton to the new train depot. So the farmers was taxed either way."

"Made me want to spit when I heard about it!" Jackson said. "Just anything to make life harder for the farmer."

"Old George refused to pay the tax," Lee continued. "So they took him to court a couple of times, and he paid the fines. But after that, he wouldn't do it. Tobe Domingus, the sheriff, beat him with a billy club and arrested him."

Jackson shook his head in disgust.

"The only reason I was in Dothan last October was because I wanted to earn some extra money. We was done with the harvest, and I heard there was some jobs down there."

He glanced at his mother.

"There's this girl, and I wanted to get enough money together to buy her a present."

Sophronia smiled and commented, "She's a sweet gal. I told him I saw her admiring a bonnet in Eufaula. I thought she might like to have it for her birthday."

"Anyhow, I wanted to earn extra money. I couldn't find work in Eufaula, so I went down to Dothan on the 14th."

"My boy didn't know that on that very day a bunch of farmers was at the courthouse trying to help Stringer,"

Jackson said. "They was all a-sittin there with shotguns on their laps, and the judge had enough sense to adjourn."

"And then, that evening," Lee said, "Tobe and his deputies met up with George and his friends on Main Street, and somebody started shooting. I just tried to get out of the way. Tobe was badly wounded, but — I have to give him credit, he ain't no coward — he kept on a-firin till it was all over. George and another fellow was kilt, and me and several others was wounded."

Jackson chewed on his lip as Lee described the fight and then said, "You know, Julia, here I have always felt blessed that none of my boys'll have to go to war. Then my son goes into town just looking for work and gets his leg shot up as bad as my friend Jimmy Bridger's was at Petersburg. It don't make no sense!"

Julia sensed his soul-deep anger over the wounding of an innocent noncombatant.

"And this Toby fellow — " she said.

"Tobe," Lee corrected her.

"What happened to him?"

"He was tried for murder and convicted."

"The first time," Jackson said. "He got a second trial and was found not guilty."

"And you think he was?"

Jackson sighed.

"Who knows? From what I hear tell, everybody was a-shootin at everybody — just like in any battle. But what I do know is that my boy dang near lost his leg, and it took a long time for it to heal. And then all through the spring he could hardly work, hobbling around, in pain, helping me and William as best he could. And none of them city folk that just had to tax the farmers offered to pay Lee's doctor bills or hire me some help while he was a-mendin."

"But I'm fine now, Papa," Lee offered as soon as he could get a word in. He did not want this Yankees lady feeling sorry for him.

"And if you hadn't been so set on earning money to court your lady friend with," Sophronia said in a teasing voice, "you would've stuck to your chores here and not got hurt in the first place."

"Aw, Mama," he said, as Julia detected a blush across his cheeks.

"So how long you staying for, Julia?" Jackson asked.

"I'm on my way tomorrow — boarding the stagecoach in Eufaula early in the morning."

"Well, now, I'm sorry to hear that. I know Papa and Mama would be glad to see you."

"And I them. I so enjoyed that fine meal the last time we were together. And Mr. Knightley's Indian tale. What a brave young man he was, fighting those fierce Indians when he was only nineteen years old."

"To hear him tell it, fighting Yankees was child's play compared to coming up against them savages. He was brave, all right."

Julia took Jackson's hand and looked steadily into his eyes. "You tell your parents I am sorry we could not have a visit. And you — you just keep on taking good care of this wonderful family."

Jackson surprised her by giving her a brief hug.

"And you take care of yourself, too, Miss Julia Tenpenny. You are one of us. You might be a teacher, but you have a farmer's heart."

Tears moistened Julia's eyes as she nodded, then gave Sophronia a hug.

"Please ask Rebecca to write with news of the new baby. What will you name it, by the way?"

"Lucinda or Nathan."

"Beautiful names."

Ilsa said her goodbyes as Julia retrieved their bonnets.

"Oh — and I hope you finally get that niece," Sophronia said.

"I hope so, too," Julia wistfully replied. "But it'll be another boy, I'm sure."

WHEN THE TRAIN pulled into the Boston terminal, Julia spotted Hubert Tenpenny standing on the platform. She was surprised to see his wife, Clementine, as well, because generally Hubert came alone to collect her and drive her to her home. As the porter helped her exit the train, Hubert and Clementine came forward, and she noticed that Clemmie was dressed in black, a color she hated, a color she only wore if — Her heart lurched as Hubert took her hand and Clemmie embraced her.

"Come, my dear," she said. "Hubert will see to your luggage."

"Just as soon as I get the two of you settled in the carriage," he said. "Come along, Julia."

He took firm hold of one elbow while Clemmie grasped her other arm.

"You know, I am not that fatigued, Hubert. I am perfectly capable of walking under my own power. Please — I know something is wrong. Please tell me what's wrong."

Hubert did not say anything until he had handed both of the women up into the carriage. His grave face terrified Julia.

"I - I must make arrangements for your trunk to be delivered."

There were tears in eyes. He looked pleadingly at his wife. She nodded her head, and he returned to the terminal.

"He cannot speak without crying. He cannot tell you. I said I would."

She put her arm around Julia's shoulders.

"For God's sake, Clemmie — what has happened?"

Clemmie's eyes misted over, and she wiped away the tears.

"We lost Louisa, dear."

Julia sat stupefied, unable to speak.

"She passed away this morning. She asked for you again and again in her delirium. You were in her thoughts to the end."

"Are you telling me, Clemmie, that my sister has *died*?"

Clemmie nodded.

"I am so sorry. We are all in shock. It happened so quickly."

After a stunned pause, Julia demanded, "What happened? I don't understand. She was fine when I left. How could she be dead?"

"The child came early — in the hospital. And then suddenly Louisa became very ill."

"But I thought she was going to be safer there, better cared for."

Clemmie sighed.

"Yes, we all thought so. No one told us there had been a rash of deaths from childbirth fever there in recent weeks, and that it's extremely contagious. No one explained any of that to John when he took her there. The child was born three days ago, and within a few hours after the birth Louisa became ill. The doctor explained nothing to us, but a nurse took us aside and told us the hospital was infected with that dreadful fever. She said — she said Louisa would have been safer at home."

Clemmie's anger overcame her grief as she exclaimed in an emotional voice, "To think she might still be alive if we had not urged her to go to that horrible place! And now she's dead, and John and their poor children — "

Julia vehemently shook her head.

"But she can't be dead! She can't be! She is my own sweet baby sister. Louisa cannot be dead!"

Clemmie embraced her through her wrenching sobs as Hubert joined them, fighting tears. He gripped Julia's hand.

When she was able to draw breath and gain control of herself, Julia murmured, "Where — where is she? Where is Louisa now?"

"At the house. We're taking you there with us, Julia. John and the children are expecting you. But you will stay with us through the funeral and for as long as you wish to."

Julia weakly leaned her head against Hubert's shoulder.

"And the child — I suppose he died as well?"

"Oh no, no!" Hubert said. "She's just a little mite, but quite healthy. We're looking after her for the time being, because John's maid has her hands full with the other children. Robust set of lungs on that child. You can hear her crying clear up to the second floor!"

Julia looked up from Hubert's lapel, damp from her tears. "*She?*"

"Oh yes," Clemmie affirmed. "John and Louisa finally got the girl they've always wanted."

Julia was amazed.

"Louisa gave birth to a *daughter*?"

Clemmie managed a smile.

"She named her Julianne, after you and your mother. While she was still lucid she held her daughter in her arms and said, 'Every time we say her name we will think of two wonderful women.' And so you not only have a niece, Julia — you have a namesake."

JULIA FELT SURE John Atwater would marry very soon after Louisa's death. He was in desperate need of a mother for his children and a housekeeper. And while Julia and his family could provide urgently needed assistance for a few months, they all had demanding responsibilities of their own. Julia enjoyed spending time with her nephews, and she felt her grief diminish every time she held Julianne in her arms, but she could not long neglect her teaching duties.

Certainly finding a wife would present no difficulty for John. In Little Turnbridge alone there were two other spinsters Julia's age, both attractive, intelligent women without an income of their own and dependent upon their families, who, she knew, would willingly marry her brother-in-law. Both women had always been close to the Atwater family, and both were on good terms with John.

She speculated as to which of the two spinsters he would choose, relieved to think that they were nearing the end of their childbearing years, because there was a limit to how many dependents her brother-in-law could support. She was shocked, and her fellow spinsters were profoundly disappointed, when he began squiring twenty-year-old Melissa Gordon about the town, and within six months of Louisa's death they were married. A year of mourning was *de rigueur*, and some people disapproved of what they considered a hasty marriage. But Julia simply pitied Melissa the heavy domestic load now on her slim shoulders, which even with the help of a maid and a cook was formidable. She also feared John would sire another eight children. Or more. At their wedding she bitterly reflected, Louisa's dear face sharp in her mind, *I hope John's fertility does not kill this poor woman, too.*

Chapter 9

THEODORE AND NORA

IN THE FALL of 1890, just a few days after Miss Tenpenny's departure, Theodore Waldron borrowed pen, paper, and ink from Miss Hattie Grimes and composed a letter.

> Dear Miss Tenpenny,
>   I hope you had a pleasant journey home. I suppose up there in Massachusets the leaves are very beautiful now. I have heard that autumn is phenominal in New England.
>   I have enjoyed my visit to Crossvine very much, but tomorrow I am going home. As I suppose you know, no trains go to Eufaula, so my uncle is taking me home on the stagecoach. Some day I hope to ride the train that runs all the way from Dothan to Montgomery. My uncle says the train is wood burning, and sometimes the tender runs out of wood before you get where you are going. Then the passengers have to get off the train and help find pine limbs to light a fire under the boiler. If that ever happens when I'm on the train, I can really help out, because I am good with an ax, just like Abe Lincoln.
>   I just finished reading *Great Expectations* this week. I felt very sorry for Pip's poor benifactor, the convict.

He was treated very cruelly. But I'm glad things turned out all right for Pip and Estella.

I am looking forward to hearing from you.

                          Sincerely, Theodore Waldron

The letter, delivered to Julia one morning at the Atwater home while she was rocking her niece, was a tonic. She was amused by the misspelled words in nonetheless well-written sentences and impressed by his choice of reading material. Few of her students tackled Dickens at his age. And she smiled over his description of the kind of train trip only a boy would enjoy.

She kissed Julianne and turned her over to the maid. Then she donned her shawl and bonnet and, for the first time that season, went for a stroll along the lanes near her home, marveling at the spectacular autumn foliage she had been too grief stricken to see.

That evening, she sat down at her trestle table and replied to Theodore's letter. She could not resist pointing out the misspellings but praised his writing skill. She asked him to tell her all about his family and the farm, and she sent her regards to his parents.

Julia and Theodore became regular correspondents. Over time, he painted a vivid, detailed picture of life on the Waldron farm, his growing interest in horticulture, and his deepening desire to become a preacher.

THEODORE WALDRON'S PARENTS, James and Bess, rented 147 acres of farmland in the Chinkapin community for eight years before purchasing the property in 1882, the year the town of Dothan was incorporated. Tee was the youngest child, with one brother and two sisters. Like most of the farmers in the area, the Waldrons were self-sufficient, growing their own food, often bartering for goods they needed. When it became apparent early in his life that Tee had a scholarly bent, his family encouraged him in his studies. While presents were rare, when they had the means his family gifted him with pen and ink and a package of foolscap. Most Christmases, he received a book, which he added to those furnished by Julia Tenpenny.

Whenever a letter arrived from Massachusetts, Tee entertained his family by reading it aloud. James and Bess sometimes had questions for the Yankee lady — what crops do they grow up there? How much does wool cost in Boston? How far is Boston from New York City? And Julia never failed to supply the answers. On her end, she was glad Theodore's family was supportive of his scholarly pursuits. Without that support, she knew that her small efforts on his behalf would be of no avail. Encouraging him to read and study, the Waldrons enabled Theodore to develop his abilities.

However, neither Theodore's studiousness nor his slight build excused him from farm work, which had never appealed to him. Long hours of manual labor in the fields left him little time throughout the day for reading or his other passion, the cultivation of flowers. But blessed with an industrious and determined nature, he read and studied by lantern light most evenings and before heading out to the fields each morning nearly always managed to water his flowers, add mulch and manure, uproot weeds, or plant a new bed.

From childhood, Tee had had a green thumb, and under his magical touch flowers appropriate to each season brightened the Waldron place year round: camellias in winter, daffodils in early spring, followed by red, white and pink azaleas, forsythia, bright blue morning glories and geraniums, and daisies and sunny golden day lilies through the summer. Flowering trees decorated every corner of the yard. Dogwood and pear trees briefly flaunted their mantles of pink and white in spring, lazily relaxing into various shades of green within weeks, as if, it seemed to Tee, blooming was just too exhausting for them. But his crape myrtle trees flowered June through September, putting forth buds and brilliant blossoms month after month, only relinquishing their last flowers when fall was on the horizon. This avocation satisfied Tee's soul, but he knew it could not earn him a living. Neither, he feared, could his chosen vocation.

Tee's brother John seemed content to farm, and his sisters, Nadine and Dinah, had no ambition beyond finding husbands who could support them. But by the time he was fifteen, Theodore knew that he wanted to be a preacher. A new church, Divine Truth Baptist, had been constructed in the Chinkapin community on an acre of land donated by the Waldrons when Theodore was twelve years old. He was regular in attendance and was frequently called upon to read scripture and lead the hymn singing. He had a powerful, pleasing voice that people enjoyed listening to, and by the time he was seventeen his knowledge of scripture surpassed even that of the preacher. But he knew these qualifications would not earn him a position at an urban church, and it was unfailingly true that most country churches could only pay a small stipend to the preacher. Like most members of Divine Truth, the current preacher, Reverend Tom Carpenter, was a farmer. And so Theodore was stumped. Even if a preaching position were offered to him one day, how could he become a minister and still earn a living, unless he remained bound to the farm? He took Julia's advice to pray on it, put it in God's hands, and continue to hold fast to his preaching ambition.

In the early spring of 1896, Divine Truth Church was invited by several black churches throughout the region to participate in a revival in Mobile that June. The deacons agreed that the preacher and one church member would take part, with the understanding that church funds would be used to pay only part of the travel expense. Theodore was excited when he was chosen to accompany Reverend Carpenter and immediately set about earning his train fare. With James's permission, he worked for several weeks as a hired hand at Comfortroot Farm. John willingly covered his share of the chores at home to enable him to earn the money. Comfortroot was owned by the descendant of a pioneer Dale

County family, the Carltons, who had settled the land when Creek Indians still occupied southeast Alabama and had peacefully co-existed with them. Now it was rumored that Barney Carlton and his wife planned to retire from farming in a few years, sell Comfortroot, and move to Birmingham to live with their daughter. They had always been hard working people, ready to lend neighbors a hand, and they treated their hired hands and the several tenant farmers on their property fairly, so everyone, including the Waldrons, would be sorry to see them go. Who knew what kind of people might take over Comfortroot? But for now, Theodore was grateful the Carltons had provided him the means to journey to Mobile.

James was proud his son had been chosen for this mission, but Bess was hesitant to give her full consent. Theodore was her baby, no matter if he had turned eighteen and appeared several years older, with his receding hairline, spectacles, and ministerial bearing. What pitfalls awaited him in Mobile she tried not to envision. Sinful Mobile was known for its scandalous Mardi Gras festivities each February, during which ungodly activities, long restricted to secret white societies, were now engaged in by black folks as well. Theodore assured his mother that one visit to a city where debauchery sometimes reigned would be enough for him. But he was wrong.

REVEREND CARPENTER AND his young assistant enjoyed the hospitality of several families during their two-week-long stay in the Mobile area. Revival meetings were held in several locations, from a large church in the black section of Mobile to tent meetings in rural areas. Not only had some souls been newly saved, but backsliding souls had been brought back into the fold. Theodore felt the call to preach stronger than ever before. And for the first time in his life, he was invited to deliver a sermon. The minister scheduled to preach at a tent meeting far out in the country had been prevented from coming by flooding caused by tropical rains that had lashed the countryside for several days. Even though the rain had now eased to a drizzle, with scattered thunderclouds, the roads on the minister's side of the county were impassable.

After enjoying an evening meal at the home of Tate and Etta Garrison, on whose property the tent had been erected, the Divine Truth brethren had an easy, if damp, walk to the service. Reverend Carpenter could have filled in for the absent minister, but decided that tonight was as good a time as any for Theodore the Preacher to debut. The Garrison household, with eight children, a grandfather, and an aunt, provided a large enough congregation to proceed with the service. But they were joined by half a dozen other families who lived in the unflooded side of the county and braved thunder, lightning, a still brisk wind, and drizzling rain for the rare privilege of attending a revival.

As people arrived, they removed wet outer garments and spread them on chairs or on the ground to dry. In view of the torrential rainfall, it crossed Theodore's mind to preach about the Ark, but he was not experienced or confident enough to try out an impromptu sermon on his audience. Instead he preached a sermon he had carefully prepared at home, in case just such an opportunity as now presented itself should arise.

During the opening hymn, "Amazing Grace," sung a cappella and led line by line since only the preacher had a hymnal, Theodore noticed a young woman sitting with her family near the front. She wore a multi-colored head scarf, from which unruly ringlets escaped. She did not have a strong voice, and she was not especially pretty. Her large, slightly prominent, hazel-brown eyes were arresting, true, but what engaged him was the sweetness of her expression and the way she kept her arm around a little girl chilled by the rain, possibly her sister, in an effort to keep her warm.

As he delivered the sermon drawn from Matthew 5:13-16, which he had entitled, "Believers: the Salt of the Earth, the Light of the World," he could not help noticing that the young woman was completely attentive. Half way through the closing hymn, he determined that he would make a special effort to introduce himself to her. There was certainly nothing self-serving in this, he told himself; it was his duty to become acquainted with everyone and invite them to attend the second meeting to be held at that location the following night. He stepped forward to shake hands with several folks and then wended his way to the main person he wished to meet. He took her offered hand, small but strong, which fitted perfectly in his.

"Nice to meet you, Reverend Waldron. My name's Nora. Nora Freedman. And them's my folks," she said, as she gestured toward her parents, sister and two brothers, who were socializing with the other worshipers. "My parents' names is Burl and Amalie. And then they's Henry, Mattie, and little Burl."

Theodore glanced at her parents, returning their smiles, and reluctantly released her hand.

"Please, Nora, I'm not a reverend. Not yet. My name's Theodore. Or Tee. My friends and family always call me Tee."

"All right, Theodore ."

"Tee," he said firmly. For some reason it was important to him that Nora address him like a close friend. He was on the verge of inviting her to sit down and chat for a bit when a commotion pointed them in another direction.

"Come quick! Come quick!" a drenched newcomer shouted. "They's been a accident!"

Several people moved toward the tent entrance, Nora and Amalie among them.

The distraught man ran through the drizzling rain toward a wagon several yards off turned on its side. A woman was screaming, "My boy Luke's under there!" while two young children wailed and clung to her skirts.

Several men put shoulders to the wagon and righted it. A wheel had come off, and the wagon had turned over in the slippery mud. Most of the family had been thrown clear, but a boy of about twelve lay unconscious where he had been pinned to the ground. Burl took command. He gestured to Tate Garrison.

"Go get some blankets — and the rest of y'all — get back and let my wife and daughter tend to this boy. Don't nobody else touch him!"

The boys' parents kneeled in the mud beside their son, hands clenched in prayer, while Theodore and Reverend Carpenter stood next to them, ready to give any aid they could. One of the Garrison girls quickly returned from the house with blankets, and Tate brought a lantern.

After finding the boy's pulse, greatly relieved, Amalie briefly glanced at the parents and said, "He breathing, but we gots to see how bad he hurt."

As she was speaking, she was examining the child while Nora gently cradled his head on her lap. Both women were oblivious to the rain and mud, so focused they did not even flinch when a thunderclap startled Theodore and others.

"Some broken ribs. And — nothing else I can feel. But bad bruises. Us can only pray they's no bleeding inside."

She directed Burl and Theodore to carefully slide the boy on top of one blanket and then covered him with the other one. She and Nora followed them into the house, where he was laid on a bed. The boy began moaning, struggling into consciousness. With the help of his mother, Amalie got him undressed and Etta supplied them with cloths and a bucket of water to wash away the mud. Amalie tore an old sheet into strips. With Nora's help, she tightly bound Luke's chest. One of the Garrison daughters made tea, and Nora coaxed Luke to sip it.

"My daughter and me best stay here tonight to tend to the boy," Amalie suggested to the Garrisons. They readily agreed, inviting the entire Freedman family to spend the night. It had already been arranged that Theodore and Reverend Carpenter would bed down in the tent, and blankets had been put there for that purpose. It was suggested that Burl and

Luke's father stay the night there, as well. Nora and Amalie, Luke's mother and her other children, were invited to spend the night in the house — if they did not mind sleeping on pallets, since the family had no spare beds.

"Us can manage," Amalie responded.

Theodore had no doubt they could. He was impressed by Amalie's knowledge and skill and the coolheaded, selfless manner in which she and Nora had handled the situation, even in the worst moments of the crisis. Luke was their patient, and neither the ugly weather nor their own discomfort swayed them in the least from doing everything in their power for him.

What strong women these are, Theodore found himself thinking, just as Nora glanced up and looked directly at him, causing him to reflect upon what fine eyes she had. Simultaneously it occurred to him that he had never heard a prettier name, a name more pleasing to the ear, than Nora.

First being careful to open a ceiling flap to vent the smoke, Burl Freedman made a fire in the tent with the skilled ease of a blacksmith. The men removed their outer garments to dry and sat around the fire rehashing the day's events and speculating on the likelihood of more flooding. Burl was a tall, heavyset man, with muscular arms developed over a lifetime of blacksmithing. It occurred to Theodore that Burl could have lifted the overturned wagon by himself. It also occurred to him that Nora probably admired men like that. Theodore was no weakling; after all, he could handle a team of two headstrong mules. But there was no escaping the fact that he was not a strongman.

Theodore asked Burl to tell him about Amalie's healing abilities, and he described his wife's skill in reducing fever, treating stomach ailments and croup, healing rashes, and easing sore throats and other aches and pains. She understood how to extract medicinal substances from a host of plants, knew whether to use the roots, bark, sap, flowers, or leaves for her concoctions, and understood how to prepare the right dosages for her patients. But even more important than this knowledge was her healing touch, which calmed and soothed even those who were traumatized.

"Now, Amalie don't never claim to be able to cure everything, and they's many a time all she can do is hold a dying person's hand and give comfort to his family. But she got the healing touch, all right, and what they is to know about cures, she know. And Nora gone be just like her. I ain't ever understood how my womenfolk learns all that curing business and keeps it in they heads and don't never let the sight of a sick or injured person scare them."

"They are mighty courageous," Theodore offered, "and gifted. You must be very proud of them."

Burl smiled and nodded in affirmation.

When the fire was reduced to smoldering embers, Luke's father went to check on his son and came back to report that he was sound asleep.

Theodore awoke to a brilliantly lit dawn, sunshine rapidly flooding the tent, and quickly brushed the hay off his clothing and refreshed himself using the bucket of water, bar of soap, and towel Etta had thoughtfully provided. He stepped out into a glorious morning, the earth scrubbed clean, the sky a vivid blue, with small scudding clouds all that remained of the storm.

It was not only the delicious cooking smells emanating from the house that quickened his step and brought him into the kitchen well ahead of the other men; it was also the thought of a pair of pretty eyes and a charming smile that beckoned him.

The Garrisons insisted on their guests eating first, so Theodore was offered a chair at the table next to Amalie and across from Nora, who was wearing a different scarf this morning, vivid purple with touches of gold.

"Us already said the blessing," Amalie commented, "but if you wants to add anything — "

Theodore was a bit embarrassed by this assumption that he was in charge of religious matters when he was merely Reverend Carpenter's assistant.

"Oh, no. Please — continue eating."

Nora was just finishing her meal, so he hurriedly engaged her in conversation.

"How's Luke this morning? Is he awake?"

"He be all right. But he gone be in pain for a while,"

Amalie nodded in agreement.

"His mama gone stay here with him till he be better," she said. "Best not to move him just yet. He be hurt pretty bad, but still, Luke one lucky child. Did he land on hard earth, that wagon would've crushed him for sure. Thank the Lord for them rains that softened up the ground."

"Amen to that," Theodore said. "Are you and Nora staying with Luke today?"

"Just me. Nora gots to get back to our place with my husband and the other chillun. They gots livestock to tend to, and Burl worried they might be flooding up by the house. They be leaving soon as he ready to go."

At that moment, Burl and Luke's father arrived. Burl explained that with Tate's help they had already re-attached the wagon wheel.

Theodore sipped his coffee, disappointed to learn that Nora was leaving. He knew the family planned to return in the evening for the second service, but he had looked forward to spending some time with Nora during the day. Something nudged him to tell her so.

"I'm sorry to hear you won't be staying the day, Nora. I was hoping we could — I thought perhaps we might — "

Might what? At home, he could have shown off his flower garden. But here what was there to do here? Slop the hogs together? Milk some cows?

"Us might go walking in this here mud," Nora suggested with a smile.

He chuckled.

"Exactly. Why not?"

And so while the famished men ate their breakfast, Theodore and Nora set out on the relatively dry path Etta pointed out to them. They inhaled the clean, sweet-smelling air. Honeysuckle was in bloom, and Theodore pointed out some wild white roses almost hidden in the brush. They enjoyed the sight of a couple of calves chasing each other and petted a friendly horse that wandered over their way.

"I've never owned a horse," Theodore said. "They're beautiful animals."

"Us gots four of them. Papa say he need that many to practice his shoeing. But me and Mama know he just love horses."

They could not keep Burl waiting, but both were reluctant to end their walk. As they started back, Nora said, "You be a mighty fine preacher, Tee."

"Well, I hope to be one day."

She stopped in her tracks for a moment.

"And you talks so pretty. Where you learn to talk like that, Tee?"

"Oh, I guess I just paid attention in school. I had some good teachers. And a kind friend I correspond with has helped me a lot. But I only went to the seventh grade, so I'm not really an educated man, Nora."

She shook her head.

"That ain't true. You about the educatedest man I ever met!"

Theodore laughed.

"Well, thank you, but — "

"No buts about it, Tee. You be a fine preacher and the smartest man I knows."

The admiration in her eyes somewhat eased his regret that he was not, and never would be, a strongman.

The Freedmans lived nearly nine miles distant, near a settlement called AfricaTown, but kept their promise and returned for the evening service, preached by the visiting minister who had been absent the night before. Theodore tried to pay attention, but his thoughts kept wandering to Nora. It was not only her large eyes and sweetness of manner that appealed to him: Nora was full figured, and he could not help noticing her feminine curves, even though the bodice of her gown was demurely buttoned all the way up to her throat. He chastised himself for noticing. Nora also had trouble casting her eyes anywhere but at Theodore. Finally they gave up and openly smiled at each other.

After the service, Amalie determined that Luke was on the mend and could be left to the care of his parents. As the Freedmans prepared to take their leave, Nora and Theodore found one another.

"I sure enough wish you live closer," she said with a wistful smile.

Theodore took her hand.

"So do I. I would really like to see you again, Nora."

"You means you gone come back for another visit?"

Returning to Mobile was something Theodore had never planned to do, even if the city had proven not to be the cauldron of sin he had expected. But now there was Nora. And to get to Nora, one had to return to Mobile. Unhesitatingly he said, "Yes. Yes, I do expect — plan — to come back. And in the meantime, we can write to one another. Would you like that?"

Nora seemed to give the matter careful thought, smiling shyly as she pleated a fold of her skirt with her fingers. When she finally nodded her head, Tee was relieved, having feared she was going to reveal the existence of a gentleman friend and dash his hopes.

"Then that's settled. Where do you receive your mail?"

She frowned as if in concentration.

"Well, now I thinks on it — Beeker's General Store at Gator Pass. That be close to us. I seen people get mail there."

"Fine, Gator Pass. I'll remember that."

"But Tee — I needs to tell you — "

"Yes?"

"I needs to say — "

He smiled encouragingly, but she only glanced down at the floor and softly murmured, "Never mind. It ain't important."

He gently squeezed her hand, not daring to kiss her.

"We'll write to each other, Nora — and I'll come back, I promise."

Then suddenly, before God and everybody, including her giggling sister, Nora kissed him on the cheek.

ON THE LONG train ride back to Dothan, Theodore reflected on his and Nora's promises to write to each other. This was the beginning, he felt, of a mutually enjoyable correspondence that would allow them to get to know one another better. At home, he addressed an envelope to "Miss Nora Freedman, c/o Beeker's General Store, Gator Pass, Alabama," and posted it in Dothan the next day. He was confident he would receive a reply within a couple of weeks. But a month passed with no response. Disappointed, he concluded that the letter had gone astray and wrote another. And then another. The summer was almost gone when he posted the fifth letter. He consulted Reverend Carpenter on the matter, hoping he knew of some other way to contact Nora, but he had no more information about the remote area where the Freedmans lived than Theodore did.

"I'm concerned something may have happened to her or her family, Reverend."

In response to the reverend's knowing smile he added, "And — yes, I guess it's obvious. I'm concerned that maybe she didn't really want me to stay in touch with her."

"Nobody who seen the way that girl looked at you would believe that, son. And has you forgot the kiss?"

"A sisterly kiss. I'm sure now that's all it was."

Reverend Carpenter shook his head reassuringly.

"I expect either those letters going to the wrong place or they not being picked up and brung out to her house."

"But how will I ever know that?"

Reverend Carpenter counseled patience.

"They's talk of another revival in the spring — along about May. I think just maybe us can make another trip down there."

Theodore sighed. May was a long, long way off. An eternity. And so to help pass the time until then, and just in case the unanswered letters were the result of misdirection and not rejection, he continued to post one or two letters a month to Miss Nora Freedman of Gator Pass, Alabama.

MAY HAD NEVER arrived more slowly in Theodore's lifetime. Farm work kept him busy, and he planted a new variety of rose from seeds Julia Tenpenny sent him, and he was now preaching a sermon once a month, all of which kept him occupied. But the trip to Mobile was always uppermost in his mind. March crawled and April dawdled. But finally May showed up.

On the morning he left for Mobile, Bess followed him out to the barn where James was hitching up the mule for the ride to the train depot. This trip she was not afraid her baby would be ensnared by sin in Mobile; she was afraid his heart would be broken.

"You a fine young man, Tee. Us is proud of you," she said.

Then she repeated the remark she had made several times in recent months.

"And if that young lady you been writing to don't appreciate you, then you needs to put her right out your mind."

Tee threw his bag in the wagon, climbed up on the seat next to James, and reached down for his mother's hand, which he held for a moment in both of his.

"Now, you know you're my one and only sweetheart, Mama. There's not another woman on earth who could hold a candle to you. You open your mouth with wisdom, and on your tongue is the law of kindness. Your worth is far above rubies."

She smiled and waved him off, thinking, *Quoting scripture ain't gone save your poor heart from the scorn of a coldhearted girl.*

AFTER A THREE-DAY revival in Mobile, Theodore and Reverend Carpenter once again were driven out into the country by Tate Garrison for another revival on his property.

"Us expecting a bigger crowd this time," Tate said. "With this fine weather, ain't no telling how many folks might show up."

Theodore could not bring himself to ask, but Reverend Carpenter did.

"You thinks the Freedmans will make it?"

"Not sure. Ain't seen them in some months. But I left word about the revival at Beeker's General Store. And lots of other folks coming."

He began listing names and providing little histories of this or that family while Theodore asked himself why on earth he had journeyed such a long way, only to be ignored by the one person on earth he most wanted to see. Then, ashamed of himself, he responded to Tate's comments with, "We appreciate all you've done to make the revival a success, Tate. I'm looking forward to seeing everyone again and meeting all the folks who couldn't make it last year."

Theodore was no pessimist, but he had little hope that Nora would appear that evening. And even if she did, what would he say to her? She had ignored him for a year. He had maintained the fantasy that she cared about him but had never received his letters, but deep down he realized that was only a way to salve his ego. As they were setting up for the revival he was reflecting on his own foolishness when suddenly it dawned on him that, if in fact his letters had never reached her, she would believe he had not kept his promise to write to her. She might have hurt feelings and stay away from the revival for that reason. She might even be angry with him.

As Tate had predicted, the fair weather encouraged a large crowd of people to attend. There were few chairs, but Theodore and the other men brought barrels and hay bales from the barn for seating, and quite a few folks simply spread out the blankets they had brought and sat on the ground. As they arrived, old friends greeted one another, and newcomers were introduced.

Theodore was brushing hay off the new frock-coat he had saved up for for a year when he saw her. She walked in arm-in-arm with her sister, as Amalie followed, carrying a couple of blankets. Nora was wearing a sprigged muslin gown that looked new, her head adorned with a brightly flowered, intricately wrapped scarf. Theodore stood stock still, gazing at her, as Amalie nudged her daughter and pointed in his direction. Nora looked his way, and their eyes met. He drew a deep breath, which did nothing to stop the pounding of his heart. Was she angry with him? Or indifferent?

Her broad smile instantly told him that she was neither of those things. She released Mattie's arm and came to him, offering her hand.

"You finally here, Tee, you finally here!"

"Finally," he responded with a smile and pulled her to him in a gentle hug. Amalie approached him, and they hugged as well.

"Us be so glad to see you, Tee," she said. "It been too long."

Ever afterward Theodore was not sure how he got through that evening without making a fool of himself. He was in such an elated state that any silly statement might have come out of his mouth. But Reverend Carpenter, thoroughly amused, assured him that he had spoken appropriately, if with a wild exuberance that the congregation probably interpreted as revivalist fervor.

Tee reluctantly parted with the family that night but was invited to come visit them the following day. They had seemed pleased to see him, which was a relief, but it also puzzled him. No one mentioned anything he had commented on in his letters, nor the reason Nora had never responded.

The next day Tate lent him a horse, and he left shortly after daybreak, eager to get an early start because he was afraid of becoming lost out in the country. He was directed to go by way of AfricaTown, due west of the Garrison farm, and then head four-and-a-half miles north to the Freedman place.

AfricaTown, he was told, was the home of quite a number of ex-slaves who had been brought to Mobile in 1860 in defiance of the federal law ending the slave trade in 1808. During a civil war in Ghana, the winning tribes had sold the conquered tribes into slavery. Dahomey warriors raided a village where the enslaved tribesmen were held and sold the survivors of the raid for $100 each. They were taken to the United States aboard the *Clotilde*, built by Timothy Meaher, a wealthy Mobile shipyard owner.

In Mobile Harbor, the ship captain sent the slaves to shore on a riverboat, hid them in a canebrake, then burned and sank the *Clotilde*. In 1861, Meaher and others were charged with illegally importing 103 natives of Africa, but nothing could be proved against him and the Civil War was beginning, so the case was dismissed.

After the Civil War, fellow tribesmen joined those who had been transported on the *Clotilde*. They and their descendants formed a community in which they were able to preserve their African heritage and culture, including speaking their native tongue.

Theodore had never met an African and did not expect to do so now. He had only ridden by way of AfricaTown because it was en route to Gator Pass. However, when he reined in the horse and paused to get his bearings, he was approached by an elderly, dignified gentleman, who held up a hand in greeting. His hair receded more than Theodore's. He had a neatly clipped white beard and wore a welcoming smile. He was clearly a village elder.

"You be lost, friend? This be AfricaTown, not Mobile."

He spoke with an accent but was easily understood.

"I don't think I'm lost quite yet, but I might be without a little help, sir."

A couple of children ran up and petted the horse. A woman standing in the doorway of a small, tin-roofed house called them back, but Theodore smiled and indicated it was fine for them to befriend the horse.

"I be Cudjo Lewis," the gentleman said.

Theodore got down from the buggy and shook his hand.

"Theodore Waldron. Headed for a place near Gator Pass. I think it's near here?"

"Four, five miles maybe. Not far. Especially when you be so fortunate as to ride instead of walk!"

Theodore chuckled.

"Riding a fine horse is not my usual way of traveling," he admitted. "At home I either walk or ride in a wagon drawn by a mule. Today my friends were kind enough to allow me the use of the horse."

"Where you from, brother?"

"Clear on the other side of the state. Near Dothan."

"Never hear of that place."

"I'm not surprised. It's not a big city like Mobile."

"You welcome to stay and visit here for a while."

The offer was tempting. It would be an enriching experience to sit among native Africans and listen to tales of their homeland. But even without pausing along the way, he had little time to visit with the Freedmans.

"That's very kind, but I have to get over to Gator Pass and back before nightfall. Perhaps some other time."

Cudjoe nodded and proceeded to explain the quickest route to Gator Pass.

IT WAS MIDMORNING before Theodore sighted the general store where Burl would be meeting him, and the intensely humid heat had long since caused him to remove his frock-coat, carefully fold it, and put it in the saddlebag. He was thankful for the shade of his broad-brimmed hat. A slough ran beside the road, and he noticed a sizable alligator, half-submerged, that appeared to watch him as he passed. He slowed down to observe this imposing creature.

"So are you the fellow this place is named after?" he politely asked.

The gator slid into the water, apparently annoyed by the attention.

Theodore was relieved to see that Burl was there waiting for him when he arrived. He was also on horseback, and they immediately headed for the Freedman place, Theodore carefully noting the several twists and turns they made so he would not be lost on his return that afternoon.

The Freedmans owned fifty acres of land on which they grew their own produce and kept a sizable collection of livestock. Although the Freedman place seemed remote, even desolate, to Tee, and Gator Pass was a more primitive settlement than Chinkapin — which, the Lord knew, was no metropolis — he learned from Burl that there were numerous farms in the region. Burl was the only blacksmith, and this skill provided enough income for the family to buy whatever they could not produce. He also explained that Amalie earned income as well. She was well known throughout two counties as both a healer and a midwife. For black and white families alike, many of whom rarely ventured down into Mobile, she was the only person with medical knowledge they ever saw.

Amalie and Nora had the noon meal prepared soon after Burl and Theodore arrived. The table conversation mostly consisted of his answering their questions about his family, the farm, and Divine Truth church. The evening before, Tee had wondered why the eldest son, twenty-year-old Henry, had not attended the revival. Now he learned that Henry had been hired as a dock worker in Mobile and was living there with the family of his future wife. But twelve-year-old Mattie and eight-year-old Little Burl were thrilled to be present for the preacher man's visit. They had their suspicions about his intentions towards their sister and figured on catching him out by listening to every single word he said. So far, though, the conversation had been boring.

After dinner they sat in the small, simply furnished living room. Theodore was burning to know about the letters but could not bring himself to raise the subject. Then suddenly Nora said, "I needs to thank you for all them letters, Tee."

He was dumbstruck.

Into his silence Amalie commented, "Nora got them letters put away in that trunk over there. They be precious to her."

After a few seconds, during which pleased surprise vied with puzzlement, Tee found his voice.

"But you never responded, Nora! Why didn't you write back?"

She shook her head, clearly embarrassed.

"I ain't never learned to read. I tried to tell you so, but — I'se sorry, Tee. I just couldn't." Then her face brightened. "Miz Beeker — her husband run the general store — she can read. She was gone read the first one to me and write you back for me, too. But then her mother took sick in Mobile, and she went down there sudden like and ain't come back yet."

She walked over to a wooden trunk by the wall, took out a folded scarf, and unwrapped the packet it contained — all of Tee's letters, tied with a red ribbon. As she picked them up, Nora recalled her excitement the day Burl returned from the general store with a letter addressed to her. She had never received a letter in her life and neither had anyone else in her family.

"I opened every letter when it come and looked at your pretty handwriting. But they wasn't nobody to read the words to me."

Tee's heart lurched as he pictured Nora staring at the meaningless symbols in the letters, yearning to know what they said. It had never occurred to him to ask if she were literate. He assumed anyone as obviously bright as she was could read. But then, where could she have learned, in this isolated place?

"Us'd sure like to hear you read them now, Tee."

Amalie nodded and smiled at him. The letters would be fine entertainment for all of them, and she was almost as eager as Nora to know what they contained. She settled in a rocking chair with some mending. Nora invited Tee to sit next to her on the cushioned wooden bench that served as a sofa. Burl was whittling a wooden boat for Little Burl, who was sprawled on a braided rug next to wide-eyed Mattie. Her expression seemed to say, *Now we're getting somewhere!*

Theodore was the only uncomfortable person in the room. Everyone else waited expectantly for him to amuse them with the reading of missiles he had intended for Nora's eyes alone.

Thankful he had not expressed the depth of his feelings for her in any of the letters, Theodore cleared his throat and began.

Dear Nora –

"Hold on, Tee," Nora said. "You forgots to read the date." Tee started again.

3 July 1896

Dear Nora,
  I have been home nearly a week now. While I was gone, the crape myrtles blossomed, and the orange and golden day lilies bloomed. The bright colors are something to see, especially with the morning light on them. I wish I could pick a bunch and bring them to you. They make me think of you and the pretty head scarves you wear.
  The crops are coming along well, and it appears we'll have a whole lot of corn and potatoes, okra, tomatoes, and squash by summer's end. Oh, and watermelons and cantaloupes. The Lord has blessed us with plentiful rain — but thankfully not the deluge we had down there!

My church is trying to raise money for a small organ. I do not play, but a member of our congregation can, and she is eager to begin playing for our church. Mrs. Ida Wright belonged to a large A.M.E. church in Dothan before moving out into the country and mightily misses her music. She has organized bake sales, and the ladies have had some success with selling their knitted garments and some truly beautiful quilts.

Also, it surprised me very much that some white folks came by the farm one day and bought nearly all of the rose plants I had set out, and I put aside that money for the organ, too. It appears that someone told them I was good with roses. But of course, when a flower blooms that is God's doing, not mine.

We have no doubt the Lord will help us as we help ourselves, and we will have our organ before the year is out.

Nora, I do hope that you and all of your family are well. I so admire the work you and your mother do with the sick. Such a fine calling.

Please give my regards to your parents,
                Yours truly, Theodore Waldron.

P.S. Please write when you can.

The P.S. caused Tee some embarrassment, now that he knew Nora was illiterate. He smiled at her, thinking, *That is something I can remedy.* He picked up the second letter and began to read.

THE WIREGRASS WAS blessed with just the right balance of rain and sunshine to produce bountiful crops that summer. The Waldrons had a special reason for appreciating this good fortune. There was money for the bride and her family, including brother Henry and his new wife, to travel by train from Mobile to Dothan; there was money to pay the preacher and the church organist (that July the new organ had arrived, and Mrs. Ida Wright at last had her music and joyfully shared her talent with the congregation); there was money for a sit-down dinner in the Sunday school room. But no money was needed for the flowers. Divine Truth had been the scene of several weddings in the seven years of its existence, but never had it been decorated as beautifully as on this October wedding day. Many of Theodore's plants had luxuriantly bloomed into the first days of fall that year, and the altar and pew ends were decorated with a profusion of flowers. The bride's bouquet of white and yellow roses, ivy, and a new plant Theodore had just begun cultivating, Queen Anne's lace, caused more than one young lady to wish for one exactly like it when her turn at the altar came.

Nora wore a pale green gabardine gown with long sleeves puffed at the shoulders and fitted to the wrist, the bodice trimmed with lace. The dress was a gift from her parents, purchased in Mobile over her protest, because even in one of the less expensive shops it cost the equivalent of several weeks of Burl's blacksmith income. But it could also be worn for special occasions at the church and was thus a practical choice for the assistant pastor's new wife.

Nora had inherited Amalie's soft, springy curls, and on her wedding day her hair was combed up, tamed with hairpins, and adorned with tortoiseshell combs, a gift from her new mother-in-law.

As they said their I-do's before a beaming Reverend Carpenter, Nora tried to grasp the reality of becoming the wife of such a kind, educated man, and Theodore remembered the day he had finally been granted what he had been praying for since he first set eyes on her.

The marriage proposal had taken place at the conclusion of the letter reading. Gazing at Nora as he put down the last one, seeing the loving expression on her face that could not be misread, feeling the warmth and good will radiating throughout the room, Theodore's heart was so full, his love for this young woman so deep, that any shyness about his intentions vanished, and he asked for her hand in front of them all. Nora smiled and tearfully nodded, Amalie wiped her eyes with the handkerchief she had been mending, and Burl stood up to shake his hand and give his consent — necessary because Nora was only seventeen. Mattie and Little Burl assailed their future in-law with boisterous hugs.

No date was set that day, but it was agreed they would marry before the end of the year. There was another revival meeting that night, which the Freedmans would attend, but the following day Theodore would have to return home. The Freedmans possessed neither paper, pen, nor ink, so Theodore had to wait until he returned to the Garrison place to use his own supplies for writing a note to Mrs. Beeker, who was expected to return any day. He asked Nora to give her the note, which requested her to read his letters to Nora as they arrived and to send him Nora's responses, and expressed his deep appreciation for her help.

Mrs. Beeker had complied, happy to assist in the romance, even adding comments now and then, such as, "Your letter has made Nora very happy today!" or "Amalie asked me to be sure to send along her regards to your parents." At the conclusion of the correspondence, when Nora was at last his own, abiding with him in Chinkapin, Theodore gratefully sent Mrs. Beeker several packets of his favorite flower seeds.

And the marriage of Theodore and Nora, like his garden, flourished.

Chapter 10

King Cotton

WHILE THEODORE WALDRON dutifully labored on the family farm, he continued to pray for the opportunity to cultivate his garden, which grew more extensive every year. With the loss of his brother John to pneumonia in 1901, with his sisters unable to assist because they were struggling to raise large families of their own, and with the realization that his father was too frail to work in the fields any longer, the family agreed it might be best to sell ninety acres and allow Tee the opportunity to use the remaining fifty acres for his nursery business. Waldron's Gardens was launched in 1903. Through hard work, his natural horticultural talent, and Nora's unfailing help, the business thrived.

But for most farmers, the story was different. At the dawn of the twentieth century, the average Wiregrass farmer became not more independent, but less so. Once almost completely self-sufficient, as the craze for cotton growing swept the region farmers were ensnared, not enriched, by King Cotton.

When the first settlers arrived, the vast pine forests provided a livelihood for any hardy individual who had the stamina to swing an ax or man a saw. The ancient beauty of thousands of loblolly and longleaf pines was sacrificed to the production of lumber for houses and fences and railroad ties. With the development of the naval stores industry, armies of men intent on draining trees of resin, their life's blood, advanced on thousands more trees, with no thought for the consequences of destroying the habitat of countless creatures to harvest the fluid used in the production of pitch and tar, essential to shipbuilding.

Pine resin was also used in the manufacture of a foul-smelling, yet extremely useful, substance: turpentine. As a solvent, medicinal elixir, ingredient in cleaning products — even an additive in gin — turpentine was more highly valued than towering pines. By the 1890s, turpentine stills were a common sight, and Dothan had become the largest inland shipping point for turpentine in the world.

But the denuded land remained fertile enough to produce richly diverse crops, with no crop planted to the exclusion of others. Barring catastrophe or illness, farm families always had ample food on the table, with enough left over to barter for all of their needs. Wiregrass farmers had thrived without cotton from the 1830s, when settlers first put down roots near Poplar Head, the spring where various tribes of the Creek Confederacy once camped, until the late nineteenth century. But when they acquired the knowledge that by adding nutrients to the sandy soil they, too — like the rich planters in the Black Belt running through Central Alabama — could be cotton farmers, they became convinced that they, too, could achieve wealth.

Farm after farm gave over fields once devoted to the production of food for the family to the production of this fleecy whiteness, this delicate fluff, which they exchanged for greenbacks and, they reckoned, a better life. The Wiregrass finally had the potential to produce a cash crop that would raise family incomes above subsistence level.

As they reaped the plenitude of plants they had sown, bent over down the interminable rows, dragging their long sacks, their hands bloodied by the prickly burs, their backs and arms aching, their eyes almost blinded by sweat, the cotton farmers — black and white, male and female, from weathered veterans of the fields to young children — dreamed of what cash, real honest-to-God cash, could do for them. What none of them envisioned was a small insect native to Mexico with the Latin name *anthonomus grandis*, which in 1892 had begun crossing the Rio Grande hundreds of miles southwest of Alabama, invading Texas cotton fields. Small though the creature was, it possessed a voracious appetite.

In 1915, not yet aware that the weevil had at last reached the Wiregrass, the cotton farmers hauled their creaking wagonloads to be ginned and rode home with fistfuls of dollars. The younguns, who had delighted in bouncing on the soft piles of cotton en route to the gin, now had to be content with sprawling on the hard wagon floor, wondering how best to convince their parents of the need for a game or a toy or a new bonnet when it wasn't even Christmas yet.

Chapter 11

NEMESIS

*A*NTHONOMUS GRANDIS speaks to the people of the Wiregrass . . .

I am not a predator. I do not sting. I do not bite. I do not spread disease. Yet I am despised, reviled, and persecuted. My kind are routinely slaughtered. Why?

For millennia, we lived contentedly in warm countries below the Rio Grande. We were unmolested. Then you invited us to join you north of the river by sowing your land with a crop which is the one food above all others Nature intended for the sustenance of me and my young: cotton. And Cotton beckoned to us, saying, come, feast; be fruitful and multiply.

And so we left our first home, beloved though it was, and did what we thought you intended us to do. We joined you. In 1892, we came together in swarms on the south side of the Rio Grande and bravely swam across. We crawled ashore onto the new land and traveled from Texas through Louisiana and Mississippi until, wearied but rejoicing, we found the lushest cotton fields ever grown, right here in the Wiregrass. We believed you would also rejoice, because we came to devour the plants you curse as you sow, curse as you tend, curse as you reap.

And then, inexplicably, the killing began. First, it was a single farmer with his little can of poison, then fifty farmers, then squadrons of farmers, all banding together to find the most effective means of exterminating us.

But we are here now. And your pitiful thousands are no match for our young, in their billions. We are here.

Chapter 12

The Tanner Family

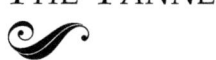

MILLICENT TANNER SATTERWIRTH, wife of the owner of the largest feed and seed store in the area, did not have to concern herself with the often futile battle against the boll weevil and other pests that consumed so much of her neighbors' energy and strength. Financially better off than either of her close friends, Abigail Knightley and Josephine Yates, she did not have to perform farm chores like Abby, or raise her own vegetables like Jo, whose husband was a cotton oil factory worker. And she was able to employ a maid to handle most of the cleaning and laundry. However, managing her three sons — eight-year-old Willoughby, sixteen-month-old Roger, and two-month-old Gerald — cooking the large meals her husband demanded, and serving on numerous church and community committees as expected of the wife of a prosperous business owner, she had little leisure time.

But on a March afternoon in 1928, with her chores done, Willoughby at school for another two hours, and her babies taking a nap, she could relax for a while. Reading was her favorite leisure activity, and she settled happily into a comfy chair with a glass of iced tea and dived into one of the library books she had picked up the week before, Helen Hunt Jackson's popular tale of a Scots-Indian maiden, *Ramona*, set in 1850s California. She enjoyed the romantic yet tragic story of Ramona and Alessandro and was touched by the hardships inflicted upon them because they were Indians.

She could relate to the story because her father Joseph was a halfbreed who had been teased and called names as a child.

If she ever had a daughter, Millie reflected, Ramona would be a suitable name for her because, after all, she was herself one-quarter Creek Indian. Lacking even rudimentary knowledge of her Creek forbears, she did not realize that their Muscogee language did not encompass Spanish names.

Between the births of her eldest son and her babies, Millie had suffered two miscarriages, and she and Harold had been glad to finally welcome Will's brothers. But with each pregnancy, Millie had hoped for a daughter, and she experienced a twinge of envy over the fact that Abby now had two daughters. Josephine, the mother of two sons, also had a daughter, Gerrilyn, about a year older than six-month-old Nobella.

Millie loved her boys, but she sometimes wondered why she seemed fated always to live in a household of males. Not only did she lack female offspring, she had never had a sister, either. As Roger roused up and sleepily wandered into the room in search of a drink, Millie smiled at the memory of how she had tried to remedy her sister-less state with the help of Abby Coltayne.

BORN THE SAME YEAR, Millicent Tanner and Abigail Coltayne had been friends from early childhood. Millie had six brothers — three older, three younger. Abby had three elder sisters and one elder brother. She was born at the end of her mother's childbearing years, ten years after the birth of her youngest sister. During that time three other children had been born to Victoria and Tobias; none had lived past infancy. And so it seemed a kind of miracle that Abigail, born when Victoria Coltayne was forty-six, had survived.

Abigail's father Tobias had farmed the family property in Barbour County with his brother Grayson for many years. But in time it became apparent that the land would not accommodate both of their growing families. In 1905, Tobias and Victoria decided to invest in good farm land farther south, in newly formed Houston County. The Tanner property, which had been in that family for decades, when it was still part of Dale County, was a few fields over from the Coltayne land.

By the time Abby was ten years old, all of her sisters had married and moved away. Thus both she and Millie lacked a strong sister relationship and decided to forge one of their own. On Sundays, plump, dark-haired Millie and slim, pale-haired Abby sat side by side in the small Methodist church near Dothan attended by both families. They daydreamed over the dresses and hats in the Sears Roebuck catalog together. They spent many hours in one family kitchen or the other assisting in every stage of preserving peaches, figs, and blackberries, and then, literally, enjoying the fruits of their labors. Learning to make the perfect biscuit, they doused each other with flour and lobbed bits of dough at each other, collapsing in giggles until reprimanded by whichever mother was in charge.

In summer, the friends went walking in the surrounding woods and waded in several creeks that crisscrossed their families' properties. Wild fruits were everywhere, and they sampled them all — blackberries, scuppernong and muscadine grapes, plums, crabapples, persimmons, and many others. In the fall, they went nutting. They caught glimpses of deer, squirrels, raccoons, turkeys, and wild pigs foraging for nuts, but still easily filled their buckets. Black walnuts, hickory nuts, and pecans — the most easily shelled of the nuts — lay on the ground for the taking, as well as one of their favorites, the small, sweet chinkapin.

It seemed to their parents that Millie, the only girl in the family, and Abby, the youngest in hers, were growing up much too quickly. One day they were playing with their corn shuck dolls, and then, but an eye blink later, it seemed, they were wearing long skirts and begging their mothers to unplait their pigtails and give them a grownup hairstyle. With their long hair brushed up into the pompadour style in vogue, the girls did indeed look like young women.

It was soon after they had graduated to long skirts, when they were fourteen, that Millie announced, "Abby, I know how we can be true sisters."

"How?"

"You can marry one of my brothers. Then we'll be sisters-in-law."

They were at the Tanner place. Millie was mending yet another of the boys' unending supply of shirts. Abby was rolling a skein of yarn into a ball at Mrs. Tanner's request. Like Victoria, Harriet Tanner did not believe in letting young fingers be idle, even if the fingers belonged to the child of a friend.

Abby was not too sure about Millie's brainstorm. Marriage was not something she intended to jump into.

"Well — I don't know. Which one?"

"Don't matter. Pick one. I've got six of 'em."

"All right." She considered for a moment. "Jacob ain't bad looking. But don't you dare go and tell him I said so."

Jacob was actually fine looking, in ways different from other boys of her acquaintance. Abby knew that the Tanner children were one-quarter Creek Indian. Of all the Tanner children, he most clearly bore the stamp of his Muscogee Creek ancestors. His thick dark hair was poker straight and his skin was faintly tinctured with sienna, so he was never pale, even in the midst of winter. His slightly oblique, deep brown eyes lit up when he smiled. He had a perfectly beautiful smile. Abby had often noted this. But she always concealed her admiration well.

"Of course I won't tell him." Millie hid her pleased expression by holding up the mended shirt in front of her face to examine her stitching.

One morning not long after this, when they had run out of things to do at the Coltayne place, Abby suggested they test an old custom that held if you found an odd-colored hair on a girl's head, that would be the color of her future husband's hair. Millie winced as Abby yanked and pulled out a pale hair not at all like Millie's dark locks.

"You husband will have blond hair," she announced.

"My turn," Millie said, and after some searching found an odd-colored hair and yanked.

"Well now, this cain't be right," she said.

The hair was reddish in color. She held it up for Abby to examine.

"Looks like my husband will have red hair."

"Now Abby, you know nary a one of my brothers has red hair!"

"Well, maybe I ain't supposed to marry one of your brothers," Abby commented without concern.

Millie was stung. She was counting heavily on Abby marrying into her male-dominated family. But apparently that was not important to Abby. Apparently Abby did not really want to be her true sister after all.

"Well, who cares anyhow," said Millie. "You can marry anybody you gol-durn please." And she stomped out of Abby's house and marched home, leaving Abby standing on the porch staring after her.

That afternoon, Millie was vigorously churning butter on the back porch when Jacob came striding up from the field, where he and his brother Matthew had been raking up cut grass into stacks of hay, to get some water. He grabbed the well bucket, lowered it and filled it, and then dumped it over his head. Then he repeated the process and took a long drink out of the bucket. Millie's energetic churning caught his attention as he stepped on the porch to grab a towel from the railing to dry himself.

"You're going to churn that butter till it's hard as a brick, Sister. Don't you think you should slow down a little bit?"

"I have been churning butter since I was four years old, Jacob Tanner. So don't you tell *me*. But I will tell *you* one thing for sure — Abby cain't have you!"

As soon as the words were out of her mouth, Millie regretted having said them. Despite her anger at her old friend, she still cherished the thought of having Abby as a true sister. And bagging Jacob as a husband was meant to be a gradual but surefire process, like slowly sneaking up on an animal in the woods and snaring it with a net before it knew what was happening.

"What do you mean, she cain't have me?"

Millie lowered her head to hide her red face.

"I don't mean nothing."

Jacob bent down to look into her eyes.

"Has Abby been talking about me?"

"Why would she talk about you, you conceited jackass?"

Jacob shrugged.

"Makes no difference to me whether she does or not. Why should I care?"

"Because you'd be plumb lucky to have her for a — "

"For a what?"

Millie made a face at him.

"Never mind. Now leave me be."

Jacob grinned and walked back toward the field he was plowing. He whistled a cheery tune and thought about Abby thinking about him. It was a pleasant thought.

IT WAS GENERALLY known that Millie and Jacob's father, Joseph, was a halfbreed and that the bad half was Creek. But their grandfather, Ephraim Tanner, was a responsible member of the farming community and his family were practicing Methodists, so the taint of Joseph's Indian blood was pretty much overlooked.

Five years after the Civil War ended, twenty-six-year-old Ephraim Tanner was a restless Confederate veteran who could not readjust to farm life. He heard about the silver rush in Caribou, Colorado, and the faraway, untamed sound of the place called to him, so he went. By the time he arrived Caribou was mined out, but he found another kind of treasure.

On the way back east he camped out in the Creek Nation in Oklahoma, arid home of the exiled Muscogee Creeks. A young girl, perhaps seventeen years old, caught his eye, and he found himself watching her — the agile way she moved, the way she laughed. He knew the history of the Creeks, of course — savage enemies of his people, thieves and brutal fighters who were rightfully evicted from the state of Alabama. Thanks to Andy Jackson, nicknamed Old Hickory for his toughness, he had never met one at home. A fiery Indian fighter, Jackson and his troops had annihilated the Red Sticks at Horseshoe Bend on the Tallapoosa River, and sixteen years later, as President, he had ordered the removal of every last hostile to the West.

But now here was this girl, who increased his heart rate with every glance in his direction. He tried to pack up his gear and move on but found he could not. Good sense took a back seat, and he wondered if that bottle of whiskey in the bottom of his saddlebag would serve the purpose he had in mind.

It did. Forty-eight hours after wandering into Creek territory, Ephraim used the liquor to purchase Shining Stone from her father, Bold Fox, a man with too many daughters on his hands. Ephraim knew he would be in a lot of trouble with the Indian affairs officials if they knew about the whiskey, but he did not care.

Shining Stone was slender and graceful, and when she smiled at him she partially averted her face in an appealing, shy manner that caused him to grin in response. Her teeth were alabaster against her dark skin, and her luxuriant black hair was so long she could sit on it. Ephraim loved the way it held the wood-smoke scent of the cooking fire. She was equally fascinated by his wavy auburn hair and pale blue eyes.

It did not occur to him to marry her in the white way, but he accepted the commitment implied when Bold Fox placed her hand in his and whispered an ancient Muscogee blessing. He then said to Shining Stone, "Be a good wife — feed him well and give him sons," this last part uttered in a wistful tone.

Doubtful of a warm reception in Alabama, Ephraim stayed on, deciding they would figure it all out as they went along. Living with the Creeks, he had trouble adjusting to this dry, dusty land so unlike verdant Alabama. He wished he could take Shining Stone there, to her ancestral home. Bold Fox, a survivor of the Trail of Tears, had been born there in the year the stars fell.

But Shining Stone died giving birth to their son Joseph. Although Ephraim had never troubled to find a preacher to marry them, when she died he rode two hours through a chilling rain to the mission church in search of a preacher to bury her, weeping the whole way. On a stark February morning they laid her to rest, dressed in the bright beribboned cotton gown she loved. After her people had provided her with valuable pelts and trinkets and parcels of food for the journey to the hereafter, the preacher conducted the burial service, and Shining Stone's relatives, most of whom were Christians, joined in the hymn singing.

No longer able to stay where every sight reminded him of Shining Stone, Ephraim decided to go home. All of Shining Stone's sisters offered — indeed begged — to take Joseph and raise him as Creek. And Bold Fox's stoicism was shaken by the prospect of losing this male descendant. But Ephraim could not leave him. The Creek women provisioned the new father with a milk cow and cloth teats, which they instructed him how to fashion in order to feed the newborn. They taught him how to swaddle the child and counseled him not to cut his hair or nails until four moons had passed so that he would retain strength.

Ephraim attended to every bit of advice they gave him and finally set off in the wagon he had purchased at a trading post, the tethered cow plodding steadily behind, nervous about his ability to care for this tiny bit of humanity. But from birth Joseph proved to be as hardy as the pioneers and the warrior Creeks whose blood coursed through his veins.

Ephraim's family welcomed him home and took the dark-eyed infant into their hearts with color-blind love. But Ephraim doubted that Shining Stone would ever have been accepted. He soothed his bitter thoughts with his memories of her, his gratitude that he had had the privilege of loving her.

He eventually married a sensible, kind girl who accepted Joseph as her own and bore Ephraim five more children. But he would miss Shining Stone's soft, Muscogee-accented voice, her bewitching smile, and the woodsy scent of her beautiful hair until his dying day. And sometimes, with wry humor, he would reflect that Old Hickory would roll over in his grave if he knew that Ephraim had brought Creek blood back to Alabama.

JACOB AND MILLICENT Tanner and their brothers lived in nearly complete ignorance of their Creek ancestry. They knew the Creeks had been run out of Alabama and that their paternal grandparents had met in Oklahoma. They knew the Creeks were considered an ignorant, savage people. They did not know that when their Muscogee forbears were rounded up and corralled at Ft. Mitchell, then marched off to Oklahoma at bayonet point, they left no stream or river polluted, had hunted no animal to extinction, had never leveled forests or overfarmed the land until it eroded.

Their father Joseph's knowledge was limited to the little Ephraim Tanner told him: that his mother Shining Stone died giving birth to him and that his grandfather Bold Fox named him Harjo, after an uncle of his who had died in the Battle of Pea River Swamp at the age of fifteen. Ephraim gave his son the name Joseph as well, in keeping with the missionaries' opinion that each child should be given a Bible-derived name to offset his or her pagan one. Thus Shining Stone's other name was Mary, and her father's other name was Isaiah. Few of their teachers or preachers made an effort to pronounce the Muscogee version of Shining Stone or Bold Fox, and so the Creeks used their Muscogee names only among themselves. Ephraim was privileged to know their Indian names only because he had, so to speak, married into the family.

To their credit, some of the missionaries and the teachers learned Muscogee, and the former translated Christian hymns into that language. The missionaries struggled to impart vast amounts of Bible history to the Creeks, and the teachers taught them the impressive history of the conquerors who had subdued them. However, being uninformed in such matters themselves, they did not teach them about the native people's nearly 15,000-year history on the American continent, or about the fortified cities, socially stratified societies, and trade networks that had flourished centuries before the first European crossed the Atlantic.

Instead, the non-Indians labored to bury Indian memories and put an end to pagan practices. They could not turn their charges into white people, but they could adjure them to dress white, act white, and adopt the English language.

Jacob and his siblings knew their father had been taunted, sometimes even shunned, as a child and that their mother's family, the Eastons, believed themselves magnanimous in allowing their daughter Harriet to marry him. According to family lore, an Easton had fought at the Battle of Horseshoe Bend, where he had personally killed several warriors, and had participated in the torching of several Creek villages which had resulted in the deaths of whole families. All of his relations were proud of him for having done so. While Harriet's parents, Deke and Lizzie, begrudgingly acknowledged that Joseph was a hardworking farm boy who spoke perfectly good English and was raised Methodist — his family belonged to their own church — they could not fathom how their daughter could choose a halfbreed for a husband, and they did everything they could to discourage the match.

Harriet and Joseph had known each other all their lives, and she had loved him since she was thirteen years old. Both their families had farmed in Dale County since the 1830s. Because Ephraim Tanner and his wife Jo-Beth were respectable people, their son Joseph was tolerated. But his parents' respectability did not qualify him as a suitable husband for any of the farmers' daughters. In the summer of 1891, seventeen-year-old Harriet learned that twenty-year-old Joseph had proposed to Nellie Sopwell, who lived near the county seat at Ozark. He was chased off the Sopwell place by Nellie's enraged father and two of her brothers, who threatened dire consequences if he ever came near Nellie again.

Nellie was unquestionably a very pretty girl, while Harriet, in her own view, was not. It was true she had long-lashed, deep blue eyes and beautiful, blond-streaked brown hair, but that did not, in her own opinion, make up for her ordinary face and her slim figure, too thin for the beauty standard of the day; and in summer time she was cursed with freckles that no preparation could make disappear. And so she perfectly understood why Joseph had fallen for Nellie and not her. Why shouldn't he have a beauty for a wife, when he was the handsomest man in the county, probably in all of Alabama? Why should he ever pay any attention to the likes of her?

While her parents were appalled at Joseph's nerve in proposing to a Sopwell, Harriet worried about Joseph's hurt feelings. What if he were so upset he upped and left the county? Such thoughts dampened her usual optimism and compelled her to overcome her shyness in Joseph's presence and reach out to this poor suffering soul — as, after all, any Christian should. But it was not easy. Her hawk-eyed mother warily watched her as she served Joseph a dish of blackberry cobbler at a church social. The smile this kind act produced cause her to blush head to toe, but she managed to address the object of her pity in an appropriate tone, which she felt sure did not betray her inner turmoil.

"This is fresh baked, Joseph. I thought you might like to try some."

"It looks delicious. Your mother's?"

"Oh, no. I baked it myself."

Clearly impressed, he made short work of it and grinned his appreciation. He was somewhat puzzled by Harriet's attention because until tonight she had quickly lowered her head or looked away whenever they chanced to meet. She was either shy or had been told to avoid him. But now she seemed eager to chat, and he found himself enjoying her company.

Gradually Harriet realized that he was not dying of a broken heart. In fact, he said something that surprised her and planted a spark of hope that he could some day forget Nellie Sopwell.

"Noticed you in Ozark the other day. You were wearing a mighty pretty blue dress. About as blue as your eyes."

"That old thing? It's a hand-me-down from one of my sisters. It's too long for me. I tripped on it."

"It's pretty, though."

But I'm not, Harriet thought. And then, as she enjoyed the tender expression on his face, an amazing thought brightened her mind and caused her to smile. Maybe she wasn't pretty like Nellie. But maybe, to Joseph, that didn't matter.

A few weeks later, alarmed when Joseph began dropping by the house bearing flowers or a book or an invitation to visit the Tanner place, behaving in a manner that made it clear he was courting their daughter, Harriet's parents had a serious discussion, and her father laid down the law. She was never to see Joseph again.

Once again Joseph retreated, this time at least politely turned away at the door instead of being chased off with a shotgun. Once again, he manfully informed his parents that he would not be marrying any time soon, after all. At this juncture in his life, the stoicism he had inherited from Bold Fox stood him in good stead. But Ephraim was angered, and Jo-Beth, who was devoted to Joseph, shed sorrowful tears as she prepared his favorite dinner that night.

When Harriet and Joseph met at church in the following weeks, each grew somber at the sight of the other, and she knew that his heart ached as much as hers when he glanced at her and then, after the briefest of nods, turned away. She took to skipping church as often as she could on the pretext of a headache or some trifling illness, but her staunch churchgoing parents usually saw through these subterfuges and required her attendance. While she and Joseph were courting, Harriet had sat with his family, but now she kept to the Easton pew, anguishing over what his family must think of her. They had been so welcoming, so happy about the match, so eager to accept her as daughter and sister. Surely now they must hate her.

Initially Harriet grieved quietly. She did not want to distress her parents. She knew that they could never see or understand what she saw in Joseph: he had the soft tread of the hunter, the lithe movements of the panther — his mother's clan. The smoke of Indian fires darkened his eyes. His sharp-featured face, softened by his warm smile, haunted her in fevered dreams.

Joseph was forbidden fruit, for which she yearned more intensely with each passing day. She came to realize that she would have him or die.

And so the obedient daughter's quiet grief turned into a desperate girl's noisy sorrow. She became subject to crying fits at the most inappropriate times. When Deke sat down at the table and said grace, his thanks to the Lord were drowned out by Harriet's loud sobs. When her sisters sat happily gossiping in the parlor with friends in their sewing circle, Harriet suddenly began wailing for no apparent reason and fled from the room, leaving her dismayed sisters to try to stem the tide of gossip about their own sister sure to follow this suggestive behavior.

One Saturday she sat so long without taking a bite of the rice pudding she loved, prepared especially for her, that Lizzie wiped her eyes with her apron and went out on the porch to have a talk with her husband.

That afternoon, tall, stoop-shouldered Deke summoned Harriet to the parlor to make one more appeal, which he believed would stop this nonsense. He motioned her to sit down and then made himself comfortable in his favorite chair. A broken heart did not exempt her from chores, so Harriet had been helping to preserve blackberries and plums and was dressed in a gray work blouse with the sleeves rolled up to her elbows and a blue skirt faded from many launderings that barely reached her ankles. This outfit, and the fact that her gold-brown hair was braided in pigtails, made her look about twelve years old. This was not going to be easy for Deke. After an uncomfortable pause he said, "I see you are still mooning over that fella."

"Yes, Papa."

"You think you love him."

"I do. I do love him."

Deke sighed and ran one hand over his balding head, then rested his elbows on his knees. He leaned forward, putting his chin on his clasped hands. This was a delicate matter, which fathers did not usually discuss with daughters. But he felt that it could not be left to Lizzie. Paternal sternness was required. A florid-faced man, his deep blush could not be detected as he cleared his throat and straightened up, taking a deep breath before he ventured, "Now, if you marry this fella, Harriet, you will have Indian babies. Did you ever think about that?"

This was such a potent argument against the romance that Deke had not bothered to come up with another one.

Actually, Harriet had *not* thought about that. Her virginal dreams had not progressed beyond thoughts of herself in Joseph's strong, muscular arms — something that had never happened in the glaring light of her parents' scrutiny. But now that her father had brought it up, she *did* think about Indian babies. And she realized that, if the babies looked like Joseph, they were exactly the kind of babies she wanted to have.

In the silence that followed his question, Deke concluded that she was capitulating. He was sure she would momentarily lower her eyes and tearfully go to the comfort of her mother's arms.

"Well?" he finally prompted. "Have you thought about that, Daughter?"

Harriet responded with a sunny smile. There was neither contrition nor defeat in her voice as she said, "Yes, Papa, I have."

And so she wore her parents down and got their consent.

The night Deke and Lizzie gave in, Harriet barely slept a wink. As the younger sister who shared her bed watched, she inspected her two best dresses and decided on the blue one Joseph liked so much. She took it out of the wardrobe, threaded a needle, and, while her sister drifted off to sleep, spent more than an hour hemming the voluminous skirt by lamp light so she would not trip over it again. Then she borrowed a pink sash from another dress to go around the waist. Finally satisfied with it, she surrendered to sleep long past her bedtime.

Despite her lack of sleep, Harriet outdid her sisters in helping to prepare breakfast the following morning, personally pouring coffee for her parents and solicitously supplying them with bacon, hominy grits, and cornbread. Her lone brother, five years younger but observant, wondered at this change in his mopey sister's behavior, but, noting his parents' serious demeanor, was afraid to ask about it.

At church, adorned with her best bonnet and carrying the purse Joseph's sister had crocheted for her weeks before, Harriet slipped into the Tanner pew. She was greeted with nods and smiles, and Jo-Beth reached over and squeezed her hand. One of Joseph's brothers changed places with her so she could sit next to Joseph, who found her hand in the folds of her skirt. Sharing a hymnal, they managed to hold hands throughout the service, even while standing for the singing.

On the church steps, it was decided that Harriet would accompany the Tanners home for Sunday dinner. As

Ephraim drove the wagon away, Deke had to shake his head, wondering what his grandfather, Lemuel Easton the Indian fighter, would have thought about a descendant's betrothal to the son of a sworn enemy. Ephraim, on the other hand, could picture Shining Stone shyly welcoming Harriet, smiling as she shared in the young folks' happiness.

Chapter 13

MISS TENPENNY RETURNS

IN THE SPRING of 1928, as he kneeled on the greenhouse floor, Theodore Waldron took a moment to massage his stiff left arm. Being a man who was always grateful for God's blessings, he thanked the Almighty, as he often had, that polio had not damaged his right arm. And his afflicted limb was not completely paralyzed; he could use it, albeit clumsily.

He was examining the azaleas which Solomon, who had become his right-hand man in the nursery, had repotted the day before. Solomon shared Tee's love of flowers and interest in all things horticultural, unlike Tee's eldest son, James Henry, who was now a factory employee in Chicago. Solomon's twin, Samuel, likewise disdained the nursery. He earned decent money contentedly providing shaves and haircuts in a Dothan barbershop.

Once Tee's youngest boy, Joshua, had been as avid a gardener as Solomon, eagerly anticipating the arrival of spring, the fun of digging in the dirt and planting the fragrant, colorful flowers he loved. By the age of seven, he understood the need to wait until the last frost had passed before planting annuals and the fact that bulbs buried in the fall would not send shoots up through the earth until the following spring. He knew that gardeners, like farmers, always watched the skies for rain, in the absence of which they laboriously provided water by the bucketful. At the age of nine, Josh had planted a small dogwood tree and nourished it through a drought, uncomplainingly toting water from the well to keep it alive. Today Tee glanced at that tall tree, with its spreading branches just beginning to form buds. Each year its bountiful white blossoms brought pleasure to everyone who saw them. But by the time he was fourteen, Joshua had discovered music in the form of a secondhand trumpet, and the garden, once his primary concern outside of school, had become marginalized, pushed to the far periphery of his life.

Joshua was enrolled in a church-funded school, Southeast Alabama Seminary High School — or Seminary, as it was called — in Dothan. Samuel had recently rented a small house in town, and Josh stayed with him during the school week to avoid the four-and-a-half mile trek to town and back. Although Dothan High School had been founded in 1889, the city school system still did not provide education beyond the seventh grade for black children. Seminary was established in 1921, organized by Rev. P. J. Hill under the auspices of Alabama black Baptist churches. Rev. Waldron's congregation, like dozens of other black churches, continually helped raise money to support Seminary. His daughter Jerusha had graduated from Seminary, but neither of the twins had been interested in attending the school. Joshua was a sophomore and a fairly good student, even if the only class he really enjoyed and excelled in was band. He was indifferent as to academics, and Tee struggled to turn his head around.

"After you graduate, Josh, you can go to Tuskegee College or Alabama State. You have opportunities your mother and I never did. My formal education ended at the seventh grade in a one-room country school, and she never had one day of classroom instruction."

In most of these sessions, Joshua's dented but serviceable trumpet, which Tee had reluctantly purchased for him, was at hand, because he was seldom without it.

"I'm going to be a musician, Pops," he would wearily respond, tired of defending his goal to his parents. They could never accept his determination to be a musician. And the fact that his band teacher told him he had talent did not impress them at all.

Tee always mastered his exasperation as best he could, hoping — and praying — that Joshua would come to his senses one day. If he aspired to teach music, as Jerusha had, that would be different. But Joshua apparently pictured himself performing with — well, Tee found his ambition hard to visualize, because it was so foreign to everything he knew. Did the boy say he wanted to play in a band, or was it an orchestra? On a stage? Or, God forbid, in one of those smoke-filled speakeasies Tee had heard about, where sinners imbibed illegal alcohol while being entertained by musicians — probably intoxicated themselves — playing those discordant notes they called jazz. Tee shook his head. He would have to pray hard about this.

He stood up and brushed the dirt off his hands, then went outside to check on the progress of some spring flowers just beginning to bloom: begonias, daffodils, and tulips. His one yucca plant displayed a creamy white blossom. The yucca was not for sale — not only because there did not seem to be a market for this type of plant here, but also because it always reminded him of his good friend, Julia Tenpenny, recently turned eighty-two and thriving in her small cottage in Little Turnbridge, Massachusetts.

It occurred to him that he owed her a letter. The previous fall, he had sent her the briefest of notes informing her about his daughter's death, and she had written to him and Nora to express her condolences. Tee had still been in deep mourning when her letter came, only now beginning to rebound, and so had never answered it. Today he found himself remembering her one visit to Chinkapin in 1914, at another stressful time for his family.

JULIA TENPENNY AND Theodore Waldron had remained correspondents through the years, so he knew she was retired, and she knew he was pastor of Divine Truth Church, married to a woman as highly regarded for her healing arts as for her role as minister's wife. In 1914 they had five children ranging in age from one year to fifteen.

For several years after they met in 1890, when Theodore was twelve years old, Julia had been his teacher, helping him to develop his natural aptitude for the English language by correcting papers he sent her and encouraging him to read books on a broad range of subjects. Eventually Julia no longer felt the need to instruct him in English usage or to help him hone his writing skills; she recognized that he had as good a grasp of the English language as she did and was unquestionably a better writer.

Of all the topics they read and exchanged letters about, theology interested Theodore the most. As the daughter of a clergyman and a devout Episcopalian, Julia was well grounded in Christian teachings and gladly shared her knowledge with such an eager pupil. In mutual enjoyment they delved into the intricacies of the Old Testament, analyzed the Gospels, and compared notes on the Epistles of Paul.

Julia had hoped Theodore could attend a university, but family obligations prevented him from taking advantage of her offer to raise the necessary funds through affluent friends. His brother John died of pneumonia in 1901, and his two sisters were each struggling to raise large families when his parents became frail. So it fell to Theodore to look after them. He did so until their deaths. By that time he was twenty-seven years old, with a wife and two children.

But from earliest childhood, Theodore loved learning. He was seldom without a book, even in the field, poring over a text as he ate his mid-day meal. He had read the Bible through several times by the time he was a teenager and borrowed books wherever he could. He also began a personal library with the books Julia sent him from her extensive collection.

Benefactors such as Julia's friends, Caleb and Ilsa Royal, contributed to the young farmer-scholar's library, as well.

Disappointed though she was that her protégé would never go to college, Julia encouraged his self-education by sending him a copy of Frederic Douglass's famous lecture, *Self-Made Men*, and by reminding him that neither Benjamin Franklin nor Abraham Lincoln had any formal training. In fact, she pointed out, Lincoln's formal education, though extended over several years, consisted of not more than one full year in the classroom.

It was surprising to no one that Theodore's learning and gift for preaching made him a unanimous choice as pastor at Divine Truth Church when the position became available.

Julia knew that Theodore had stopped farming and become a nurseryman. Gardening was her favorite pastime, and she and Theodore swapped gardening tips, occasionally mailing packets of seeds to one another and sharing the details of gardening experiments.

When Theodore turned twenty-one, Julia insisted he no longer referred to her as "Miss Tenpenny." When he responded that he could not bring himself to call his venerable mentor by her given name, she proposed a compromise. "If you insist on a title," she wrote, "then let it be 'aunt'."

She always enjoyed hearing from Theodore, but in early September 1914 she received a letter which deeply disturbed her. The handwriting was barely legible, and the letter was uncharacteristically brief.

> Dear Aunt Julia,
>
> I apologize for taking so long to respond to your letter of 24 May. Early in June, I became very weak and ill, and was diagnosed with polio. I am glad to report that, while still confined to my bed, I feel much stronger. Nora of course takes wonderful care of me, and the children have been very considerate and tiptoe in and out of the sick room. Thanks be to God, no one else in the family has been afflicted.

When I am recovered, I will respond in greater length to all of the points you raised in your last letter. I so enjoy our explorations of the Scriptures.

Sincerely, Theodore

Julia was deeply affected by the letter. She had always meant to see Theodore again one day. Now it might be too late; polio was a potentially fatal illness. She resolved to make the long trip back to Alabama and within a fortnight was on her way. En route she stopped in Eufaula to visit with the Royals, who were getting along in years now as she was. They had been strong supporters of her teaching efforts in rural Alabama after the Civil War. They had used their considerable influence to raise funds for the education of colored children, and on several occasions had visited the one-room school where she had taught literacy, arithmetic, geography and history.

She was fond of the Royals and delighted to see them again, enjoying their hospitality for three days. She regretted that she was unable to see their children again. Their son practiced medicine in Atlanta, and their daughter was married to a merchant in Mobile.

Julia had always admired Eufaula's tree-shaded streets, with its stately homes ranging from neo-classical to Greek revival to hipped-roof plantation style, and during this visit she viewed them for the first time from the seat of an automobile, Caleb's prized Chevrolet. Caleb and his grandson treated her to a leisurely rowboat ride on the Chattahoochee River, during which she felt very much the grand dame as she sat on a cushioned seat holding one of Ilsa's ruffled parasols to ward off the sun.

Her trip would not have been complete without a visit to the Crossvine Community, naturally by buggy since the roads outside the town were still primitive, little more than cow paths. She was heartened to see that New Road School was still operating, now a part of the Barbour County school system, with two added rooms and well-kept grounds. Caleb had also pointed out the colored school in Eufaula, which appeared to be as well built as the white schools she saw; but he told her that the black children's books and other educational materials were invariably hand-me-downs from the white schools. Coming from an area where not only blacks but also Italian, Irish, and other ethnic groups were looked down upon and routinely denied housing and employment opportunities, she knew that prejudice also flourished above the Mason-Dixon line. But at least there it was not sanctioned by law. And it was apparent to her that the instigators of Jim Crow, whose defense was that educational facilities were "separate but equal," were dedicated to enforcing "separate," while lax about ensuring "equal."

JULIA HAD ONCE again corresponded with Jackson Knightley, whose son Nathan wrote telling her that she would be most welcome. Caleb was able to drive her in the car this time, because there was a graded gravel road all the way to the Knightley place. Dr. Royal still practiced medicine, and the family continued to regard them as their family doctor, so he felt at home in their household.

The young man who had written to Julia was seventeen years old, the baby of the family. Nate was an attractive fellow, above middle height, slender, with wavy red hair and light brown eyes. William, Bryce, and Nate farmed alongside their father, while Lee had moved to the Florida Panhandle and become a sheriff in Holmes County.

"He's running for judge," Jackson proudly told her. "And I think he's a-gonna win."

Julia remembered Lee's encounter with armed citizens during the Dothan riot shortly before her last visit and concluded that this experience must have convinced him law and order might be a good career.

"And the girls? Have they all moved away?"

"Every one married," Sophronia supplied. "Rebecca and Lillian each have three younguns, and my youngest girl, Lucinda, married last fall. But they all live close by."

It was mid-morning, and, like Nate, William and Bryce had left their chores to come in for dinner and say hello to their visitor. Glancing at Bryce, Julia recalled the mud-splattered little boy who had been in trouble for jumping in rain puddles, whom William had regarded as such a nuisance. It was clear from the way the two of them now interacted that they had become good friends. They were both married, as well, and had built homes of their own on the Knightley property.

"And what about you, Nate? Are you planning to build your own house one day, too?"

Nate looked at his father as he said, "Well, not here. I think Papa has other plans."

"Latched on to some right good property down in Houston County," he said. "Planning to set Nate up on that when he comes of age and finds him a wife."

Jackson could not imagine anyone attempting to farm without a helpmeet.

"Oh, I think he's already picked out his wife," Sophronia declared with a smile.

"Abigail Coltayne," William volunteered when Nate stood shyly silent on the subject. "Abby's one of our second cousins — a kissing cousin, so to speak."

"She's a sweet gal," Jackson said, "but until she's said yes and the preacher has made it official, it's still an open field. Right, Nate?"

Nate did not answer. He knew his heart would break in two if Abby did not accept his proposal. But he also knew that she flirted with Jacob Tanner as much as she flirted with him, so he was by no means confident he would win her. No sense saying so in front of this crowd, though, especially with Miss Tenpenny and the doctor here. They both seemed to be enjoying this conversation, which in fact made him quite uncomfortable. It was time to change the subject.

"Miss Tenpenny, I'm glad I finally got to meet you. Papa has told me about how your fiancé fought at the Battle of Cold Harbor during the war. He says he was a brave man who oughtn't to of had to die. He always says he's glad none of his boys've ever had to fight. Don't you, Papa?"

Jackson gravely nodded, watching Julia's face. Why on earth did Nate have to dive into such an unpleasant subject?

With a gentle smile she said, "It was tragic that any of those boys had to die, on either side. And yes, it's a blessing that boys of your generation don't have to endure what those young men did. I know all of us are thankful for that."

After a slightly awkward pause Nate announced, "Well, best get back to work. Nice to see you, Dr. Royal."

Caleb shook his hand.

"Now, you remember what I said the last time I saw you — you need to eat a little more. You need to gain some weight."

"Yes, sir."

As they headed back to the field, Bryce reached over and touseled Nate's hair.

"I'm telling you, boy, you better grab Abby before somebody else does!"

"By durn it, I'm working on it, Bryce. I cain't 'grab' her — I have to court her. But believe you me, one of these days I will marry Abby Coltayne."

JULIA BOARDED THE Dothan train in Eufaula on a Saturday morning, Caleb promising to collect her upon her return the following week. She would visit with the Royals for another day or so before journeying back to Massachusetts. But for now she was glad to be on her way to Houston County. As enjoyable as her Eufaula visit had been, Julia's thoughts had kept turning to Chinkapin, where her dear friend might be fighting for his life. Theodore's letter had distressed and saddened her. Polio was a frightening disease, with often devastating effects. And Theodore, as she recalled, had been a frail little fellow, small for his age and quite thin, despite his mother's and sisters' continual efforts to fatten him up.

What would happen to him and his family now that he had been afflicted with polio?

The jerking motion of the train pulling out of the station jolted her out of her reverie, and she glanced around the white-only car. She sighed. As she viewed the monochromatic array of faces, she realized that among them she might discover someone with an interesting narrative to while away the time, but exclusivity always riled her. She could not remain sitting in this pocket of white privilege.

Hooking the handle of her reticule over one arm, she carefully maneuvered down the aisles of several passenger cars, braving the jarring motion of the connecting passages, until she came to a colored car. No one was surprised to see her there. Whites customarily seated themselves in any vacant seat in a colored car when the train was overcrowded.

She leaned over a vacant seat to address the woman sitting by the window. She was holding a boy about five years old on her lap.

"Is this seat taken?"

"No, ma'am."

"Oh, good. Then may I sit here and visit with you and your little boy on the way to Dothan?"

The woman smiled and nodded.

Julia sat down, arranged her long skirt, and set her reticule in the small space at her feet. She removed her hat and placed it on her lap, revealing her untidy, spun-sugar white hair, which was loosely waved around her face, with the longer hair pulled into a bun at the nape of her neck.

"My name is Julia Tenpenny."

"I'm Helen Jarvis. This is Richard."

"Nice to meet you. May I ask where you're headed?"

"Mobile."

"You've got quite a way to go, then."

Richard impulsively leaned over and touched her hair.

"Richard!" his mother admonished. "You know you don't — "

"It's all right. He's just curious. Now then. Let me think, Richard. It's been a while since I visited with someone your age, but I just might have something you would find interesting."

She reached into her voluminous bag, felt around, apparently picking up and rejecting several items, then brought out a bright tin soldier with a vivid red-and-blue uniform.

Richard's eyes grew large as she handed it to him.

"I can't think why I've been carrying that fellow around. I have no use for a tin soldier. Would you like to have it? That is, if your mother says it's all right."

Richard nodded, his fingers busily exploring the details of the soldier's face, uniform and sword.

"Say thank you, Richard."

"Thank you, ma'am."

"You're quite welcome."

An hour outside of Dothan a train conductor came through. He noticed Julia and stopped next to her.

"Ma'am, the white cars are up ahead. There's plenty of room."

"Thank you for that information, sir."

"Would you like me to escort you to another car?"

"No, thank you."

"But ma'am — "

Julia understood that he was just trying to be helpful. But his well-meant interference annoyed her.

"Is there any law against my sitting here?"

"Well, no, ma'am. Of course not. There's no law against *you* sitting *here* — "

"I thought not. And I do not believe anyone here objects to my presence."

She glanced about. A couple of people shook their heads.

"Therefore, I shall remain here. I have been having a fascinating conversation with my seat companion, Richard, about how to bait a fish hook."

"You got to hold the minnow real tight," Richard offered, "or it'll slip right out of your hand."

"So you may carry on, conductor," she said.

The conductor tipped his hat.

"Yes, ma'am."

As the train pulled into the Dothan station, Julia looked with disapproval at two women making slow progress along the platform, their steps severely hindered by fashionable hobble skirts cut ridiculously narrow around the ankles. Julia had never been a slave to fashion and had no intention of shedding her comfortable, loose-fitting skirt. She had, after all, been known to wear bloomers when she was young, enjoying the freedom of the split skirt as she rode her bicycle all over town, blithely ignoring the disapproving looks of offended matrons and the amused smiles of gentlemen alike.

For a few moments as she watched the women descend the platform steps, hoping their confining skirts would not cause them to fall, her thoughts turned to her niece, who was their opposite. Twenty-four-year old Julianne Atwater had inherited her parents' good looks and her Aunt Julia's mettle. She had participated in numerous suffragette rallies and had been jailed twice, which only made her the more determined. Sometimes Julia felt anxiety for Julianne, who was like a daughter to her, but remembering her own journey into enemy territory during Reconstruction and her lifelong penchant for defying convention, she could not discourage her.

She looked about and saw shiny horse-drawn hacks from every hotel at the station, including Albert House, where she had reserved a room. But Theodore had assured Julia that his son would personally welcome her and transport her to the hotel.

As a porter helped her deboard, Julia spotted a young man in bib overalls and a white collarless shirt who matched Theodore's description of his fourteen-year-old son, James Henry, who she knew would be meeting her at the station.

He immediately headed for her, no doubt because she, too, matched Theodore's accurate description.

"James Henry?"

"Yes, ma'am."

She held out her hand, and he shook it.

"I'm so pleased to meet you at last."

"Nice to meet you, too, ma'am."

He was tall for his age, with a stocky build, quite unlike his father. Theodore had told her that James Henry was the image of his grandfather, Burl Freedman.

Her trunk of clothes was at the Royals' residence. She had only the reticule for her stay in Dothan, and he quickly retrieved it and put it in the mule-drawn wagon. He handed her up into the seat.

"Papa wanted to come, too, but he wasn't up to it."

"Oh, of course not," she said.

She pictured Theodore lying helplessly in bed, his thin frame wasted, skeletal, with a gaunt face scored by suffering. She was dreading the first sight of him, fearful that her grief at his condition would make him feel even worse than he had before. But then, she had always been good at reining in her feelings. And she simply had to see him before he —

"Giddap, mule! Giddap!"

James Henry's shouted commands broke through her anxious thoughts. The stubborn animal finally started off after the fourth "Giddap." Julia smiled. There was certainly no danger it would bolt and gallop headlong down the road as a horse might. She was fond of mules. When she had taught school down here, she had sometimes traveled in a wagon pulled by a faithful mule. Mules were patient and dependable, and they always got you where you wanted to go — eventually.

"What's this fellow's name?"

"Buster. Oughta be Hardhead."

"Do you ride him?"

"No, ma'am. I'm too old for that. But my brothers and sister do."

He glanced at her.

"Papa says you live in Massachusetts."

"Yes, I do. In a little town you've probably never heard of. It's very close to Boston."

"Gets mighty cold there, I reckon. Lots of snow and ice."

Julia was familiar with the Alabama child's yearning for snow. She had often described snow scenes to her pupils in Crossvine.

"Oh, lots. But I remember you do get snow here, occasionally. I believe your father wrote me last winter that you had some snow."

"A few sprinkles. Didn't stick."

Disappointment was evident in his voice.

"So, when will it start snowing up there where you live?"

"In a few weeks — probably by October. And James Henry, if I could send some to you, I would. We get awfully tired of snow up there. You have to shovel it all the time, you know, so you can walk out the front door."

"But still — it's pretty, though."

"Beautiful. Some day you must travel north and see it for yourself."

James Henry nodded. A trip north had long been one of his goals.

When they pulled up at the Albert House Hotel, he reiterated his parents' invitation for Julia to spend the night at their home. The offer had been made and declined in an exchange of letters about the trip. The Waldrons were a family of seven in a seven-room house. She could not imagine where they would put her overnight.

"I cannot put your family to that trouble. We'll all have lots of time to visit tomorrow."

The plan was for James Henry to return to the hotel the next morning, a Sunday, and bring her out to Divine Truth Church. She did not expect that Theodore would be able to attend the service. She was invited to share in a potluck dinner at the church, after which she would visit with Theodore at their home until time for James Henry to take her back to the hotel.

As they reached the hotel, Julia turned to James Henry and asked, because she had to know, "Your father — can he — is he completely confined to his bed? Is he able to sit up at all?"

James Henry rared back in surprise at such a question.

"*Sit up!* Why, this past week he's been walking around all over the place. Even got outside to check on his crape myrtles and calla lilies."

Julia was astonished.

"He can walk?"

"Oh yes, ma'am. Course his left arm's stiff. And he can't bend the fingers on that hand, so it's about useless now. But he gets around pretty good. Mama fusses at him for trying to do too much, but Papa can't ever sit still."

Julia's eyes brimmed with sudden tears, partly from relief, partly from gratitude to God for this healing. She took a handkerchief out of a pocket and dabbed at her eyes.

"I'm so glad he's well, James Henry."

A bit embarrassed by her tears, he helped her down, grabbed her reticule, and walked her in the door and up to the front desk. The polished black-and-white tile floor gleamed, and the wainscoting was a rich walnut color. The lobby was cooled by half a dozen gently whirling ceiling fans. An ornate chandelier hung over the reception area, the cut glass winking in the sunlight that poured in through tall windows.

James Henry was well aware that the front desk was as far as he ever dared go, even if he had the money in his pocket to pay for the most expensive room in the place. The resentment that was never far from the surface so goaded him that it was hard for him to return the parting smile of his father's old friend.

"Thank you so much for meeting me at the station," she said. "I'll see you in the morning. Nine o'clock all right?"

James Henry nodded and went back to his place — on the seat of that dang old wagon behind that dang old mule.

DIVINE TRUTH CHURCH was the typical clapboard structure that housed so many churches in every region of the country. There was a steeple with a bell that must have taken years to save up for. Julia knew from correspondence that the current goal was to replace the plain glass windows at the back of the church with stained-glass depictions of New Testament scenes. Out of her teaching pension she had set aside what was for her the princely sum of five dollars to put in the collection plate toward that goal today.

When she entered the church she was pleased with its simple beauty. The oak pews with their deep red cushions, the red-carpeted aisles, the organ — all bespoke years of faithful stewardship of this small sanctuary. Then she saw Theodore sitting on a bench near the pulpit. He stood up as Julia entered the church.

It had been twenty-four years, and she only had the one photograph taken of the Waldron family five years earlier, but she could have picked him out in any crowd — the slender build, the spectacles, the wide grin, the scant hair.

"Aunt Julia! At last you're here!"

But the voice, now — deep, resonant — that was a surprise.

She was down the aisle and up the step to where he was standing in an instant, and the two old friends embraced, each fighting tears. Nora, ever the caregiver, offered Julia a handkerchief which she had foreseen would be needed.

"Thank you, Mrs. Waldron."

"Nora," she insisted.

"Then I must be Julia — or, if you prefer, Aunt Julia."

Nora gave her a hug.

"Welcome to Divine Truth. And I hopes you has a good appetite. Folks bringing lots of good food. Tee say you likes southern cooking."

"I cannot tell you how much I've missed it all these years. I've been looking forward to this dinner all the way down from Massachusetts."

Nora smiled, then excused herself to help set out hymnals on the pews and put fresh flowers on the communion table next to the pulpit.

"Come, come sit down. Sit here," Theodore said.

He beckoned her to join him on the bench, holding his left arm with his right hand as if to steady it.

"You are healed. What a miracle, Theodore."

"I praise God every hour for it."

He looked at her in apology.

"James Henry told me how concerned you were, how worried that I was completely paralyzed. I'm sorry my letter caused you so much distress."

"Nonsense."

She took one of his hands in both of hers for a moment.

"What your letter accomplished was to convince me I must come and see you with my own eyes. And I will get to hear you preach, as well, a blessing I did not expect to enjoy. I suppose it will be an Old Testament text this morning?"

She was thinking of Job and his sufferings. Because even though he had come through relatively unscathed compared to many polio victims, he had still suffered and would always be disabled.

"Oh, yes — Old Testament," he confirmed.

The organist approached him with a concern, and a congregant who had arrived early came forward to request a special prayer. Seeing that he would be occupied with duties until time for the service, she excused herself and strolled about the shady grounds.

AS JULIA ENTERED the church, James Henry guided her to the front pew where she joined Nora and the other children. Six-year-old Solomon and Samuel scooted over to make room for her, while nine-year-old Jerusha, who held baby Joshua on her lap, shyly smiled in her direction.

Robed in dark purple, the choir led the processional hymn, "I Will Sing the Wondrous Story," as they marched up the center aisle, while Julia marveled at the strength, the passion, and the beauty of their voices, which seemed to emanate from the depths of their souls.

After a deacon had made the announcements and special prayers had been said for several individuals, Rev. Waldron introduced Julia as "my old friend and mentor, Miss Julia Tenpenny, of Little Turnbridge, Massachusetts," asking her to stand and be recognized.

"She took me under her wing when I was a boy, and we have been correspondents for — how long, Aunt Julia?"

"Almost a quarter of a century." She glanced about the congregation and smiled. "And I have saved every letter he has written to me."

"Well, just ask my wife how many of your letters I have ever thrown away."

Nora shook her head.

"None of them. And the very first one you ever sent, we gots framed on the wall."

Julia was touched.

"Why, Theodore — I cannot believe it!"

"Yes, indeed. The one in which you praised me for writing so neatly on Miss Hattie Grimes' paper, using Miss Hattie Grimes' ink, and corrected my misspelled words."

"But in recent years," Julia said, again addressing the congregation, "Rev. Waldron has become the teacher. He has broadened my understanding of several passages of scripture."

As she sat down, the organist began playing "I Love the Lord; He Heard My Cries," and Julia, while lending her faint singing voice, mostly listened, enjoying the sound of hymns rendered, not in the sedate fashion she was accustomed to, but in the robust way their composers had probably intended.

Rev. Waldron's sermon that day was not drawn from Job, but from Psalm 30. In his stentorian voice, he quoted:

I will extol You, O Lord, for You have lifted me up;
And have not let my foes rejoice over me.
O Lord my God, I cried out to You,
And You healed me;
O Lord, You brought my soul up from the grave;
You have kept me alive, that I should not go down to the pit.

From there, he took the congregation with him as he soared into ringing praise of God and thankfulness for his miracles, then brought them to earth with the acknowledgement that there are times when despair can threaten to defeat us.

"The psalm touches on our despair when we are overcome with troubles — 'Weeping may endure for the night,' and we may be sad and sorrowful for a time. But then the psalm lifts us up with God's promise that despair cannot triumph, as it so jubilantly declares — 'But joy — *joy* — comes in the morning!'"

Julia's heart filled with pride for the delicate little boy she remembered, now transformed into this gifted preacher whose physical frailty was overcome by his spiritual strength.

THE POTLUCK DINNER was even more delicious than Julia had imagined it would be. Afterwards, she and the Waldrons strolled to their home. Soon after they arrived, Theodore took her on a tour of the nursery.

In a sizable greenhouse, seedlings were nourished in neat rows of variously sized pots on two long tables. Tee pointed out Nora's medicinal herb garden thriving in large pots sitting on the floor, among them button snakeroot, used as an expectorant; rose geranium, a treatment for diarrhea; and stone root, an antidote for poison oak. Gardening tools, wheelbarrows, work boots, gloves, and sacks of fertilizer took up the rest of the space. Like all true gardeners, Julia could enjoy the scent of rich soil while ignoring the strong smell of fertilizer that permeated the air.

Outside, Theodore gestured into the distance, to where his land ended and farm land began, and explained that his family had sold ninety-seven of their original 147 acres to fund the nursery. The original farm house sat on the acreage they had retained. The former Waldron farm land was now owned by a man who did not work the land himself, but parceled it out to several sharecroppers who tried to eke a living out of their small portions.

"I know just how hard it is to farm on that land because my family and I did it for years. And we owned it and could profit from it. But those poor souls, who rent or borrow everything from the owner, will be lucky to feed their families and house them in shacks on what they are able to earn, and at harvest they will have nothing to show for their labors."

He shook his head as he gestured towards his former land.

"Those poor folks — well, I do pray for them, Aunt Julia, I do."

He led her to a section of the nursery devoted to flowers and shrubs.

"As you see, the crape myrtles and calla lilies are still in full bloom, and we have an abundance of late roses. We also grow hibiscus and camellias and lots of annuals — like gardenias, verbena, and salvia. Oh, and look — these are the coneflowers I grew from the last packet of seeds you sent."

"Yes, I love those. The varieties of color are amazing. And what on earth is this strange-looking plant? We have nothing like it up north."

"Interesting, isn't it? That's a night-blooming yucca — *yucca filamentosa*. Its cream-colored flowers open when the sky darkens. Some folks call it Adam's Needle. They are native to Dale County up the road but grow well here, too."

"Fascinating. I would love to amaze my neighbors with it, but it would never thrive in Massachusetts."

Theodore led her away from her examination of the yucca to another section of land. "This is where we cultivate most of the fruit trees — fig, plum, peach, pear. We sell the trees and a lot of the fruit, as well. And Nora puts up jams and preserves, of course, which we sell for ourselves as well as to benefit the church."

Julia looked about. "No scuppernongs?"

Theodore smiled.

"I remember your writing to me about how much you enjoy those. But we haven't gotten into cultivating grapes as yet. If you look around, though, you'll find other interesting plants — like those wild persimmon bushes and guava trees. We don't sell those, but we preserve the fruit."

"Your family has a veritable Garden of Eden here, Theodore!"

He smiled broadly.

"Why yes, I believe we do."

IT WAS GROWING late, the sun beginning its descent. There was just enough time for a visit with the family. Nora showed Julia the framed letter, in a place of honor on the living room wall, then led her to a worn but soft, comfortable chair. Enjoying Nora's sweet potato pie with a cup of coffee, she took the opportunity of getting to know the children.

As a teacher, Julia had always stressed to her pupils the benefit of using standard English. While dialects interested her, she had continually taught and reinforced the importance of standard English to all of her students, of whatever ethnic background. Now she noted that the Waldron children were, in a sense, bilingual. They invariably used standard English with their father and with her, but they usually spoke to their mother in dialect.

James Henry, she was told, hated gardening, but loved to putter with anything mechanical. He could fix clocks, repair a pump or a harrow or a plow, figure out how to take apart and put back together nearly anything. Solomon, two inches taller than his fraternal twin Samuel, loved swimming in the creek, while Samuel hated swimming but loved to fish. They also loved to fight with each other and did so almost the entire time Julia was there.

Jerusha was Nora all over — sweet tempered, gracious, soft spoken, concerned for others — "Can I get you some more tea, Miss Tenpenny? Do you need a fan?"

Nora could not help bragging on Jerusha's lovely singing voice, and at Julia's insistence she sang several verses of "Sweet Hour of Prayer."

Eighteen-month-old Joshua was one of the prettiest children Julia had ever seen. She could not know that the beauty of his ancestor Ivy, the lost one, was reborn in his perfectly symmetrical little face. But it was clear to her that the entire household, including Theodore, was wrapped around his little finger.

Julia shared with Nora and Tee her experiences in serving as a surrogate mother to her niece, Julianne Atwater, after the death of Julianne's mother. She told them how proud she was of Julianne's participation in the struggle for women's rights and that she was even more proud of the fact that she had become a nurse.

"I wish she could meet you, Nora," she said. "I'm sure you could give her a lot of valuable advice from all of your years as a healer and a midwife."

Smiling, Nora declared that she would equally welcome swapping experiences with Julia's niece.

As Julia hugged them all goodbye, she felt grateful that she had finally had the opportunity to meet Theodore's wife and children. And as she clasped Reverend Waldron's hand in farewell, she reflected that, in her heart, he had always been her favorite pupil.

JULIA USUALLY CARRIED a couple of books on the train to occupy herself, but on this trip she also perused several newspapers purchased along the route home, all of which carried front-page news about the war in Europe. The week before, the French, assisted by British forces, had halted the German advance at the Marne River near Paris. From what she had gathered since the outbreak of hostilities in August, the general belief was that the war would be over in a brief time. But she well remembered a similar attitude among the American populace in 1861, when the country was on the brink of four years of unprecedented slaughter.

Julia chose not to gainsay the optimists, thinking, *I fervently hope they are right.*

She felt pity for the families of all of the soldiers engaged in this new war, but shared her countrymen's sentiment that it was fortunate no American troops were dying over there.

As they neared Boston terminal, Julia thought about her niece, who had promised to meet her at the station. While Julia had had the complete support of her parents in her decision to become a Freedman's Bureau teacher, Julianne's father was appalled, if not downright outraged, at the activities of the suffragettes and thoroughly disapproved of his daughter's participation in the movement. On two occasions, she and half a dozen of the women he considered rabble had been jailed. John Atwater had more than once commented to Julia that his late wife would never have condoned Julianne's participation in this crazed determination to upset the social order.

Knowing John's obstinate opposition to anything that might upset his comfortable world and the futility of arguing with him, as well as his annoyance with her that she had accompanied her niece to some of the rallies, Julia forebore replying to assertions in this vein. But finally she said, in a chilly tone, "What my sister would have felt about Julianne's willingness to fight for women's rights, even at the risk of losing her own freedom, we shall never know, John, since she died without the opportunity of crusading for suffrage herself. But I have little doubt she would have been extremely proud of her daughter."

"And do you think I am not? I only ask that she apply her considerable talents in appropriate ways — managing a household, helping her husband to succeed in his work, and raising a family."

Of course, Julianne did not have a husband, and that was largely Julia's fault as well. Raising a second brood of children, John was grateful that Julia had helped finance his daughter's medical education. But the unsatisfying result of all of that education was that Julianne was now employed as a nurse in Boston, independent, and apparently content with her spinsterhood. While a nursing career was considered suitable for a woman, a year at a finishing school would certainly have sufficed, providing her with all of the social skills necessary for a wife.

Julianne by no means lacked for admirers, a couple of whom had tried to convince her that she would find fulfillment as a helpmeet. Vanquished by her scorn, they had sought out more pliable young women. But one of the men she had enchanted, Edward Ronan, professed to believe in equality in marriage.

"Equality within the four walls of our home would be meaningless to me, Edward," she had informed him. "When women have the vote, perhaps I will consider matrimony."

Believing that women's suffrage might be decades away, Edward joined the ranks of those men who supported suffrage, and he lived on the hope that someday this strong, passionate woman would consent to marry him.

Chapter 14

OF WIREGRASS BRIDES AND BABIES

KEZIAH CATES AND Nora Waldron both came to the Wiregrass as brides: Nora after her marriage to Theodore in 1897 and Keziah as the bride of Daniel Cates in 1904. Daniel was a member of Divine Truth Church, and Keziah joined upon her arrival in Chinkapin. She and Nora soon became friends, and each knew the detailed history of the other's family.

Nora shared with Keziah the story of the tragic loss of her young grandmother, Ivy, to a slave trader and tales about her uncles who fought for the Union in the Civil War. She told her that her mother, Amalie Freedman, had lived in the home of Henri Bouchard, her slave owner father, up to the age of eleven. She often described how Amalie had trained her in midwifery and the healing arts in the small community of Gator Pass near Mobile.

Keziah frequently talked about the Dollarleaf community where she grew up. She was proud of her parents, who, while still teenagers, wisely rejected the harsh life of the cotton fields and established a decent home for themselves and their children near Columbus, Georgia. Keziah's two brothers had moved to Atlanta to work for the railroads, while both of her sisters were married and living close to their parents. All of them had completed the seventh grade, and one sister operated a beauty parlor in Columbus.

Nora knew that Keziah would have preferred that she and Daniel have a farm of their own, but because they had a decent employer who treated them well and a comfortable dwelling, she had adjusted to life at Comfortroot Farm.

Few of the mothers whose children were delivered by Midwife Nora knew how her own babies came into the world, but Keziah did. When they met, James Henry was five years old, and the next year Jerusha was born, followed by the twins in 1908 and Joshua in 1913. Amalie traveled all the way from Gator Pass for each birth, bringing her daughter Mattie with her for the last two births. Each of these occasions was an opportunity for a long visit.

Keziah came to know Amalie Freedman well and soon understood the source of Nora's knowledge, strength, and compassion. On one late summer day, not long after Jerusha's birth, Nora asked her mother to attend to a family where three children were suffering from the croup. The Pyeburns lived about a half mile distant, and Keziah walked with Amalie to show her the way and to provide assistance, even though she considered herself no nurse. She helped Amalie heat water on the wood-burning stove to fill a tin tub, in which each child was soaked for a time and then warmly wrapped up. She helped her dose the poor coughing children with hot tea and honey and repeatedly treat them with hot poultices applied to the throat. Through what became a twelve-hour stint, Amalie comforted each child and bolstered up the flagging spirits of the exhausted, sleep-deprived mother.

Assisting Amalie in every way she was directed to, Keziah watched this woman with growing admiration. What pride Amalie's mother would have felt, she reflected, could she have seen her daughter, torn from her as a newborn, now serving others in this selfless way.

When the coughing finally lessened, Amalie gave each child a smile and reassuringingly hugged the mother as she prepared to depart. Quite unaware of Keziah's appraisal of her, she noted her tired face and said, "You be plumb wore out, little Keziah. You needs some rest."

Keziah smiled, realizing that Amalie had to be every bit as tired as she was herself.

"I'm fine. I'll walk you back, and then Tee'll drive me home in the wagon."

Knowing the circumstances of Amalie's birth, Keziah sometimes wondered about her upbringing in the home of Henri Bouchard, the man who had victimized Ivy, and his wife Lavinia, the woman who had sold her away. She would never have been insensitive enough to ask about it, but one day, as Nora rocked Jerusha and Keziah tucked a sleepy James Henry into bed, Amalie began to reminisce about those times.

"Burl and me's chillun, and these two babies here," she began, reaching over to stroke Jerusha's head, "ain't never lived in a big fancy house, and most likely never will — but Lord, they lives is so much better than many a chile what has."

"Tell Keziah about living in the big house, Mama," Nora suggested. "She be curious about that."

"It's true I'd like to hear about those times, Amalie, but only if you're sure you don't mind talking about them," Keziah said. "And nothing you say about rich folks can surprise me. I almost went to work in a fancy home in Columbus when I was a young girl, but after I learned what kind of folks lived there, I turned the job down."

Amalie chuckled.

"Ain't hard to understand a spunky girl like you doing that, little Keziah. But of course, I was just a baby when my papa, Henri Bouchard, ask my Granny Reba did she want me to grow up in the big house, and much as she despise Lavinia Bouchard, she say yes, long as I sees my grandchile every day. Granny say Bouchard search everywhere for my mama, try everything he could to get her back, and because of that she let him take me into his house. Granny know Miz Lavinia wouldn't have nothing to do with my raising, anyhow, and sure enough, Tatty, a servant Granny trust, took care of me.

"It sure was a mighty fine place, with big rooms and high ceilings and fancy hanging lights and fireplaces in 'most every room. 'Course Tatty and me stay in a little room at the back, near the kitchen. But by the time I'se four years old, I'se doing chores, so I tag along with Tatty through all them rooms. Sometimes I pretends I live in the prettiest one — with pink-and-blue stripe wallpaper made out of silk and fancy furniture with flowers carved on it. That room belong to Miss Adelais, the oldest sister.

"Once I remembers Bouchard look hard at my face and say, 'you're nothing like her, you look just like me.' Well, time wore on, and I suppose I look more and more like the Bouchards, just a shade or two darker and with curls instead of that wispy straight hair. And Miz Lavinia study me, too, and seem like every time she really look at me she find some kind of excuse to slap me. And the older I gets, the harder she slap me. And whenever Bouchard was away, she do terrible things to me. She burn up a pretty dress he brung me clear from Mobile, and she laugh at my tears while I watch it burn. She take my china doll he give me and break it all to pieces."

At this point Keziah could contain herself no longer.

"Well, didn't you just hate her? Didn't you try to run away?"

Amalie shook her head.

"And where I could go in them times? And anyways, how I suppose to leave my poor Granny Reba, who never stop grieving for my mama and love me the same as she love her? No, I stays and comforts her and does what I can for her. And Tatty help me all she can. And then they was Miss Abrielle, who us call Miss Billie. She wasn't nothing like her mama or her older sister. Miss Adelais was hateful as Miz Lavinia — I hear tell she was alongside Miz Lavinia when she snatch my poor little mama away. But Miss Billie took up for me and other folks.

"When I turn eleven, in 1862, Miss Billie marry a older gentleman name of Noah Stern. I cry and cry when she leave. Mr. Noah run a store and don't own no slaves. He say he ain't gone fight in the war. Miz Lavinia talk something awful about him. Her oldest boy a soldier, but seem like she forget her youngest son pay another man to fight, maybe even die, in his place. She still carry on about her daughter marrying some no account that won't fight for the cause and don't own a single slave. And so one day, when Bouchard gone from the place, Miz Lavinia put me in the wagon and drive over to her daughter's new home, about three miles away. When us gets there, I almost jump up and down I'se so happy to see Miss Billie again. Then Miz Lavinia grab my hand, hard, like, and drag me up to the door and shout at her daughter.

"Miss Billie open the door and give me a hug and stare at her mama."

"'You loves her so much,'" she say. "'Well, now you can have her. And if that spineless husband of yourn don't want her, why you can send her to the devil, for all I care.'"

Anger flared in Keziah's heart over the treatment of eleven-year-old Amalie. She frowned as she asked, "So Billie Stern finished raising you?"

Amalie nodded.

"And did she know you were her half-sister?"

"Lord, yes. Everybody be knowing that. And her and Mr. Noah say they be glad to have me. But just a few days after Miz Lavinia brung me to they house, she show up again and demand her daughter give me back. I was afraid and hid behind Miss Billie."

"But why did Lavinia want you back?" Keziah asked. "Clearly she hated you."

"They's a lot I'se too young to understand back then. But later I thinks, Bouchard was furious about her taking me away, even if it was just to Miss Billie, and he tell her to try and get me back."

"And so you think this *Bouchard*" — Keziah said the name as if it left a foul taste in her mouth — "actually cared for you?"

"Oh, no. That man never care about nobody but his own self. I thinks he just want me in the big house so his wife got to look at me every day — not to remind her of what she done to my mother, but of what Miz Lavinia done to *him*. Once I hear him tell a gentleman friend about how she done made a fool of him by selling a slave away behind his back. So he make her look at me every day for revenge. And I thinks he bought me pretty things just to spite her."

Keziah shook her head in disgust.

"So when Lavinia came after you, what did Billie do?"

Amalie smiled broadly.

"I well remembers that day. And I remembers word for word what Miss Billie say. She look that old woman in the eye and she say, 'Mother, I'd walk through blood in hell before I'd give Amalie back to you.' So her mama get back in her wagon, hopping mad, and I never seen her again, except from a distance."

"How long did you live with Billie?"

"Almost five years. During all that time, the Sterns makes sure I sees my granny every week or so. Then I meets Burl, and right soon us marry and takes Granny Reba to live with us at Gator Pass. Miss Billie come visit us now and again up till she die of yellow fever the year Mattie born. She was a good woman with a big heart, and I misses her to this day."

Keziah regarded her thoughtfully.

"But the rest of them — the Bouchards. You must hate them."

Amalie sighed and shook her head.

"Hate ain't ever made nothing right, Keziah. Evildoers gets what coming to them, one way or another. Bouchard die a terrible death, some say of poison. The oldest son die in the war, and the other boy sell the property and run away to Canada, leaving the womenfolk to fend for they selves. The mean daughter marry a gambler who spend up all her money from her share of the land and then leave her, and she live with her spiteful old mama in a rundown place over in Clarke County. They both long dead now. Did I set out to make them folks miserable, I couldn't never make them so miserable as they made they selves."

She took the sleeping Jerusha from Nora's arms, kissed her on the forehead, and gently laid her in the cradle, just as Theodore came in from pruning some plants and offered to take Keziah home.

KEZIAH GREW FOND of each of the Waldron children, although it was no secret that Jerusha was her favorite. Keziah's siblings back in the Columbus area all had children, but she was seldom able to visit them. And so Nora and Tee's children became surrogate niece and nephews. Nora was also separated from her sister Mattie, her brothers Henry and little Burl, and their children, and was glad to have Auntie Keziah, as she came to be known, nearby.

Because of Nora's expertise as a midwife and healer, it was natural for Keziah to talk with her about her disappointment that she and Daniel did not have children. Assuming that the reason Daniel and his first wife had had no children was because Matilda was barren, Keziah, and Daniel as well, remained hopeful for many years that they would have a child. Keziah continued to blame herself, but eventually Nora gently suggested, in her kind and understanding way, that perhaps the problem lay with Daniel, not with Matilda or Keziah. Keziah had often wondered if that might be the case, but even after this discussion with Nora she never suggested such a thing to Daniel, who, to his credit, had never blamed Keziah, either. Their love for one another remained strong, and their marriage was a happy one, only occasionally marred by the usual misunderstandings and disagreements between husband and wife.

Any disappointment Keziah felt about being childless was ameliorated by her fondness for the Waldron children, which was enthusiastically reciprocated. Auntie Keziah was the one who brought sweets purchased on shopping trips in Dothan, as well as the inexpensive toys she loved to buy. Nora and Tee seldom bought toys, determined that their children would not be spoiled. But Keziah now and then convinced them that a small cloth doll, a top, or a paperback book or two, would not undo all of their teachings against selfishness and self-indulgence. The children, after all, worked in the household and in the nursery as soon as they were old enough — that is, by the age of five — and had school work to do as well. Surely a few small toys would not hurt them.

For many years there were no constraints against spoiling children at Comfortroot Farm, because, for more than a decade after Daniel and Keziah arrived, there were none.

Pierce Tomlin was a self-contained man who rarely displayed emotion. He had had a wonderful wife. He had lost that wife. And their son. He made it clear to Keziah, the only person he ever confided in, that, as God obviously intended him to be single, then he would, by God, remain single. This was always said with an angry scowl. And so despite the obvious attempts of several women to ensnare this attractive, affluent widower,

Pierce remained staunchly, it could even be said defiantly, single, in the face of the community's almost unanimous belief that he should marry. "Why, he must get powerful lonely in that big house," a man might be heard to remark. "But without any womenfolk it must be so — peaceful," another man might wistfully respond. "He needs him a wife! And children!" a woman would counter. And so it went through the years, while the recalcitrant widower minded his own business, just as he wished everyone else would.

And then he met that pretty, ethereal, fair-haired young woman at church, as lovely as any picture show actress, too refined to play the vamp, but perfectly able to overcome this older man's defenses with her flirtatious smiles, her slim body dressed in the prettiest of frocks, and her cultured Montgomery speech reminiscent of the accents of his well-educated Richmond relatives. Within two years of their meeting, Pierce Tomlin and Rowena Crandall were married. Three years later, in 1915, their daughter Amelia was born.

Like Nora and Keziah, Rowena settled in the Wiregrass as a bride. However, unlike them, she never felt entirely at home there. It was always apparent to Keziah that young Mrs. Tomlin preferred Montgomery society to the life of a farm wife. She clearly loved her husband and never expressed any regret at marrying him, but she often spoke wistfully, even longingly, about her parents' home in Montgomery.

The duties performed by Keziah and part-time help freed Rowena from the household chores she was not trained for — she could hardly boil a pot of water, let alone cook or bake or can vegetables. Nor could she sew, producing, as the average farm wife did, a substantial part of the family's wardrobe. But she was not completely lacking in skills. She could embroider and crochet. She was a charming hostess, giving parties several times a year to which one or two farmers, but mostly city folk from Dothan or friends from Montgomery, were invited. She was an accomplished pianist, and Keziah enjoyed listening to her play. And a few times, greatly amused, she watched Rowena's unsuccessful attempts to convince Pierce to dance to tunes on the Victrola. Like Pierce, Keziah realized that Rowena would always think of Montgomery as home. But she was a devoted mother, sweet tempered, and earned Keziah's respect.

The year that Amelia was born, Keziah's forty-five-year-old husband succumbed to pleurisy. The efforts of one of the most respected doctors in Dothan, summoned by Pierce, were futile. Nora and Theodore Waldron, himself only recently recovered from polio, stood by Keziah as the disease squeezed the life out of Daniel's lungs.

Keziah thought of returning to Columbus, but Pierce and Rowena would not hear of it. They sat with her in the Tomlin parlor to discuss it.

"Why, what on earth would I do without you, Keziah?" Rowena asked. "You can't leave, you just can't!"

She was tearful, and Keziah caught a note of panic in her voice.

Pierce put his arm around Rowena's shoulders and commented, although not with much conviction, "But Keziah might need to be close to her family now. Don't you think it's selfish of us to keep her here?"

Rowena dabbed at her eyes with a dainty hanky.

"I guess that's true. But oh, Keziah — whatever will I do without you?"

Keziah thought it over for several days before making a decision. Both of her parents were still living, but they were well looked after by her siblings, so she was not really needed in Columbus; and she was able to visit her family and old friends in Dollarleaf several times a year. Here in Chinkapin, she was especially close to the Waldrons and had many other warm associations at Divine Truth Church. She also knew the Tomlins would not only provide her a home, but do so with respect; and, at least on the part of Rowena and Amelia, affection. Keziah could never imagine Pierce feeling affection for her, but neither could she imagine him being unappreciative or unkind.

Thoughts of Daniel also influenced her decision. She reflected on the loyalty he had always shown to Pierce and Comfortroot Farm; she knew he would want her to stay. And she hated the thought of not being able to visit his grave at Divine Truth Church whenever she wished.

And then there were all the Wiregrass children she treasured — James Henry, Jerusha, Samuel and Solomon, adorable toddler Joshua, and now baby Amelia.

And so Keziah decided to stay, not in the cottage, but in a comfortable room Pierce and Rowena offered her, with a fireplace and two windows, one with a window seat perfect for reading. With her housekeeping duties, her reading, her quilting, Keziah was always busy. But never too busy for the Wiregrass babies she loved. And like Theodore and Nora, she encouraged all of them in their educational pursuits, especially Jerusha, the most scholarly of them, who they hoped would attend college one day.

Two years after Daniel's death, Lorraine Tomlin came along, giving Keziah another excuse to shop for toys. And in 1919, Benjamin arrived — a child who touched Keziah's heart and soul as she had never imagined any hardheaded little boy could ever do.

Chapter 15

JAMES HENRY

FROM THE TIME he was five years old, James Henry worked alongside his father and eventually his younger sister and brothers in their nursery business. But even though planting and tending flowers and shrubs was far less demanding than cotton farming, requiring less stoop labor and sparing hands and fingers from the cuts and scrapes of cotton burs, the Waldrons, like every rural family, raised vegetable crops for their own use, so he had more than a passing acquaintance with the mule and the plow. Through these physical exertions, he developed his muscles, growing tougher and stronger every year, although never as tough or as strong as his idol, world heavyweight boxing champion Jack Johnson. And he developed something else: an intense desire to find a different way to make a living.

Since rural Green Sedge Elementary School did not accommodate black students, James Henry attended a colored school on the west side of Dothan which included grades one through seven. His father took turns with other families in transporting their children by wagon to and from the school, some three miles distant from Chinkapin. Seventh grade was the highest level of education available for black children.

James Henry was looking forward to graduating. Like most farm children, his agrarian duties had caused him to miss school to the point that he was nearly fifteen when he graduated in May 1914.

That year the teaching staff planned to have a concert as part of the graduation. There were a dozen graduates, and the two-room school would not easily accommodate them and their families. Daniel and Keziah Cates were members of Divine Truth, and Daniel, for more than a decade one of Pierce's most trusted workers at Comfortroot Farm, decided to approach Pierce Tomlin about locating an appropriate place for the event.

Tomlin unhesitatingly agreed to help. He prevailed upon Jonas Holt, a Houston County official, who arranged for the event to be held at the courthouse.

On graduation night, the graduates and their families wore their Sunday best, and practically all of the family members attended, from young children to grandparents.

As they left the building, a girl of about seven years of age sharply cried out, holding her head. Blood trickled through her fingers where a rock had struck her. Seconds later another child was struck on the arm and a stone missile hit a teacher's eyeglasses, shattering one lens. Holt, who had been closing the doors to lock up behind them, heard screaming and shouting and came running out.

"What on earth — " A small rock stung his cheek.

There was a small group of laughing white folk, adults and children, who called them names and shouted at them.

"Get on out of here — y'all don't belong here!"

Holt waved the lantern he was carrying at them and shouted back,

"Stop this instant. You're trespassing on county property!" He was a large man, over six feet and heavy set. Most in the crowd knew him and would not relish going up against him. The whites were a small group of fewer than a dozen, and there were close to forty black people coming out of the school.

With a few more spiteful remarks they dispersed, a pitiful bunch who had nothing better to do with their time than harass some school children and their families.

"I'm sorry, folks," Holt said.

In his mind, there was not even a remote possibility that black children would one day attend the better equipped white schools, and he would not wish them to. But he had sincerely invited their families to avail themselves of this county facility, making them welcome for this special occasion, and he was ashamed of the treatment they had received.

Theodore Waldron, quick to appreciate any kindness on the part of a white man, was the first to speak.

"It wasn't your fault, Mr. Holt. That's just how some folks are. We thank you again for having us."

"It was a nice program, Reverend," he responded. "The young people did well. I heard some pretty singing in there."

Then, considering he had done all he could, he extinguished the lantern, set it back inside the courthouse corridor, locked up, climbed into his one-horse buggy, and set off for home.

Tee, Nora, and the other adults had quickly examined those struck by the rocks and found that, except for the little girl with a slight cut on her forehead, no one was injured. Nora borrowed a crisp new white handkerchief, bought for the child's brother for this dress-up occasion, and pressed it to the girl's forehead, urging her mother to clean the cut thoroughly and brush it with iodine when they got home.

Gray-haired, reed-slim Miss Starnes, the teacher whose glasses were broken, held them in her hands and wondered where in the world she would find the money to have them repaired. She was grateful the one lens was not shattered, because her vision was extremely poor. Then she rallied and raised her voice to get the students' attention. She had a throaty, high-pitched voice that carried far, and they were used to obeying it.

"Now you all listen to me. Don't any of you let what happened spoil your graduation. You are all achievers, you hear me, *achievers*, and you have acquitted yourselves well. Don't you go letting somebody's bad behavior make you forget that."

"No, ma'am," most mumbled. But as she was leaving, someone said to her retreating back, just loud enough for the students around him to hear, in the dialect she strove mightily to train out of them, "Us is achievers, all right. Us is achieved the right to be white folks' maids and white folks' shoeshine boys!"

James Henry snorted in agreement, though he dared not voice this opinion in front of Tee — that strong believer in the ultimate redemption of the white devil.

JAMES HENRY WAS a thorough malcontent. And would have been even were he not a black person confined to a narrow space in a white world. Because he hated muck and manure, he hated the unending bending down to plant and water and weed and doing so in any kind of weather, fighting off God's abundant varieties of stinging and biting insects. And he also had no desire to perform any of the menial work he could find in town. Even the nursery, dissatisfying as it was, was better than that. But try as he might, he could think of no options.

Then the war raging in Europe, of which he was only vaguely aware, provided his ticket out of Alabama and out of the nursery business. Shortly after his eighteenth birthday in July 1918, the draft notice came. His parents were upset. He was thrilled.

There were no training camps for blacks in Alabama, so James Henry was assigned to the all-black training facility at Fort Dodge near Des Moines, Iowa. Before his cross-country train trip, he was feted with a going-away dinner at Divine Truth Church, where he was the recipient of many hugs and unanimous good wishes, and listened during the evening church service that followed as his father expressed his deep pride in his eldest son and fervently prayed, with every member of the congregation, for his safe return. At home after the service, he was presented with a pocket New Testament, to be kept about him at all times, and a new fountain pen for writing letters, with an admonition to write as frequently as possible. At dawn the following day, Tee put him on the train in Dothan.

As they rolled through the countryside, the train passed field after field of people hoeing cotton. At this time of year the cotton had already been chopped, the unneeded thin cotton plants that resulted from standard overseeding removed. As in that operation, armies of workers were needed to hoe and pull up grass and broadleafed weeds that abounded in the rich soil throughout the summer months. To most train travelers the farm workers were part of the landscape, of no more interest than the monotonous rows of plants. But James Henry really saw them.

A young black woman with an infant snugly strapped to her chest in a sling fiercely hacked at stubborn weeds or stooped to yank them up with her hands. He could feel the strain on her muscles, the burning blisters on the palms of her hands. A scrawny white boy no more than six or seven years old raised up to watch the troop train pass by. Young as he was, this was probably not the first year he had worked in the fields. He grinned and waved his straw hat. A grizzled old man who could have been the boy's grandfather wiped sweat from his brow with the back of his hand, stared for a few moments, then turned back to his task. James Henry could feel the relentless heat that scorched the old man's back.

James Henry felt sorry for each and every one of them, of whatever age or color. He wished he could reach out and rescue them, say to them, Come away from those soul-withering fields, come away from the heat and the hard labor and the grinding necessity to get up tomorrow morning and do it all over again. He wished he had the power to release them from their toil.

The train with its cargo of raw recruits was rocketing out of the south into the Midwest. Before them was the most vividly beautiful sunset he had ever witnessed. Deep cerulean was overlaid with streaks of bright beaten gold. Staring out at that glorious sky, unsure of what lay ahead, James Henry promised himself that when his duty was done he would never work in the dirt again.

AT FORT DODGE, James Henry was assigned to the 809th Pioneers, which was commanded by both white and black officers, the latter being restricted by Army regulations from commanding white troops. Stringently exercised, drilled in rifle practice and trained in the use of a gas mask, James Henry sometimes smiled to himself (out of range of the sergeant's hawk eye) over the ease of basic training compared to sweating behind a plow.

In August, the 809th was ordered to France. Like most of the men in his unit, many of whom were also fresh off the farm, James Henry had never been aboard a ship. Sent to New York City to board the massive *President Grant*, the members of the 809th were amazed to find themselves among 5,000 soldiers, a number of individuals greater than the populations of many of their home towns.

While the soldiers had seen photographs or read newspaper accounts of the tens of thousands of lives lost, the incalculable damage inflicted by new and terrible weapons, dread of what lay ahead in war-decimated Europe was lessened by the anticipation of a sea voyage which many believed would be the adventure of a lifetime. And to cruise out of New York harbor aboard the *President Grant*, headed to France, a country they had never dreamed of seeing; to hear the multitudinous crowd shouting their farewells and giving rousing cheers as a band played a military march and the great ship, with several long blasts of its horn, set off; was the greatest thrill many of them had ever experienced.

A group of soldiers near James Henry began a rousing rendition of "Over There." James Henry and all of his buddies joined in and did not stop until the Statue of Liberty was completely out of view.

Settled in his bunk that first night, lulled by the sea, James Henry fervently wished that his family could have stood on the New York shore and seen the great ship, teeming with thousands of young Americans who had sacrificed the safety and comfort of home and were ready to fight for freedom — however long, however difficult, however perilous that fight might be. In his cramped quarters, oppressed with the heat of that late summer evening, he sensed that, to a man, each soldier felt an overriding sense of pride which diminished the inconvenience and discomforts of shipboard life.

By the next day, James Henry was thankful that he was not seasick, like the many who staggered on wobbly legs from their bunks to the head, or simply leaned over the deck railings in misery. He had not expected to be a good sailor, but surprisingly, after a few mild bouts of nausea, he found he had an iron stomach and steady legs.

Within a couple of days, most of those suffering from *mal de mer* had recovered and were gradually regaining their appetites. They were able to enjoy the sight of the vast ocean, marveling at things most had never seen — leaping dolphins or an occasional whale spouting a greeting.

Most chose not to think of the modern weapons making life a hell for civilians and comrades already in embattled Europe. Never before had war been waged with machine guns, hand grenades, poison gas, and bombs dropped from the air. But the men had been rigorously trained in combat, including the black soldiers who would primarily be assigned to labor battalions in the Service of Supply. And all had been drilled in the use of gas masks to protect themselves from the often fatal, lung-searing damage of poison gas. So they believed themselves prepared for what lay ahead.

But not half way to France, one soldier after another developed a cough, then a high fever, bone-rattling chills, and severe body aches. The troops soon learned the terrifying truth that a killer as deadly as any bullet, one no gas mask could deter, stalked the ship — invisible, undetectable, present in every breath of air the men breathed. The vicious Spanish flu virus had traveled out of New York harbor aboard the *President Grant*. Half the 5,000 troops were stricken. The medical staff, some of whom were ill themselves, were poorly equipped to care for hundreds of flu victims. It fell to those soldiers impervious to the virus to help their comrades any way they could — trying to keep them hydrated, bringing them meals and coaxing them to eat, cleaning up after them when they could not keep food down, and offering them words of comfort.

Many victims died during the Atlantic crossing. The unafflicted soldiers were assigned the somber tasks of collecting each deceased soldier's ID, swaddling the body in a sheet, and carrying it on deck for burial at sea. To James Henry it seemed that these men would have had a better chance of survival in a cold, muddy, rat-infested trench, with bullets whizzing over their heads, than they had had as victims of the unseen enemy that had silently invaded their bodies.

In early September, the *President Grant* docked at St. Naizaire, France, a critical port because many American soldiers disembarked there. James Henry was one of the men chosen to bury seventy-five additional victims of the flu. With this grim assignment accomplished, the men of the 809th set to work constructing hospitals for wounded American troops and completing extensive repairs to the infrastructure.

Although spared the grueling experiences of the men in foxholes, the men worked hard, sometimes subsisting on meager rations when food supplies did not arrive on time. But occasionally James Henry and his comrades were allowed to go into town on leave, where the inhabitants took a lively interest in the "black Yankees," as they were called. Many of the black Yankees were southerners and amused by the misnomer.

During James Henry's first foray into town, he was led, against his will, into a restaurant where the only blacks were his fellow soldiers. A grinning companion urged him inside, while James Henry nervously glanced around, expecting at any moment the long arm of Jim Crow to reach all the way from the States and toss him out on his ear. It took him some time, and more than one calming drink, to realize that Jim Crow did not exist here.

An aging French *chanteuse* winked at him, shocking him and causing him to glance around fearfully at the unconcerned whites tippling at the bar. She slid her eyes over his finely muscled body and smiled and raised an eyebrow at him in as frank an invitation as a man was likely to get. He hastily downed his drink and moved away toward the safe haven of his circle of buddies. Just out of the corner of his eye he saw her shrug and teasingly smile. Years later, he would wonder — what if he had taken her up on her offer? He could ever after have bragged about the time he spent with a bona fide French woman, an experienced woman with a siren's voice. But by then he had met Tilda, his wife, the sweetest and prettiest brown-skinned girl a man could ever hope to have. Adieu to thoughts of *femmes fatales*, he smiled to himself soon after they met. Hello to American brown sugar.

ON NOVEMBER 11, 1918, Jacques Bonet, a spare-framed Frenchman who had taken several of the men of the 809th Pioneer Infantry under his wing and instructed them in the French language, came running down the road with three bottles of cognac shouting, "*Celebrons mes amis! La guerre est terminée!*" Thanks to Jacques, the men perfectly understood what he said and began cheering and then, because he was the harbinger of such amazing, such fantastic news, a couple of soldiers hoisted him up on their shoulders and paraded him around until the desire for a taste of fine French liquor overcame their giddiness.

Sprawled under some trees by the road, the men sang for hours — they sang patriotic songs, drinking songs, sentimental songs, silly songs. And in and around the singing they talked about home.

Like all of them, James Henry yearned to see his family. But he had no unrealistic expectations about the welcome he would receive in the Wiregrass. Southeast Alabama would be sodden with rain this time of year, and just as mired in prejudice as it ever had been.

In France he had been treated as an equal. For the first time in his life he had not been barred entrance to restaurants and night clubs because of the color of his skin. And here white people had not, like the typical southerner, treated him as if he were a child — and an ignorant child at that.

"Home" was on everyone's lips as they celebrated. James Henry wanted to go home, too. But he was not sure exactly where home was.

THE WALDRON FAMILY was deeply thankful for James Henry's safe return from France. But the likelihood that he would remain with them decreased with each passing day. He frequently spoke of this or that soldier friend who lived in the North and had encouraged him to move there. The discrimination and inequities he had experienced in Houston County all his life were no longer bearable.

Going to war had made James Henry a man; coming home had made him an angry man. Why was he welcome to spend a portion of his mustering-out pay at the drug store but forbidden to sit at the counter and have a drink? Why were business owners eager to take the money he had earned by going to war, while barring him from any job other than janitor?

"I risked my life for my country!" he stormed to his father. "Come home, and still not treated any better than a yard dog!"

His preacher father counseled patience and Christian forbearance; his mother prayed that her son's attitude would not get him into serious trouble.

After an evening in a colored restaurant in town, James Henry was headed home, planning to walk to a friend's house and catch a ride out to the Waldron place. He had just crossed Burdeshaw Street when a familiar voice called out his name. He turned to see Tommy Harchester and his girlfriend Mavis.

Tommy and his two brothers had disappeared soon after draft notices began arriving. It was rumored they had gone to some other city to join up. In truth, they had hidden out in the Florida back woods with relatives and returned soon after the Armistice, openly bragging about how easy it had been to avoid the draft.

"What you up to nowadays, James Henry? Heard you went and played soldier for a while."

James Henry was in no mood for a conversation with one of the Harchesters. But a black man did not walk away from a white man who was addressing him. Even if the white fellow were a half pint and the black man the size of a linebacker, the latter could clearly see in his mind's eye the whole array of white society backing up the runt — the white police force (with emphasis on force) and the white courts, not to mention the white mob. Oddly, the white man in such an encounter believed he dominated the black man because of his superior traits, seldom realizing that he was carried aloft on the massive shoulders of Jim Crow. But for Jim Crow, the linebacker would brush the runt aside like a gnat and go on about his business.

But Jim Crow reigned, and so at the sound of his name, James Henry stopped, planting himself directly in Tommy's path, which forced him to stop as well.

Tommy was accompanied by his girlfriend Mavis, a thin, narrow-shouldered girl whose teeth were a bit too large for her face. Her one asset was thick, naturally blond hair which that morning had been ruined by a bad permanent wave and reduced her to tears every time she looked in a mirror. She was not in a tranquil state of mind, and her mood was not improved by the fact that it had taken her more than hour to drag Tommy out of a speakeasy so she could go home.

"Come on, Tommy, what are you stopping for?"

James Henry did not budge, as oblivious to her comment as she seemed to be to his presence.

"Move out of the way now, boy," Tommy said.

He had obviously had too much to drink and was unsteady on his feet. He was spindly-legged with a burgeoning beer belly. At 6'1", with 200 pounds of muscle hardened by years of manual labor and intensive combat training, James Henry was capable of pulverizing Tommy Harchester but preferred not to. He did not want to cause trouble for his family and had seen enough death to last a lifetime.

"I'm not a boy," he said. His voice was low, calm, but with a menacing undertone Tommy failed to catch.

"No, you ain't no *boy*, James Henry. You're a *nigger* boy." Tommy grinned and spat a stream of tobacco juice into the dirt, where some of it splattered one of James Henry's shoes. Oblivious to James Henry's narrowed eyes and clenched fists, Tommy had no inkling of That Word's effect. If so, he might not have uttered it.

James Henry had been called That Word innumerable times in his life — and not always with hatred. He and his friends often used the term among themselves in a teasing way.

But That Word, delivered with a smirk by a physically weak draft dodger endeavoring to impress his girlfriend; That Word, spewed forth in an alcoholic haze to James Henry, the war veteran, bestirred all the bitterness that was corroding his soul, and molten rage flooded his entire body. Without thought, he clenched his right hand into a fist, swung hard, and laid Tommy flat on the pavement. For a few seconds, Tommy was unconscious. Blood trickled down his cheek.

Aware of his own strength and its deadly potential, James Henry was relieved when Tommy came to and tried to sit up.

"My gosh, James Henry," Mavis wailed, "why'd you go and do that? You could've killed him!"

She knelt beside Tommy, reaching for a handkerchief to stem the flow of blood.

He struggled to get up, but he was still too dazed. He brushed away Mavis's efforts to nurse him.

James Henry's rage subsided as quickly as it had erupted. There was no guilt in its wake and no fear either. A great weight was lifted from his mind as he suddenly realized that he was done with all of the Tommy Harchesters. And he was done with all of the white people who smiled and were polite but condoned Jim Crow.

He pulled out his wallet and dropped several dollars on Tommy's chest.

"He'll live all right," he said. "Take him to a doctor. He might need stitches or something."

"I don't need your goddamn money," Tommy sputtered. "You — you — "

James Henry's malevolent stare dared him to say That Word again.

Tommy staggered to his feet, holding on to Mavis, and wiped the blood from his face with the back of his hand as James Henry turned away.

He did not continue his journey home. Instead, he walked straight toward the train station, as purposefully as if he had been planning this impromptu trip his entire life. From a few blocks away the ear-splitting squeal of the brake told him a train was already there, waiting for him. He quickened his pace and within minutes had paid his fare and climbed aboard.

Thus, before Tommy could rally the like-minded to teach him a lesson, James Henry was headed north on a one-way ticket.

Chapter 16

LOVE AND WAR

EUROPEAN BATTLES WERE of far less concern to the people of the Wiregrass than the battle against the boll weevil that by 1915 had infested Alabama cotton fields. Healthy cotton plants still pushed up out of the fertile soil and flourished in the southern sun and summer rains, but pernicious weevil larvae devoured more and more of the linty food it seemed their purpose on earth to destroy. Nathan Knightley, working his newly established hundred-acre farm with the help of his brother Bryce and the workers his father had hired to help them, was fortunate enough to enjoy two years of good yields before, in 1917, his crop began to show signs of the weevil. Unlike the diversified family farm up in Barbour County, Nate's fields were largely given over to cotton, and in the year the country entered the war in Europe, his decades-long battle against the weevil began.

But that was not the worst of his troubles. From childhood, he had considered his cousin Abigail Coltayne his sweetheart, even though it was clear that she did not always feel the same way. There were times, at family gatherings, when she paid attention to him and sought out his company. And growing up on neighboring farms in Barbour County before moving to the Chinkapin community, they had enjoyed many of the same social activities (although, as a Primitive Baptist, Nate was not allowed to go to barn dances — dancing was a sin

— whereas Methodist Abby could, and did, dance as much as she wished).

But as they entered their courting years, Nate began to lose the confidence he had always felt that he and Abby were meant for one another. In 1918, this concern that Abby might not become his wife intensified one May afternoon when he arrived late at a dinner-on-the-ground picnic at Dewberry Methodist Church to which she had invited him. He found her in animated conversation with Jacob Tanner. They were companionably sprawled on a quilt, she looking, Nate thought, a trifle unladylike in her above-the-ankle — actually, *way* above-the-ankle — gown, the latest thing, leaning on one side, her legs thrust out, both shoes kicked off, exposing her stockinged feet. Jacob was sitting cross-legged like some Indian (which is what he was, Nate reflected), gnawing on a drumstick in between saying this or that which Abby found hilarious. Both of them were oblivious to him.

So engrossed were they in one another that Nate felt it would be an intrusion to join them. As he started to turn away, he was hailed by Jeff Grainger, one of the hands on Nate's farm, a tall, beanpole-thin fellow. He envied Nate; he had no prosperous father to buy him a farm. But he was good-natured and optimistic, young and strong and ambitious enough to believe he would own his own farm one day. Jeff and Nate had become friends and frequently hunted and fished together.

Jeff had recently enabled Nate to acquire a musical instrument, something he had always desired to do, even though he could only read the shaped notes in the Primitive Baptist hymnal. He despaired of ever being able to afford an instrument or the music lessons to go along with it, but Jeff surprisingly provided a solution one day when they were tramping through the woods in search of quail. Nate mentioned his wish to play an instrument, half expecting Jeff to tease him about it. Instead, Jeff looked thoughtful for a moment, then remarked, "My grandpa always wanted me to play his concertina — left it to me when he died. I never could stand that squeak-box music. A piano, now, or a fiddle — that'd be fine. But that old concertina — "

He paused to shoot a quail, then sent his hound to fetch it. Nate took aim, missed, then glanced sideways at his friend.

"So do you know how to play it?"

Jeff put the quail in his bag and petted the dog.

"Sort of. I know how the durn thing works, anyway."

Noting Nate's interest, he suggested, "Tell you what. I don't want the dang concertina. You can have it, and I'll show you how to use it, too, if you'll let me have that extra harrow your papa give you that's just a-rustin behind your barn."

Nate grinned.

"Deal."

Now, as Nate tried to avoid looking in Jacob and Abby's direction, Jeff distracted him by asking, "You see that gal?"

He nodded toward the church steps. A young woman about their age was chatting with the preacher's wife. She was wearing a light blue lisle gown and holding a ruffled blue parasol. Her chestnut hair was prettily swept up under a wide-brimmed straw hat. Abby, in contrast, had tossed her hat on the quilt, exposing her long, untidily pinned-up hair.

"That there's Miss Clarissa Huggins."

Jeff seemed to expect Nate to recognize the name, but he only stared blankly.

"You know — Huggins Lumber. Her daddy's rich. People from all over buy lumber from his yard."

"Oh. Them. But I thought his daughter went to some fancy boarding school someplace."

"Did. She done graduated."

As if realizing they were talking about her, Clarissa parted from the preacher's wife and daintily, in her high-heeled slippers, stepped in their direction. Once upon them, however, she gave them the slightest smile, then proceeded past them to where Abby and Jacob were ensconced. Jacob jumped to his feet, offered Abby his hand, and pulled her up.

"Why, hey there, Clarissa," Abby warmly greeted her.

Clarissa closed her parasol, set it on the quilt, and gave Abby a hug.

"Why don't you join us?" Jacob asked.

"Why, sure I will."

"Come on," Abby said. "I'll walk you over to the food tables."

Nate observed this activity without a word and seemed to forget he had come to enjoy the victuals himself until Jeff nudged him.

"Ain't you hungry? We can sit over yonder with Ma and my sisters."

As Nate filled his plate, Abby, on the opposite side of the long table with Clarissa, caught his eye and grinned.

"This here's Clarissa Huggins, Nate. Clarissa, this is my cousin, Nate Knightley."

Not "my sweetheart," he noted. Just "my cousin."

Clarissa's charming smile somewhat soothed his feelings.

"So pleased to meet you, Nate."

She gazed at him steadily through large brown eyes, causing him to shift his feet self-consciously. As she delicately drizzled gravy on her mashed potatoes, Clarissa leaned across the table and said, "Tell me something, Nate. Has anyone ever told you what perfectly lovely red hair you have? What I wouldn't give to have hair that color! Wouldn't you, Abby?"

Abby's mouse-brown hair was the bane of her nineteen-year-old existence and therefore always a sore subject with her.

"It's red enough, all right," she acknowledged a tad irritably.

"It ain't nothing," Nate modestly commented. "Lots of redheads in my family."

His embarrassment did not override his pleased surprise at the attention this attractive young woman was giving him.

Her plate filled, Clarissa turned away with Abby and strolled back toward Jacob, but before they walked off she looked back and once again smiled at him in more than a friendly way. *That gal,* he delightedly thought, *is flirting with me.*

He considered the way Abby had laughed and chattered with Jacob earlier, completely ignoring him, and concluded that Miss Clarissa Huggins just might be prettier than she was.

Jacob's sister Millie waved to Nate from the seat of Harold Satterwirth's high-wheeled buggy. It was common knowledge that Millie and Harold were as good as engaged. While the Tanner family had always been fairly prosperous, there was no question that Millie was moving up on the social ladder by marrying the eldest son of Arthur Satterwirth, owner of Satterwirth Feed and Seed.

Blond, thickset Harold and dark-haired, plump Millie were more than physically suited to one another. Both were outgoing, loyal to friends and family, and hard working. Millie, as the only girl amidst six brothers, had always been her mother's mainstay, performing unending household chores. On a daily basis, Harold hefted as many sacks of seed and fertilizer as did his father's two employees, and he generally unlocked the store each morning and closed up at night.

Now Harold and Millie sauntered over to the food tables where Millie added her contribution of a chocolate cake, and Harold spread their quilt near Abby, Jacob, and Clarissa. Nate was considering joining the group when he was greeted by newlyweds Earl and Josephine Yates.

Several years Nate's senior, Earl was another fishing buddy. Nate did not know shy Josephine very well, but he knew that she, like Millie, had come up in the world by acquiring a mate. Earl was merely a worker in a cotton oil factory in Dothan. But he had recently been promoted to a supervisory position and was the owner of a modest home outside the city limits in the Chinkapin community, which seemed the height of success to someone with Josephine's background.

Josephine Keel was orphaned at the age of three. Her twenty-year-old mother had died of a snake bite after stepping on a copperhead while taking a shortcut through a dense thicket to bring her husband his noon meal. Not long after that tragedy, her father was killed in a logging accident.

Josephine was taken in by a solvent but parsimonious great-aunt with a choleric temper, who doled out food, clothing, and affection in miserly portions. The aunt did not, however, stint on religion; while growing up, Josephine spent more time in church than she did in school.

Earl was touched by her half-starved, poorly clothed state and entranced by her large, dark eyes and timid, loving nature. She gratefully accepted his marriage proposal, viewing this kind man — rawboned, balding, and a dozen years her senior — as a kind of savior.

The day she left her aunt's household for good was one of the happiest days of Josephine's life, only slightly marred by the fact that her new mother-in-law, pudgy Hilda Yates, was equally disagreeable and even more quarrelsome than her aunt. But thankfully, Mother Yates did not live with them, and Earl, as her eldest, favorite child, could manage her so well that Josephine was not often troubled by her spiteful remarks and petty demands.

Josephine had brought a platter of fried chicken. As she placed this tasty offering on a food table, she waved to her close friends, Abby and Millie.

Earl spread their quilt near Nate and Jeff's family.

"I'll get our plates, sugar," he said to his bride. He patted the quilt. "You just sit down here."

Josephine smilingly obeyed and said not one word, which is exactly what Nate expected. Jeff's mother tried to start a conversation with her, but only received a few soft "yes, ma'ams" or "no, ma'ams" before Earl returned.

Despite all of his good qualities, Earl was not the most tactful of men.

"How come you're not a-settin with Abby, Nate? What's Jacob Tanner got that you ain't?"

Nate felt his face flush, but restrained himself from making a sharp reply.

"I reckon Abby can sit wheresoever she pleases," he said, in as indifferent tone as he could manage. "Makes no nevermind to me."

Josephine put down a piece of cornbread and looked at him through serious dark eyes. To his surprise, she opened her mouth and spoke.

"How can you say that, Nathan Knightly? Abby's my dear friend, and she told me — But maybe I shouldn't say."

"Abby told you — ?"

"Why, that y'all are a-gonna marry some day!"

Nate was silent for some moments.

"And just when did she say that, Jo?"

"Not so very long ago. Last month. Right after Earl and me got married. Abby was visiting me, and Jacob come walking along the road by our house with Dorinda Kimble, and he waved to us. That's when she said it."

Appreciative of such an outpouring of information from a person who had rarely spoken to him before, yet uncertain how to feel about her news, Nate only responded, "Oh."

Because did Abby say what she said out of love for him? Out of a real conviction they would marry? Or did she say it because the sight of Jacob with Dorinda, an attractive young woman, made her jealous, and she didn't want Jo to know it?

Jeff, sated and now clearly bored, gave his mother a hug and tapped Nate on the shoulder.

"Them bass ain't a-gonna catch theirselves, Nate. Plenty of time to get in some fishing this afternoon."

"I'm ready, buddy."

Like Jeff, Nate gathered up his plate, cup, and fork and set them with the other dirty dishes at the end of one of the tables. Washing up was women's work, and none of the men troubled themselves about it.

"Good luck, boys," Earl said. "Hope you catch a whole string of 'em. I hear trout's biting good, too."

Then, touching Jo on the cheek, he offered, "Want some cake, hon?"

She nodded and smiled, perceiving in Earl's brief question and gentle touch his love, his nurturing nature, for which she was deeply grateful.

IN THE FOLLOWING weeks, Josephine, in the throes of morning sickness, kept to the house. But Abby, Clarissa, and Millie became a threesome. They went to the picture show, sighing over Francis X. Bushman; they saw a vaudeville act at the Dothan Opera House; they donned bathing dresses and braved a dip in chilly Kelly Springs north of town. While many of the girls' conversations centered on current fashions and hairstyles or a dozen other trivial subjects, Millie was amused by the obvious interest Clarissa and Abby took in her brother Jacob, whose name frequently came up in conversation.

Millie had always hoped Abby would marry Jacob, but she seemed to vacillate between him and Nathan. Millie liked Clarissa well enough and envied her wardrobe, but the phrase "new friends are silver, old friends are gold" sometimes crossed her mind when she thought of her two friends, and she knew that Abby would always take first place in her heart.

As that golden spring of 1918 turned into summer, the war in Europe, of so little concern to them for most of its duration, began to impact even lighthearted young women determined to enjoy newfound freedoms — skirts were above the ankle and bathing dresses were above the knee; women were achieving independence as nurses, social workers, secretaries, and telephone operators. The women's suffrage movement was stronger than ever. But when America entered the war in 1917, young men aged twenty-one to twenty-nine were required to register for the draft, and now eighteen-year-olds were subject to the draft, as well. The threat of young men being called into the service of Uncle Sam and sent into the hell of war-torn Europe cast a pall over what would otherwise have been halcyon days.

Clarissa did not have brothers, and Abby's brother, fifteen years older than she, was exempt because of his age. Millie's husband was shortsighted and thus exempt, as well. The younger Tanner brothers were below draft age, and the two eldest were not called up because they were married with several children. But Millie worried about Jacob.

Both Jacob and Nathan had received draft notices, and in July Jacob was required to report for training at Ft. Hancock near Augusta, Georgia. Jacob viewed military service not only as a duty to his country but also as an opportunity to wear a swell uniform and impress Abby and Clarissa. An essentially optimistic soul, he did not imagine himself dying in a foxhole; he did imagine himself returning home as a war hero.

Nathan's response to his draft notice was not much different, except for the war hero part. Although, not unlike a long train of his male ancestors, he believed that fighting the enemy enhanced a man's appeal in the eyes of a woman, he never believed himself hero material; but he was willing to fight. When his second notice from the draft board arrived, announcing that his services would not be required because he was a Class II registrant — an essential agricultural worker — he was disappointed. His father soon set him straight.

"Give thanks to almighty God, son," Jackson said. "War ain't no game. If you shoot the enemy, whether they die or maybe just lose an arm or a leg, you got to live with that for the rest of your life. And if they shoot you, and you live, you might be blind or crippled or worse for the rest of your life. The Lord has spared you, and thankfully your brothers are out of it, too, because they're older and have families to support. I went through four years of hell in the Civil War, so I understand how fortunate, how blessed, our family is right now. And you need to understand that, too."

Nathan saw the sense in Jackson's words, but it was hard to be grateful when Jacob returned from training and strutted about in his uniform, bragging about how he would almost singlehandedly win the war. It was downright sickening the way the girls fluttered around him. Clarissa bought him a Swiss Army knife; Abby baked him a peach cobbler.

"But after all," Nate's mother comforted him, "he's going off to war. It's natural for folks to spoil him a bit. That don't mean Abby favors him over you."

"Maybe not. But she sure ain't paying any attention to me lately."

Sophronia smiled. Except for Nathan, her baby, she had seen each and every one of her children marry the person he or she loved. Sophronia was sure that Abby would ultimately choose her son, whom she considered handsome, responsible, hard working, and caring — everything a woman could want in a husband. Why would Abby choose anyone else?

Still Nate fretted. He was not much consoled by the fact that he knew Jacob had escorted Clarissa to a July Fourth celebration without Abby. And Jeff Grainger had witnessed Jacob holding Clarissa's hand as they strolled down St. Andrews Street in Dothan. But then Abby had told him she had recently spent the entire afternoon at the Tanner place with Jacob, invited to dinner there by his parents. Joseph and Harriet Tanner had known Abby since her childhood and had always been very fond of her. Clearly they cottoned to the notion of Jacob and Abby being together. And as everyone knew, any young woman would choose a fighting man over a dirt farmer. So what chance did he have?

All speculation on Nate's part came to an end when Jacob and the other recruits boarded the train which would take them to the port where they would embark for Europe. Nathan was at the station to say goodbye to Jacob and other friends, like his neighbor, Billy McCafferty, a bright fellow whose freshman year at the University of Alabama would have to be postponed because of the draft. Billy's parents,

William and Marvean, and his sister, Stella, were there to send him off. His petite mother clung to him as if she would never let him go. Stella dabbed at her eyes with a handkerchief, and as the train whistle sounded and the engine came into view, William gently pried his wife's hand from Billy's arm.

Of course Jacob's family was on hand — a tearful Harriet and Millie, stalwart Joseph, and all of his brothers. After being hugged by the whole tribe, Jacob turned to his two lady friends and platonically kissed each of them on the cheek. Abby brushed tears from her face and stepped over to stand arm-in-arm with Millie. Suddenly, Clarissa, to the surprise of all assembled, leaned into Jacob's arms, brazenly kissed him on the lips, and whispered into his ear. Apparently speechless, Jacob stared at her intently for some moments before boarding the train.

ABBY AND MILLIE frequently visited Josephine, who by August was past the worst of her morning sickness and could enjoy chatting with her friends on a Saturday as they sipped coffee and shared Jo's homemade fruit cake in her small, neatly kept home. Millie was on her second slice of moist, scrumptious cake when she mentioned that her parents had heard from Jacob — a postcard mailed from France dated August 13 stating that he was fine and missed them all. Abby wondered if the "all" included herself, since she had not heard from him.

By August 1918, the tide of war had turned against Germany. On August 8, Allied counter offensives on the Somme had pushed the German army back and into retreat. But soldiers and civilians were still dying by the thousands. No one could foretell whether or not Jacob would return, and both Abby and Millie expressed their concern.

"Well, let's pray for him," Jo insisted, grabbing each of them by the hand and fervently asking the Lord to watch over Jacob and keep him safe. She went on for some time, quoting from several Psalms and a number of New Testament verses, while Abby tried not to fidget and Millie struggled to keep her eyes off the luscious cake that begged to be eaten. At the long-awaited "amen," Millie took a quick bite and then, glancing Abby's way, asked, "So, have y'all seen anything of Clarissa lately?"

The image of that parting kiss at the railroad station, unwitnessed by Jo, was still fresh in Millie's and Abby's minds. Abby fumed whenever she thought about it. What right did Clarissa have to kiss Jacob like that? And in front of the whole world, too!

Jo responded, "I saw her to wave to a couple of weeks ago, when Earl and me was coming home from church. She was sitting in her papa's car outside their house, and I reckon she didn't see me because she kept on looking straight ahead and did not wave back."

Millie brushed crumbs from her lap and took another sip of coffee.

"The reason I ask — I visited with her a while back, and she didn't have much to say. But then Dorinda told me she heard Clarissa was planning on moving back to Atlanta soon. That's where she went to finishing school, you know. Stayed with her aunt and uncle there."

Surprised, Abby remarked, "Well, I ain't seen much of her either, but two weeks ago I ran into her in Blumberg's, and she barely spoke, said her mama was waiting for her and she didn't have time to talk. But then she declared — in that sugary voice of hers — that she'd truly *love* for all of us to get together soon. And she did not say a single word about leaving town."

Discussion of Clarissa was halted by the sound of Earl arriving in his second-hand truck.

Smiling, Jo pulled back the curtain and glanced out of the window. She quickly dropped the curtain.

"Oh, my Lord, y'all, he's got Mother Yates with him."
She sighed.
"Reckon I better start dinner. She's always hungry."

Millie and Abby hugged her goodbye, eager to avoid the critical looks and sharp tongue of Mother Yates. She would not approve of Jo entertaining company in the middle of the afternoon.

As they departed, Millie, with a guilty pang, wondered if she were wrong not to tell Abby the whole truth about Jacob's correspondence. In her brief encounter with their newfound, suddenly standoffish friend, Clarissa had revealed that she had received several letters from Jacob and that she wrote to him almost daily. Millie was not comfortable sharing this information but thought perhaps she should.

She and Abby had the use of Harold's tall buggy, and Millie was driving them home in it. After a few moments of silence, she began, "Abby, when I saw Clarissa, she told me — "

Abby abruptly cut her off.

"I do not care about anything Clarissa Huggins might have to say, Millie."

Relieved, Millie did not mention Clarissa's name again. Instead, they enjoyed a discussion about her and Harold's pending nuptials, set for mid-October, and Abigail's role as maid of honor.

SOPHRONIA KNIGHTLEY AND Victoria Coltayne had on more than one occasion lightheartedly discussed the possibility that their youngest children would marry one another. Neither was young any longer. Both hoped to live to see Nathan and Abigail happily settled in life, whether or not they married each other. Although Victoria had moved to a different county, they often saw one another when Sophronia came down to visit her son in Chinkapin.

Victoria could just picture a grandchild with Sophronia's and Nathan's lovely, wavy red hair, unlike the straight brown hair, nearly as fine as the down on a chick, that Abby had inherited from her. Sophronia would prefer that a grandchild inherit the dark, nearly black hair of Tobias and Noble Coltayne.

"Well," Victoria said one autumn morning, "if our younguns do marry, maybe we'll have us some sweet little redheads *and* brunettes."

"That would be nice," Sophronia agreed, reaching for another pecan to shell for the pie Victoria planned to bake, as her friend emptied an apron full of shelled nuts into a bowl.

"But we need one with Abby's straight brown hair, too."

Like her daughter, Victoria did not care for this trait they shared but appreciated Sophronia's effort to compliment it.

Three days after Victoria's visit, Abigail summoned Sophronia to the Coltayne home where Victoria was so ill she could not get out of bed. The next morning, Tobias and all of their children were at the bedside, along with their minister, as she died of influenza, one of dozens of victims in Houston County alone. More than 25,000 cases of flu had been reported in Alabama by early October. Despite the heroic efforts of hundreds of volunteers and the Public Health Service — a nurse was sometimes on duty forty-eight hours, with only two hours of sleep — the pandemic continued to rage throughout the country through December.

Millie and Harold cancelled their October wedding and did whatever they could to help the Coltayne family and others stricken by the disease. Millie prepared food for the sick, and Harold delivered it. Millie also assisted in caring for children whose mothers were too ill to look after them.

Nathan and Sophronia consoled Abigail through the darkest period of her grief. Jackson spent hours with Tobias, his cousin and lifelong friend, reliving memories of Victoria with tears and laughter. As they shared meals that Sophronia helped Abby prepare, Jackson prayed for Tobias and his family and gave thanks for the gift of Victoria, expressing the hope that she would be among the chosen. While appreciating this "chosen" comment from a Hard Shell Baptist, Methodist Tobias knew beyond a doubt that Victoria was in heaven waiting for him. He intended to continue avoiding sin and join her there one day.

The pandemic wreaked devastation worldwide. But on November 11, the Great War ended, reviving weary spirits. As the country rejoiced, the families of soldiers and sailors excitedly awaited the return of their young men.

One young man in particular occupied most of Abby's thoughts. As far as anyone knew, Jacob Tanner had escaped the flu and survived combat unscathed.

"So when do you reckon he'll be home?" she asked Millie toward the end of November.

Millie hesitated so long Abby was fearful something was wrong.

"He *is* coming home soon, ain't he?"

"I think — I believe he wrote he'd be back by Christmas."

"By *Christmas*! But I hear some of the other boys're already on the way home. Now why on earth would he not get here till Christmas, Millie?"

Millie had been dreading that question from Abby ever since her mama had gotten the letter from Jacob the week before. She would have given anything not to be obliged to answer it. But Abby needed to know the truth.

"Well — Come set down over here, honey," she said, indicating a comfortable chair near the fireplace, where the November chill had prompted her father to light a fire.

She sat next to Abby and took one of her hands as Abby's grey glacé eyes widened in alarm.

"Well, it's like this. Jacob ain't coming straight home because he's stopping over in Atlanta for a while. In a couple of weeks, we're all going over there to see him."

"In Atlanta? But why?"

"Well, because — because — "

Abby lost patience.

"Oh — out with it, Millie! Because why?"

Millie dropped her hand and took a deep breath.

"Because him and Clarissa's getting married, Abby. On December 14."

Astonished, Abby stared at her.

"*Married*? Him and *Clarissa* — that — that — "

Even in her distress, Abby's Methodist upbringing prevented her from calling Clarissa the vulgar name that was on the tip of her tongue. Quickly her anger gave way to tears.

"But why, Millie? Why? He cared for me — I know he did. He always did."

Millie knelt by her and put her arms around her shoulders.

"Of course he did, sugar. I believe he still does. But that — "

Millie bit her tongue. She was a Methodist, too.

"Well, she trapped him. She just trapped him."

Abby raised her head and took a handkerchief from her pocket to wipe away tears.

"What do you mean, trapped him?"

"Oh, Abby, don't you understand? Clarissa's in the family way. And the baby's Jacob's."

Under her breath she added, "At least, she says it is."

She stood up and got Abby a glass of water.

"Oh, Millie," Abby moaned. "I have been such a fool over that boy."

"Not as big a fool as Clarissa. She's ruined her reputation, and I don't believe Jacob loves her. I'll never believe it."

For a moment, Millie's concern over Abby's stress was overshadowed by her disappointment that now she and her old friend would never be sisters-in-law.

Abby shakily sipped the water, trying to compose herself. Finally she said, "Well, it don't much matter what you or me think, Millie. He's marrying Clarissa."

NATHAN WAS SURPRISED when Jacob did not come home right away to be welcomed by the fanfare Dothan provided for the other returning Houston County soldiers. As a mere male, he was not immediately privy to the information about the Tanner boy's wedding and the accompanying gossip. However, he eventually learned about Clarissa's delicate condition, which had necessitated, if not a shotgun wedding, at least a hastily arranged one. When he heard the news, his thoughts went to Abby. He was pretty sure she was not happy about it.

But the first time he saw her after hearing that Jacob was no longer on the marriage market and unlikely to return, because he was being set up in the furniture business in Atlanta by some of Clarissa's well-heeled relations, she seemed cheerful enough and in quite a friendly mood.

Sophronia was again down from Barbour County visiting Nate and had invited Abby to supper. Tobias drove her over in the wagon and visited a spell before he went back home.

"Well, well," Abby smilingly said when Nate came in from the fields, "if it ain't my dear cousin Nathan."

And then she actually kissed him on the cheek. She had brought a chocolate cake and after the meal cut him a slice herself.

While Sophronia rocked near the fire, Nate and Abby shared the sofa and talked longer than he could ever remember they had. For a good part of the conversation, they held hands, and even with his mother in the room he got the impression she would allow a kiss on the lips, and he gently complied.

Nate drove her home by starlight. He helped her down from the wagon seat and then looked into her eyes, which shimmered like quicksilver in the moonlight. Emboldened by the warmth shown him that evening, he spoke from his heart.

"Abigail, Abigail — I truly love you."

She smiled and nodded.

"I know you do, Nathan."

He saw Tobias sitting on the front porch, waiting up for his daughter, but somehow he knew it would be all right to take Abby into his arms and kiss her.

"I love you so much, darlin'," he declared. "I always have, and I always will. Abigail Coltayne, will you marry me?"

Abby touched his cheek.

"Of course I will. Why wouldn't I?"

Joyfully, Nate lifted her up and swung her around. As he set her down he excitedly exclaimed, "Let's go tell your papa!"

Later that evening, after he had shared the news with his delighted mother, Nate thanked the Lord for his future wife, never once reflecting that, when he proposed, the "I love yous" had all been on his side, with nothing more than a polite smile from Abby in return.

Millie and Harold were finally married at Dewberry Methodist Church in January 1919. A month after their wedding, Abigail and Nathan were married at Coolwater Primitive Baptist Church, with Millie as maid of honor and Nate's brother Bryce as best man.

Earl and Josephine Yates' son Jesse was born in the spring of 1919. Millie and Harold's firstborn, Willoughby, was born in October, and Bryce Knightley arrived two days before Christmas.

Bryce was skillfully brought into the world by midwife Nora Waldron. Before this, Abby had only known Nora to speak to, but at Bryce's birth, her calm nature and nurturing spirit so affected Abby that she recognized Nora was a treasure. After bathing and swaddling the baby and placing him in Abby's arms, she sat next to the bed and spoke comforting words about Victoria Coltayne, realizing this new mother was still grieving for her own mother and saddened that Victoria had not lived to see her youngest child's firstborn. Abby could not help tearing up about it, despite the joy of holding a healthy son in her arms. Although Nora's thoughts were never far from her own firstborn, who had chosen to live in a place alien to her, a big city in the frozen north, with apparently no intention of coming back home, she put aside her own sadness over James Henry to comfort Abby.

She brushed the long strands of untidy hair back from Abby's brow and took one of her hands and gently patted it.

"Now don't you fret none, honey. Your mama see your baby clear as you does. She always gone be with you and this child."

Nora's touch and reassuring tone had a healing effect, and as Abby caressed her tiny son, she felt a lifting of the grief that had burdened her since Victoria's death.

FOR A WHILE it seemed there must be a competition among Abby, Millie, and Josephine as to who could produce the most children. Letitia Knightley was born in April 1921. Calvin Yates arrived in September 1923, and Toby Knightley was born the following month. Gerrilyn Yates was born in the summer of 1926, and Roger Satterwirth came along that November. Nobella Knightley arrived in September 1927 and Gerald Satterwirth in January 1928. Although the friends were blessed with good husbands, it was mainly their friendship and constant support for one another that kept them sane and centered through the sometimes rocky shoals of motherhood.

ALTHOUGH ABBY WAS a member of Coolwater Primitive Baptist Church, which she had joined before marrying Nate, she maintained ties with Dewberry Methodist, the church she grew up in, and she and her family visited there from time to time. On a January morning in 1923, Abby and Nate sat near the back of the church in case it was necessary to take one of the children out during the sermon. Toddler Letty could usually be kept amused with a doll, but three-year-old Bryce was a constant fidgeter, and keeping him quiet and seated in the hard wooden pew was a challenge.

The youngsters in the congregation could be a sore trial for their parents during the long sermon, squirming, whispering, or nodding off until those moments when Reverend Lester Bayard, a forceful speaker, let loose with a thunderous cascade of words designed to rouse even the most complacent congregant. Then his words reverberated so loudly that even the youngest child came to attention.

In a lull between dramatic pronouncements, Abby noticed the McCafferty family seated two pews up on the right side of the church where she had a good view of petite Marvean, her husband William, and her daughter Stella. Marvean still wore black on Sundays in remembrance of her son Billy, who had died in France in 1918. Abby vividly recalled the day Billy and Jacob Tanner had said their farewells at the train station in Dothan. After Billy's death, Marvean, already birdlike in size, had seemed to shrink even smaller, and it was rumored that for weeks after the news arrived her husband and daughter had had to coax her to eat anything, and she rarely spoke. But eventually she rallied, and today she sat up straight with a smile on her face and seemed happier than she had been in the past five years.

Abby picked Letty up from the floor, where she had slid down in search of her small celluloid doll, found the doll for her, and once again shushed Bryce, who was trying to talk to a friend two pews away. That boy's mother jerked him around to face the pulpit, and the two mothers exchanged understanding smiles.

For some reason, Abby kept staring at Marvean today. Like her, she had a son and a daughter. What if she lost the son? She suddenly pulled Bryce against her side and hugged him, holding him close to her for a few moments. What if she lost him? What if, one day when he was eighteen years old, a draft notice came for him as it had for Billy, and what if, like Billy, he went away for training and was allowed to come home for just a couple of days, showing off his new uniform, before he shipped out? And what if he never, ever came home again. What if? Abby kept staring at Marvean, and her eyes brimmed with tears. *Poor woman*, she thought, *poor woman.* Nate glanced down, surprised at the tears, which he thought the reverend's words had produced, and playfully whispered, "Now, hon, you don't really think you're a-goin to hell, do you?"

Abby tried to smile and squeezed his hand, shook her head, and wiped away the tears. She was so fortunate. The Great War, the war to end all wars, had been fought and won. There would never be another war. Bryce would never have to go to some foreign land and fight. Never. He would stay right here in the Wiregrass and live to be a very old man. She leaned down and kissed his ginger curls.

MARVEAN MCCAFFERTY LIKED to sit on a fencepost and watch her husband work in the fields. She had always done so and observed nothing out of the ordinary. But in the spring of 1923 she had begun seeing Billy out there. It was some four years and five months (she had stopped counting the days) since his poor slashed body had been laid to rest in the Meuse-Argonne American cemetery in France alongside more than 14,000 other American soldiers, and until now, while she had often sensed his presence, she had never seen him. But one day there he was. It was Billy, far away in the distance, in that fallow field beyond the cornfield that had always been his domain as a youngster. He would run up one of the low hills with a stick sword and pretend he was Teddy Roosevelt charging San Juan Hill. Or he would ride his gentle, obliging horse across the field pretending he was a Cavalry officer chasing the Sioux out on the vast western plains. Or he might just sit under a hickory tree and read the book he had brought with him. He was a great reader, she remembered proudly, who loved to learn new things.

She did not understand why she had now begun to see him. For more than four years she had longed to see him again, to hear his voice, to know that he was all right. She had even participated in a séance in Dothan at the home of another grieving mother who had hired a famous medium to come all the way from Atlanta. This medium had reunited many parents with their soldier sons, it was said, and she deeply wanted to believe in the medium's chance of success in reaching Billy. It was disappointing, then, when Marvean, who was not a gullible fool, immediately realized that the moans and slurred words of her friend's son sounded suspiciously like those claimed to be produced by Billy. Disgusted, and sad for her friend, who completely bought into this hog wash, Marvean never consulted another spiritualist.

But her desire to see her son again never diminished; and now, strangely, there he was. But why was he so far away? He could not seem to come any closer. But no matter — she could sit on the post and watch him.

Sometimes, watching him, her face was crumpled with pain because she saw the German soldier run his bayonet through his chest and watched Billy fall, bleeding, in agony. But sometimes it was the other way around, and he was the one who killed the enemy. He would stand looking down at the still body for a moment, not triumphant, but slumped over, as if with regret. And then sometimes he was marching across a flowery field, and he would turn and wave at her, and although she could not clearly see his face she was sure he must be smiling. Such warmth would flood her soul that for a moment the ice-cold grief at her core melted away.

Marvean's neighbors were used to seeing her sit on the fencepost. It had never struck any of them as odd. She never sat there more than an hour or so, and it seemed to be just a diversion for her, a way of getting out of the house and showing off a new parasol or a new straw hat that shaded her from the sun. Or maybe she just enjoyed perching on a post like a bird, breathing the fresh air and taking a break from the cooking and the ironing. The neighbors always spoke, and she always responded with some pleasantry. But recently it was different. She did not seem to hear their comments, and they might see an expression of horror on her face, or, what was even stranger, a broad grin as she waved enthusiastically at the corn stalks, her husband invisible many rows away. Why was she grinning, and to whom was she speaking? Because they also heard her attempts at conversation with Billy (who never tried to talk to her, never did more than wave). People began to conclude that she was crazy. But most of them understood; grief will do that to you.

Marvean had always sat on the fencepost, but never in bad weather and only when her husband was in the field. Nowadays she sat out there whether William was working or not, and he or their daughter would have to drag her off the post in the wet or the cold.

"Come on, now, Mama. You'll get sick if you stay out here."

Marvean would reluctantly climb down from what had become her sentry post.

There came a day when she heard Billy's voice — or maybe it was the just the wind whispering. The far-off, wind-whispered voice said, "I'm going home, Mama," and she was sure he was smiling.

Marvean tried to smile, too, but she was confused. Did he say, "*going* home" or "*coming* home." Surely he was coming to her, not going away someplace. Where would he go? Out yonder? Way out in the beyond into that great expanse of blue sky behind him? He seemed to be pointing there. And the wind brought the words again, "I'm going home."

William had been watching her from the porch, and he saw her go limp and feared she would fall and hurt herself. He ran and called to Stella, and they both got her into the house. They helped her lie down on the couch where she refused food or drink or a sip of brandy.

"He says he's going home now," she murmured. "I'm so afraid he's going where I won't ever see him again."

"Who?" Stella asked. "Surely you don't mean Billy?"

"He says he's going home."

Stella felt tears welling up. She took one of her mother's fragile hands and held it for a moment.

"Billy was laid to rest four years ago, Mama. You know that."

Marvean nodded, faintly smiled, and closed her eyes. William stroked her forehead and thought of going for the doctor. But Marvean was soon deeply asleep, a peaceful expression on her face. Stella covered her with a quilt and led her father to the kitchen table and poured his iced tea.

Marvean slept on. She did not, in this world, awake again. She opened her eyes out there in the blue yonder near Billy's favorite hickory tree. He was smiling, still wearing his uniform, which was clean and pressed and bore no evidence of the bayonet thrust — no gash, no bloodstains — and he looked as dashing as he had the day he went away. He was not far off, but right there in front of her. She smiled as he reached for her outstretched hand.

"I've been waiting for you, Mama," he said. "We're going home."

Sources

Books and Articles
Long Rows to Hoe

Adams, Capt. G. B., *Reminiscences of the Nineteenth Massachusetts Regiment*, http://sunsite.utk.edu/civil-war.html

Alabama: *AfricaTown, USA (Local Legacies: Celebrating Community Roots – Library of Congress)* http://lcweb2.loc.gov/diglib/legacies/AL

Beard, Michael F., "The Battle of Mobile Bay" and "Mobile: The Overland Campaign – March-May 1865," Alabama Gulf Coast Convention & Visitors Bureau, 2003

Center of Military History, United States Army, Indian Wars Campaigns, www.history.army.mil

Center of Military History, United States Army, U.S. Army Campaigns: Civil War, www.history.army.mil

Chamberlain, Joshua Lawrence, "The Passing of the Armies," published in *The Appomattox Paroles, April 9-15*, 1865, H. E. Howard, Inc. (Lynchburg, VA) 1989

Hickman, Kennedy, "American Civil War: Battle of Cold Harbor," militaryhistory.about.com/od/civilwarintheeast/p/coldharbor.htm

Houston County – The First 100 Years, Dothan Landmark Foundation, Arcadia Publishing (Charleston, SC) 2003

Lawson, Eric and Jane, "Black Yankee: An Interview with Thomas Davis, First World War Veteran," www.worldwarI.com/sftdavis.htm, 1997

Stepp, Wendell H. and Pamela Ann Stepp, *Dothan – A Pictorial History*, The Donning Company/Publishers (Norfolk, Virginia) 1984

"The Battle of Hobdy's Creek," www.exploresouthernhistory.com

"The Creek War of 1836 in Alabama, Georgia and Florida," www.exploresouthernhistory.com.

"The Ft. Mims Massacre," The Ft. Mims Restoration Association, www.ftmims.org

The Heritage of Barbour County, Alabama, Heritage Publishing Consultants, Inc. (Clanton, AL) 2001

The Heritage of Dale County, Alabama, Heritage Publishing Consultants, Inc. (Clanton, AL) 2001

The Very Worst Road – Travellers' Accounts of Crossing Alabama's Old Creek Territory 1820-1847, Compiled by Jeffrey C. Benton, University of Alabama Press (Tuscaloosa, AL) 1998

"William/Lamochattee 'Red Eagle' Weatherford, Chief," www.geni.com/people/William-Lamochattee-Red-Eagle-Weatherford

Walker, Margaret, *Jubilee*, Houghton Mifflin Company (New, NY) 1966

Yetman, Norman, ed., *When I Was A Slave,* Memoirs from the Slave Narrative Collection, a replication of selected unabridged slave narratives from narratives originally recorded by the Federal Writers Project, 1936-1938, Dover Publications, Inc., 2002

Interviews

Many thanks to the following individuals for their first-hand accounts of southern farm life in the 1930s and 1940s:

My cousin, Max Tew, who shared his memories of picking cotton and peanuts as a child in Houston County, Alabama.

Helen Wansley Thomason, who provided detailed descriptions of growing up on a cotton farm in Elbert County, Georgia.

Museums

George Washington Carver Interpretive Museum, Dothan, Alabama

National Museum of the Civil War Soldier, Pamplin Historical Park, Dinwiddie County, Virginia

Westville Living History Museum, Lumpkin, Georgia

Acknowledgements

My deepest gratitude to my daughter, Bonnie Lisa Stroud; my grandchildren, Brianna, Desmond, and Dylan; and my brother, Robert Stroud, for their encouragement and support during the writing of this book.

Heartfelt thanks to my cousin, Sonia Calhoun Guinand, who accompanied me on numerous genealogical forays into Alabama and Florida over the years and helped me connect with my Alabama roots.

Printed by Libri Plureos GmbH in Hamburg, Germany